SEEIN(

"Enough!" The ground quaked as Gerah Maugaine's voice boomed across the landscape of the cold, gray planetoid.

Gerah grabbed the offending warlord by his armor. The front of the metal chest plate twisted like warm taffy beneath his steely fingers. As their eyes locked, the warlord's face distorted into a mask of terror, his mouth frozen open in an unending scream.

Even after all breath escaped his lungs, his body involuntarily fought to wail, above even his natural instinct to breathe.

He only managed a strained gurgle.

The remaining warlords stood transfixed by the scene as a creeping awareness of dread and emptiness surrounded them. The feeling swamped them until even the horizon was swallowed in its caustic darkness.

And as their mortal vision was abandoned, a sound – at first thin and fleeting - swelled to a crescendo, filling the shallow atmosphere of the planetoid with its supernatural fanfare; a series of notes, sung with impossible perfection by a million invisible voices.

The warlords frantically looked around, seeking any mortal anchor to ground themselves against the unreality of it all and immediately wished they hadn't.

The man they knew as Gerah Maugaine no longer stood before them. The being they now looked upon was more a projection of force than mortal. Their human minds instantly rejected the existence of such a being.

Such things were not possible.

Such things *could not* be possible.

NOTE: If you purchased this book without a cover, you should be aware that you're missing some really cool artwork and valuable stain resistant features!

This is a work of fiction. All characters and events portrayed in this novel are either products of the author's overactive imagination or are used fictitiously.

THE LAST WITNESS™

BOOK 0: THE ARTERRAN CHRONICLES

TM & Copyright ©1988 - 2012 Gerald Welch

ISBN-13: 978-0615610481 (Bookmason)
ISBN-10: 061561048X
BISAC: Fiction / Fantasy / Epic

Requests for reproduction or interviews should be directed to: marketing@bookmason.com

Official website: http://www.thelastwitness.com

Cover and other artwork by Gerald Welch
Published by BookMason Publishing. http://www.bookmason.com
BookMason is a trademark of BookMason Publishing.

Edited by Donna Courtois: http://www.donnacourtois.com

First public printing: April 2007
Second public printing: March 2012

Printed in the United States of America

THE LAST WITNESS

BOOK ZERO

THE ARTERRAN CHRONICLES
by Gerald Welch

To Valley [signature] 9-13-12

Visit the official website! Join the forums,
Download custom wallpapers and more!

www.thelastwitness.com

ALSO AVAILABLE!

- - - COMING SOON! - - -

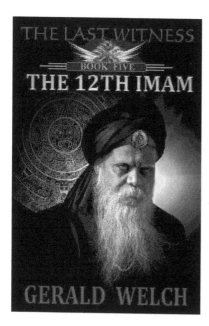 

AND FOR A CHANGE OF GENRE IN THE SAME UNIVERSE:

When Shelly met Mark, she knew she had found the man she would marry. Now she must convince Mark, her parents and their close-knit community that she has what it takes to be an Army wife. But when tragedy strikes, will she be able to convince herself?

THIS BOOK IS DEDICATED TO:

Frank Nelson, *the greatest eighth grade artist of all time;*

Jim Mullaney, *who is an inspiration to writer and fan alike;*

*To the people who most keep me company while
I am writing in the wee hours of the morning:*

Squire Parsons, *your music moves mountains.*
Sara Groves, *your music is always there for me.*
Toby Mac, *your music is my link to what's important.*
Amy Lee, *if you ever need a bass guitarist, look me up.*

And to my first fan, **Blake***...*

INDEX

QUID FUISSET, FUTURUS EST

"What have you learned?"

The man stood quietly, gathering his thoughts in the cool breeze drifting through the auditorium. He knew what the question was going to be; it had been the same question that was given to all the others; but while he had what seemed like an eternity to perfect a response, his preconceived replies melted away, leaving him alone and without an answer.

"Just start at the beginning," he thought as he closed his eyes.

"There was light and there was life. The Host of Heaven filled the skies, a unified force of angelic warriors until the rebellion of Helel. The faithful angels slaughtered the seditious demons and banished their spirits to the physical realm until the end of days."

The man stopped. That story had already been told.

"Life exists on two worlds: Ehrets and Earth," he said, balling his fists to represent each planet. "They exist in separate galaxies and are concealed from each other by a natural rift in space."

The following silence begged for more information.

"Both worlds are inhabited by plants, animals and man - both were home to the effects of original sin. And though the Christ died on Earth, His message was sent to Ehrets by vision and prophecy."

The crowd remained silent and it made him feel even more

uncomfortable than he had already been. He wasn't used to large crowds and this was the largest crowd he had ever seen.

"There is more..." the voice guided.

"Each world has had its share of disaster and tragedy," he continued, not knowing where to go with the story. "On Earth, a flood shattered the mother continent, nearly wiping out the human race...and Earth's languages were splintered when the people tried to build a tower to Heaven. Ehrets retained the original tongue, which was changed only slightly by time and dialect."

"Continue."

The man felt more comfortable and relaxed his stance.

"Ehrets was spared the flood, but their own tragedies more than made up for it. The Fall at Amagrath destroyed nearly every advance Ehrets ever claimed. Oh, Ehrets is more technologically advanced than Earth, but the price they had to pay..." the man drifted into somber silence, searching for what next to say.

"I've been to both worlds and they're nothing alike! Dinosaurs are as plentiful as orchids in the wilds of Ehrets, but on Earth they only exist as museum fossils."

"These things are all known."

The man looked dejected for a moment before returning his attention to the crowd. When he did, his face lit up and his newly discovered purpose shoved his shyness to the side.

"The office of Witness!" he almost shouted. "It was granted to men of similar nature on both worlds - at the same time – while each man was still a judge."

"Much better", the voice said, confirming his choice of topic.

"What happened to these men?"

"The judge on Ehrets liberated his people, so his power was augmented and handed down through his heirs, establishing a worldwide theocratic empire. The judge on Earth – his name was Samson - used his power selfishly and died a blind prisoner. The line of Witnesses ended before it had a chance to start, and Earth never experienced the destiny that Ehrets took for granted."

"The man who liberated the people of Ehrets?"

"His name was Arter."

"Then that is where your story shall begin…"

PRELUDE: CHAPTER ONE

1103 B.C.

His name was Arter and his shame hung heavier than the thick iron chains that bound each limb. Led like a dog to the Temple of Infidels, Arter braced himself as he entered the heart of the Dagon Empire.

The first cool breezes of the evening drifted through the rough iron manacles that bound his arms, chilling his open wounds. Arter stole glimpses of his surroundings as the weight of the shifting chains allowed, enabling the jeering crowd to better view their prize. The raucous laughter grew louder, and as he suppressed another groan, Arter realized that this new experience called shame was quickly mastering him. It urged him to look beyond the twisted faces and the violent taunts - to the ground, the sky - anywhere but at the mob surrounding him.

A moan escaped again. The weight of the iron shackles forced him to arch his back to catch each breath. The soldier behind him, seeing the pause, kicked him in the back. The pain from the boot had not disappeared before Arter's face struck the ground.

The shame urged him to stay down and cover his face.

"Look up!" commanded a small spark of the man he once was.

They were crowing now, the cowards. These were the same people who months before could not collectively summon the courage to look him directly in the eye. But now, while he was bound and bleeding and helpless, they delighted in avenging themselves for the many indignities they had suffered over the last few years.

Arter could understand the torture and humiliation. How often had he followed their retreats with mocking laughter? The parade through the masses was only a part of that shared warfare, but the Dagonite soldiers committed acts they would never have dared attempt while he possessed the power. Had they dared to escalate the warfare to such a personal level, Arter would have taken the battle into the heart of the kingdom itself – ironically, here - to the Grand Temple of Dagon, the religious and cultural soul of the Dagonite people.

The largest structure in the land, the stone coliseum was dedicated to the worship of the water god Dagon. More people than Arter had ever seen were crowded into the huge stadium. He had no experience on how to estimate the number of those in attendance, having been raised by a small band of priests in the Jusinan Temple of the One God.

Standing in the royal booth above the procession, a man who had a lifetime of experience with crowds had already determined that more than three thousand people were present. As Premiere of the Royal House of Dagon, Habideh was especially pleased to see that even his political enemies from the eastern district were in attendance with their reluctant praise.

Habideh was amazed at how quickly it had all come together. The first news he had heard of the troublesome Jue was a casual mention, the sort of offhand story that he heard in passing many times a day. Arter was mentioned briefly in a discussion of a squabble involving a woman and her parents. The only reason it was even mentioned in his presence was because the woman was a blood relative of Palheem, Habideh's chief political opponent and leader of the eastern district, which made revenge a matter of royal honor and pride.

In typical eastern district fashion, Palheem boasted before the entire council that he would make an example of this upstart Jue. The Jues would learn to fear his tribe. He didn't say they would fear the kingdom, Habideh noted; just his tribe.

Palheem's brute squad invaded Arter's village with a simple order: Return him – alive - to Palheem for torture and execution. The reports that Habideh heard were so unbelievable that he first thought they were manufactured to embarrass Palheem, who publicly dismissed the tales as weak excuses of weaker men.

There were variations, but the stories agreed that an unarmed Jue single-handedly defeated the entire armed squad sent to arrest him and described how he chased the few survivors - chariots and all - back to the capitol gates.

Habideh and the other Dagonite leaders began to take notice when subsequently larger companies met similar fates and similar stories reached not just the Palace, but other areas of the Dagonite Empire. To save face, Palheem made a pact with other political factions to bring the rogue Jue in, deliberately leaving Habideh outside of his plans.

Palheem sent more than a thousand troops. It was overkill, but that was the point. Not only would it insure minimal Dagonite losses, but it would replace a recently acquired mindset for Juish rebellion with the rightful fear of their Dagonite Rulers.

"Especially Palheem," Habideh assumed.

The troops encountered Arter while he was returning home through a field. Though he noticed their approach, he didn't try to escape. He merely bent over to pick something up. Four companies of archers immediately opened with volleys of arrows before the rest of the men advanced with swords and clubs.

The only surviving soldiers were the few who had run early and they spoke in fearful stutters. All agreed: he held nothing in his hand but the jawbone of an ass, but he shattered shields and armor alike. The battle hardened warriors spoke of waves of arrows that splintered upon striking Arter's bare skin and swords that couldn't even tear his clothing. Palheem sat back in his seat, ominously silent in defeat.

Habideh began to plan. Exaggerated stories or not, the Jue had some means to conquer scores of men. Palheem's mistake, Habideh knew, was that he was attacking Arter's strength. He hadn't gained political power by giving an enemy the advantage of attacking his strongest point. Habideh learned early to seek and exploit his enemy's weak spots.

So, instead of sending men to attack Arter, Habideh sent them to watch. He discovered that Arter visited a prostitute from Sorek whose name was Geila, and ordered his men to bring her to him.

PRELUDE: CHAPTER TWO

Geila had never been inside the palace, though she had seen it many times as a child when her family visited the capitol city. Her earliest memories were of streets full of vendors and traders, loud and smelly; bartering over fish and meal and silver trinkets, but that was so long ago. Little of the empire's glory had survived Habideh's consolidation of power.

The buildings were as tall, if not taller than she had remembered, but they had become dirty broken down shadows of their former greatness. The streets that at one time boasted the largest open market on the east coast were empty except for the occasional chariot that thundered from the palace grounds and back to the only remaining building worthy of Dagon's former glory.

The sun reflected just as brightly off the palace's golden dome as it had all those years earlier and the marbled steps that led to the front post still provided a clean, majestic contrast to the dirt path leading to it. As a child, she and her friends had often pretended to be Dagonite royalty, using clay pots for crowns and carpets for fine purple robes.

The memory normally brought a smile to her face, but Geila found no reason to smile as the soldiers escorted her through the front gates. Though not the giants she had seen as a child, these men were powerful, and since their attention was focused solely on her, far more dangerous.

Geila bowed, presenting her documentation. One of the soldiers snatched it from her and, symbol by symbol, read the lengthy document. His returning glance was one of pure disgust and it caused Geila to lower her gaze to the ground.

Women in her profession rarely saw the inside of the palace unless they were servicing foreign diplomats or were on trial. Geila shuddered. What if she was under investigation? Surely she was too low of status to be noticed by the premier.

Geila had to fight the sudden urge to run.

After a moment of discussion, one of the soldiers walked inside and returned with more soldiers. These men were even larger than the first. Instead of the simple iron and leather armor of the gate guards, these men were adorned in golden and silver armor. Their lances even had golden tips.

"This way," the first man barked.

Geila followed, her face still turned toward the ground, though she allowed herself momentary glances around. The palace was even more amazing than she had dreamed. The floors were covered with real tiles. Expensive silk tapestries lined the walls and golden filigree adorned every corner post. The interior doors were taller than her father's house.

After several corridors and chambers, they reached a hallway guarded by another set of soldiers, wearing the same type of gold armor. The doors behind these soldiers were covered with gilded images of warriors fighting a fierce battle. Geila's ability to read was crude, but even she recognized the seal of the Royal House of Dagon.

The soldiers stepped aside and the doors swung open. Geila walked quietly as she entered the premiere's personal chambers.

Habideh sat quietly overlooking his city through the largest glass window in the palace, most likely the largest piece of solid glass in the region. Had it come to this? Did victory now depend on dallying with east district prostitutes? His reverie was interrupted by a general.

"We've secured the woman, Premiere," the general said.

Habideh spoke without turning from the window.

"My time is valuable, whore. Tell me what you know of a man from Jusinan by the name of Arter."

"He...he is a judge of the Jues, my lord."

This surprised Habideh; he had assumed Arter was a soldier.

"I want to know how he - unarmed they say - defeats scores of men. What weapons does he use? How many men are in his army?"

"He needs no army. His God has given him great strength. I have not seen a physical feat that he wishes to accomplish that he can't do. Surely you heard that he pulled down the south wall of Nook with his bare hands."

"I didn't bring you hear to tell me fables. What can you tell me about *him*?"

"He does not like our people, especially our soldiers."

"Why?"

"They kidnapped his bride when he was younger and abused her until she died."

"Surely that can't be the source of this war," Habideh said.

"It is," Geila answered, in a tone that normally would have had her imprisoned. If Habideh noticed, he didn't let it show.

"What other weakness do you see in him?"

"I don't know of any weakness in him. Even while asleep, he is unharmed by swords."

Habideh cocked his head in disbelief. Geila caught a glimpse of his face, but quickly averted her eyes.

"Your soldiers no longer even try to attack him."

"You're saying that he can't be physically harmed?"

"Ask the man standing next to you," Geila said, referring to the general posted near Habideh. The man's face flushed at once with anger and embarrassment.

Habideh smiled at his general's discomfort and then turned to her, looking at Geila for the first time. She was younger than he had imagined, though her voice was light, and she was taller than most of the Sorek women he had seen. She would have made a good concubine if he'd found her before she had been sullied. Geila's eyes darted back and forth, evading his glance. Noticing this, Habideh moved toward her, softening his voice.

"I know your father's hardships have led you to the life you're living... but the law says you should be executed for your crimes. You see my predicament."

Geila froze. Habideh paused as he studied her response and then walked next to her.

"The advantage of being Premiere allows me to... overlook certain crimes as I deem necessary. All you have to do is help bring in a Jue who is guilty of murdering your countrymen."

Habideh studied Geila for a reaction. The soft lines of her face retained the worried look she had entered with. Habideh lowered his own face to match hers.

"I'm even willing to grant your father a small seat on the Council. Sorek is in need of new blood and the man responsible for assisting in the capture of Arter will be greatly rewarded."

Geila said nothing as she weighed the offer. A proposition like this would normally have been treated as an unbelievable gift to a family of such poor lineage, but the thought of betraying Arter and dealing with his wrath was unthinkable.

Habideh, offended by her hesitation, grabbed her hands and placed his face within inches of hers.

"Or I could just as easily have your entire family executed as traitors to the throne!" he snarled.

Habideh now had a spy who reported on Arter's activities and Geila succeeded where thousands of armed men failed. The source of his power resided in his hair, her report said. Shave the seven locks from his head and Arter would lose his strength. Habideh immediately called for Geila.

"You wish me to send a barber to defeat this Jue?"

"He has spoken to me with all his heart," she said, her own heart already broken.

Habideh glanced at the report again and threw it to the floor.

"They will come after midnight. But remember this: I punish failure more severely than I reward success."

Habideh sent his inner bodyguards to accompany his barber. Much was being risked on the words of an east district prostitute. The guards crept in while Arter slept and the barber slipped out his sheers, silently slicing off each of Arter's seven locks of hair. As planned, Geila, who was lying beside Arter, sat up.

"Arter! The soldiers are here!"

Arter awoke slowly, thinking all had been as it was. Eight soldiers were an irritant, not a threat, so he walked over to the men. Then, his eyes shot wide open as he saw that one of the men was holding locks of hair.

His hair.

Turning around, Arter madly leapt at Geila.

"Traitor!" he yelled, reaching madly for her arm.

The soldiers attacked Arter from behind, tackling him to the floor. Arter's arms felt slow and heavy as he tried to fight back. The soldiers quickly subdued him and took Arter to the dungeon. Habideh smiled at Arter as the soldiers bound him with chains.

Arter was taken to the whipping post to begin his punishment and Habideh turned his mind to the annual celebration. No doubt many would turn out this year just to see the Jue. He had stirred up a lot of trouble over the past three years. To further foment hatred against the Jue, Habideh would hire witnesses to make even more claims against him. The Jue's infractions would be the most pressing subject at this year's celebration.

But what would he do? There had to be some way to take political advantage of the situation; something to insure maximum turnout and political effect...

The celebration was still three months away. He had plenty of time to plan. As he mentally listed the events of the celebration, it hit him. The sacrificial ceremonies on the last day would be changed. There would be no use of pigs this year, or any year after, Habideh decided.

Jusinan's greatest warrior would become the first of many human sacrifices.

PRELUDE: CHAPTER THREE

The coliseum was packed. Habideh had hoped for a large turnout, but even he was amazed at the size of the crowd. Laws had to be passed to mandate attendance for past ceremonies, but this year, everyone coveted a seat. Each family understood that the humiliation of the Jue and the resulting loss of Juish influence would increase Dagonite power in the region.

And everyone craved a piece of that new power.

It had reached the point that middle class families were not only being turned away at the gate, those who had already found seats were thrown out to seat the upper class and royalty.

More people were present than Habideh had ever seen. In fact, he noticed that the coliseum was far too full. Next year, another coliseum would have to be built.

In his honor, of course.

Habideh gave a condescending smile to the councilmen sitting beside him, singling out the politically defeated Palheem with only a half wave of his hand. Ignoring the offensive odor and missing teeth of the new councilman from Sorek, Habideh turned his attention to the trumpets sounding at the front gates.

The gates swung open, revealing a squad of highly decorated soldiers. Recognizing the telltale red and black battle tunics of the Awven - Dagon's finest warriors - the crowd burst into thunderous applause. Each man was a battle hardened veteran, awarded for his fierceness and bravery on the battle-field. Their armor and shields glistened in the late afternoon sun glow.

Arter staggered behind in dusty Jusinan rags and chains, a sad contrast to the displayed strength of the Dagonite Empire.

Though Arter's steps were weak and measured, a second squad of Awven followed closely behind to deny any chance of escape.

Habideh hoped that the people in attendance didn't realize how badly injured Arter was. The Jue would need to live long enough to play his role in the day's festivities.

At the sound of the fanfare, Geila, who was placed in a seat of honor at Habideh's right hand, turned her face away. She couldn't bear to look at Arter, though every instinct urged her to look at her former lover.

Arter glanced around the inside of the coliseum. It was built around a fifty foot tall statue of an armored warrior with grossly twisted facial features. Its two thick arms held the main supports of the coliseum roofing in place. No one knew who had sculpted the statue, though some of the priests believed that Dagon himself carved the image with his own hands.

Arter stood facing the altar. A ten foot slab of carved marble, it sat at the feet of Dagon's statue like an empty plate waiting to be filled. The royal booth where the Dagonite priests sat was on the right side of the altar, while Habideh and his entourage sat in the booth on the other side.

Habideh turned and whispered a few instructions to the captain of the guard. The captain left and Habideh stood. The crowd's jeers subsided so they could hear their victorious premiere.

"I welcome all the worshipers of Dagon to his temple this day, for a great wrong done to our peoples has been righted by your premiere. I present to the families of Dagon, west and east alike, the man who fell before the power of our great god Dagon: the Jue Arter!"

At that, a cheer that rattled Arter's bones erupted from the crowd. The Awven shoved him down the ramp into the coliseum, and Arter fell before the mammoth stone altar. With great effort, he hauled himself - heavy chains and all - back to his feet.

"As he tried to make sport with our people, let us make sport with him!" Habideh smiled and motioned to the sentries.

The sound of grinding wood rumbled through the coliseum as the large wooden gates to the right opened. The Awven guarding Arter stepped back as children dressed in adult armor spilled out of the gates and ran toward Arter. The armor was so large that several tripped and fell, and the crowd laughed. As they neared Arter, the children dropped their armor. They picked up sticks and stones to attack Arter and the crowd cheered.

Arter tried to turn from each of the projectiles, but he never needed to evade an enemy before. Where his skin once defied physical attacks, it now bruised and surrendered his blood to the coliseum floor. The world seemed to tilt as more rocks found his skull and Arter fell. After a command from Habideh, the Awven pulled the children back, and the crowd hissed and booed.

The sounds of the brutal assault on Arter caused Geila's pity to overcome her fear and she looked at Arter for the first time since his capture. Even though he had been cleaned up, she could see that he had been savagely beaten and if Habideh's mood was any indication, he would suffer more torture in the days to come.

But something was wrong.

She looked again and a voice in the back of her mind began screaming.

Something wasn't right.

Geila looked more closely. During the months of his captivity, Arter's hair had grown; not to its former lengths, but clearly past the shoulders.

And though she was seated, the strength drained from her legs.

"His hair!" she choked out, daring to clutch Habideh's sleeve, pointing to Arter. "His hair's grown back!"

"The Jue is helpless," Habideh answered, freeing his sleeve from the whore's grasping fingers. "The chains hold him secure to the point that children can beat him senseless!"

"His hair is his bond with his God! You...you don't know what he can do!"

"This is Dagon's Temple, whore! His God has no power here!"

Geila felt the blood drain from her face.

"We're all dead," she whispered, absently rubbing her lips.

Habideh turned back to the festivities, making a mental note to rid himself of both the girl and her peasant father upon returning to the palace. The girl was mentally unstable and her father was a hopeless drunk.

The priests came before his stand and Habideh received them, and turned his attention back to the crowd.

"Give thanks to the great god Dagon for this sacrifice."

His words rung loudly throughout the coliseum, but even those close to the stand leaned forward to hear his next words to see if the rumors were true.

"Each year, we pay blood tribute to Dagon with a host of swine, but this year we have more to be thankful for. The Jue Arter has offended our people, our god Dagon and this very temple."

Many in the crowd yelled their approval and began booing at Arter, pelting him with garbage. Habideh raised his hands to quiet them. They obeyed, but it was obvious that their blood lust wasn't satisfied.

Habideh smiled. "To repay that trespass, this year - and every year henceforth - our sacrifice will no longer be paid by the people of Dagon. It shall be paid with Jusinan blood, beginning this day, with the Jue Arter!"

The crowd roared its approval as the Awven marched down the ramp with chains to bind Arter to the altar.

Arter paid no attention. He allowed his body to lie in the dust, and in a moment of self-realization that comes to a man only a few times during his life, began to cry. The murder of his wife; the destruction of his village; everything that had happened up to this point was not Geila's fault; nor even the Dagonites', he realized.

It was his own.

If he had kept his vows to the Creator, none of this could have happened. The realization broke him.

"Creator God, what have I done?" he asked the air before him. "I know that you haven't failed me... I have failed you. I've always been a believer...but I've never been a follower."

He raised his head toward the sky, but the towering stone face of Dagon stood defiantly over him. The empty stone eye sockets seemed to gloat over his situation. Arter looked past the statue to the small sliver of sky peering through the roof.

"For my offenses, I ask forgiveness and I pray that if You can, in Your mercy grant me one more chance, I will deliver the people from the Dagonites. It shall be done."

Arter allowed his head to drop to the dirt floor, the weight of the chains and the pain of his wounds finally overtaking his pride. The approaching soldiers and the laughter of the crowd no longer mattered.

"Look! He's fallen before Dagon!" one spectator said.

"Dagon has squashed the Jue and his God!" another squealed.

And in that moment of total surrender, the most curious thing happened. Arter felt two small and sharp clicks in the back of his head. He opened his eyes as the pain drained from his body. The familiar feeling of air being forced into his lungs - deep, deep into the bottom of his lungs - returned and Arter knew his prayers had been answered. He took a moment to raise himself to his knees in solemn thanks and then, with what appeared to be a giant shrug, snapped the chains that bound him.

The crowd gasped and then cheered. Their rational minds, unable to accept the supernatural reality displayed before them, strained to translate the event into something acceptable. Maybe Habideh was giving the Jue a fighting chance; perhaps the chains weren't properly secured.

But a few Dagonites began to realize the horrifying truth as the Awven reached Arter. They saw finely honed swords break as they struck bare skin, and hand carved ceremonial arrows shatter upon impact with old Jusinan wool.

The snap of Awven bones could not be heard above the roar of the crowd, but Habideh looked around the coliseum, and his heart skipped a beat as his eyes were opened to the true situation.

He hadn't beaten the Jue; he had delivered to him all of the Dagonite rulers in one place and at one time.

Arter wasn't going to escape; he was going to kill them all. Habideh shoved his personal guards down the stairs.

"Kill him!" he screamed.

"Stupid Jue!" one spectator mocked, oblivious to his own fate.

"Why is he running toward Dagon?" another asked.

"Maybe he thinks Dagon will save him!" the first howled.

Moving past the altar, Arter climbed onto the stone platform where Dagon's statue stood. Slapping aside the few Awven still hounding him, Arter stood between the statue's legs and placed one hand on the inside of each huge shin and pushed.

The stone defied him, laughing at the pitiful mortal pushing against its marbled strength. The crowd's jeers and laughs echoed all the louder in the coliseum at Arter's seeming act of madness.

Above the din of the crowd, Arter heard the cries of more soldiers coming in from the western gates. But his faith would not be denied. Looking up at the statue once more only fueled his anger. He leaned into the effort and small fractures began to feather up the stone legs.

The rows closest to Arter fell silent as small chips of stone popped from the statue's polished surface. Too fascinated by the scene to avert their eyes from their own destruction, or shocked by the unreality of the scene to move, hundreds of eyes followed the fractures, weaving around to the front of Dagon's chest. And in one shattering moment, explosive shards of stone shrapnel burst from the heart of the statue.

Only then did they truly understand the situation.

The stampede out of the coliseum began, but it was too late. The statue came crashing down. The two strong arms that held the roof aloft pulled it down on the people below, destroying the superstructure, collapsing it onto those who had reached the exits. Foundational boulders caved in, pulling in even the guards who stood outside.

There emerged a lone survivor.

A new man, ushering in a new era...

The Book of
The Last Witness:

THE ARTERRAN CHRONICLES

Midrash 34 : 22, 23

"And then Arter defeated
the enemies of Jusinan
and destroyed their gods,
uniting the kingdoms
of man from Qedem to
the shores of Hala.

And Arter judged the
people of Jusinan two
hundred and three
score years."

EIGHT YEARS AGO

If war is the natural result when men attempt to play God, then civil war must be the result when they play Satan. What then describes a civil war between father and son? The question was often asked by both men, though neither could see their own fault.

The son, Grayden Mashal asked himself once again as he walked among a pile of bodies and machinery, searching for signs of life. Whatever had killed these people had purposely stacked them like this for intimidation.

The metal had already cooled, but he didn't need his scanner to tell him that he would find no survivors. He had been late, directing another battle in an attempt to distract from this secret mission, but it didn't work. An hour earlier he had heard the last message from the group, which had smuggled out a strategic item from his father's palace.

And now, it appeared that he had lost it. But while it was important, the carrier of that item was even more important. Though she was one of the Christian cultists, Aymoon was his first and only love.

She had pleaded with Grayden to end the war, to leave with her to a remote part of Roosh, but he hadn't listened. He had only his end goal; to take the throne that was rightfully his and set Aymoon as his queen.

The flies had already begun to weave thick patterns over

the carcasses. Grayden rose above the bodies until he levitated among the flies, and raised both arms.

"Leave this place," he said in solemn concentration. The flies hovered for just a moment and then abandoned the area.

Grayden levitated carefully among the wreckage, careful not to walk on any of the bodies. As the direct descendent of Arter, Grayden shared Arter's powers and more as Witness Regent. The computer device on his arm scanned the bodies and quickly pointed out what he was looking for.

A squad of young men scrambled over the hill behind Grayden, clothed in mismatched stolen armor. They grabbed nervous glances, firearms at the ready, as they secured the area around the massacre. None of them looked at the pile of bodies, some out of respect, others out of fear they might recognize someone.

Grayden had gingerly removed the bodies and then he stopped. The sudden silence caused the men to look around. Though he was still levitating, they could only see the upper part of Grayden's torso and it was moving with the familiar heave of crying.

He reached down and moved rubble from the body of a young woman. Her gown placed her outside the ranks of the soldiers who lay dead around her. Around her neck was the object she had paid for with her life: a cheap-looking medallion, slightly scarred with blood, but otherwise unharmed. Grayden levitated out of the pile with her body and gently laid her on a soft spot on a nearby hill.

One of the soldiers securing the area suddenly bent his head down, listening to his comm signal. After listening to a few words, his face turned pale.

"General!" he shouted, running to Grayden's position.

Grayden lay down the body of the only person he ever cared for and holding back his emotions, listened to one of the few people he still trusted.

"We've got incoming! I've got a report of a company of enforcers and Maugaine is leading them!"

At the mention of Maugaine's name, the troops hunkered down, fear clearly on their faces.

"Let him come," Grayden whispered, grief overcoming rational thought. "It no longer matters."

"But sir..." the lieutenant desperately appealed. The look on his soldiers' faces returned Grayden to the present.

Damn his father.

"Get Malthus," Grayden said. "We're going to need him."

The young man turned to run, but a roar of mechanics flooded over the hill and the enforcers began firing into the squad of soldiers. Though trained to immediately respond, they were caught off-guard by the massive numbers.

Grayden was even caught unawares and smashed backwards into the pile of bone and metal, still in the fog of despair, confusion mounting on top of his anguish.

Several squads of enforcers scrambled over the hill, and Grayden's men fell. The enforcers were indeed in full force, but Grayden saw no indication of Maugaine's presence.

Before he could respond, six enforcers jumped on him, firing their rockets directly into his face. Though the discharge temporarily blinded him, the only real effect it had was to replace Grayden's despair with a broiling anger. The enforcers drew blades from their hips and began attacking Grayden with them. The blades dulled and then cracked after they attacked him, so the enforcers grabbed him en masse and self-destructed.

The explosions rocked the pile of bodies and metal, burying Grayden in pulp and gore.

Grayden staggered to his feet, making himself an instant target, but once he was aware of the attack, the full protection of the Witness Regent became effective and the shells fired at him instantly crushed themselves upon impact with his body.

He ran forward and backhanded a small group of the military androids. The enforcers flew backward into the air, but internal gyros balanced them before they hit the ground. They landed on their feet and began moving forward the instant they hit the ground.

Grayden could take no more. He screamed and then grabbed a deep breath. As his head tilted forward, he triggered the Witness power of Speed. A crack of thunder erupted as the air parted before him and the enforcers seemed to slow to a crawl as he tore through them, tearing limbs and heads and torsos from their robotic frames, easily dodging the incoming fire.

Once he exhaled, he exited Speed and returned to normal time. The rest of the enforcers had targeted him and began firing. It did them no good. Grayden tore through them one by one until the entire company of enforcers was nothing but a pile of mangled metal.

Grayden levitated down to where he had laid Aymoon's body, but it was nowhere to be found. His eyes attached on a small patch of the robe she wore, covered in dirt and blood.

He stared at it a few moments, then kissed it and placed it in a pocket near his heart.

The head of an enforcer lay on the ground nearby, mocking his sorrow with its eternal glare. Grayden picked up the nearly human-looking head and, placing his thumbs in the eye sockets, cracked the skull apart, shattering its illusion of humanity. Wires and circuits spilled out of the shell, followed by the light lubricant that served as enforcer blood.

Grayden was fighting a war with human lives and blood while his father was playing a game of attrition with his endless supply of android enforcers. It was the perfect solution; turn the already mobilized police automatons into military androids. They never slept or ate and could be easily replaced. And while Grayden could defeat them, it wasn't without great effort and his army was nearly helpless against them.

An old man stood nearby, holding the medallion in his hand. "They failed to retrieve the medallion," he said in a thin, familiar voice.

Grayden fell to a sitting position and the life seemed to drain from him. "Whatever it takes, I'm going to make him pay!"

"You are needed at Kairahb," the old man said.

Grayden looked up helplessly to Malthus, a lost soul awash in grief.

"The fortress at Kairahb is still in play and your men need you," Malthus repeated, careful not to show any emotion.

Grayden said nothing. He grabbed Malthus and the ground seemed to fall out from beneath their feet. They ascended and began moving west. The battle could easily be seen from the sky. Only two hundred miles from the palace, Kairahb was the first distraction planned in the operation to smuggle the medallion out. Enforcers were attacking the armored carriers that they had stolen from Eythan's armories at Denton. The reinforced skin of the tanks allowed them to survive long enough for Grayden to reach them.

Grayden lowered out of the sky, dropping Malthus off safely outside the battle zone and then accelerated to the battle. As he lowered into the battle, Grayden heard his men cheer, but felt no pride. Only anger burned in his veins.

"Pull back!" Grayden commanded and the tanks began slowing their advance. They were too close to the palace and temple as it was. He didn't need to trigger Maugaine's Call to defend the Temple by getting too close or there would be no reprieve.

While he could defeat as many enforcers as his father sent, there was no power sufficient to stop Maugaine. He had already killed a Witness Imperium; a Witness Regent like Grayden would be easy.

Grayden peeled the enforcers from the armored carriers, drawing their direct attention. Unlike the earlier androids who were disguised to enable them to mingle among people, these were the larger battle enforcers, much stronger than their earlier counterparts, clearly designed as robotic punishing devices. While their strength didn't approach that of a Witness Regent, together they were a force that Grayden couldn't take for granted.

Some of the enforcers ignored him, continuing their attacks on the tanks. Grayden turned toward the garrison and once he attacked the entrance, the enforcers turned toward him en masse.

Grayden accelerated into the building, tearing through the

front walls with ease. But he didn't get a chance to enter the building as the enforcers pounced on him. They were slower than their earlier counterparts and Grayden tried to grab a breath to enter into Speed, but the force of the enforcer blows were just powerful enough to rattle his concentration.

Grayden fell to the ground, covered with enforcers, who had magnetically locked onto each other, pulling him to the ground. Grayden stood to his feet, dragging the androids with him, each step stomping a new benchmark in stamina and determination. As he reached the inner chamber of the fortress, the central command center for Arterra's southern forces, the internal defenses came online and began firing at Grayden. The combination of enforcers and energy weapons was wearing him down. Despite the anger motivating his movements, Grayden's legs buckled.

As he fell to his knees, Grayden grabbed the head of the enforcer that was clinching his chest and with effort, ripped it from its torso. He quickly mashed it into a small metal mass and with all of his strength, threw it at the defense mechanism. He missed the cannons, but the dense metal still tore through the wall, damaging the computers controlling the cannons. The electromagnetic attacks stopped, but before Grayden could turn his attention back to the enforcers that wrapped around his body, several of them began to punch him, dropping Grayden to the ground. Grayden was disoriented, but somehow turned his attention to the attack.

The stronger-than-steel blade at the end of the front enforcer moved toward Grayden's eyes. It kept moving as it hit his face, reducing itself to a stump of metal as it collapsed into itself.

The other enforcers triggered an electromagnetic discharge that rendered Grayden's onboard computer useless and further disoriented him. The stab of blade probes barely registered before fifty thousand volts of electricity flooded his body.

Grayden fell to the ground and more enforcers covered his body, following up with energy attacks. Grayden took a deep breath and somehow managed to trigger Speed. The enforcers had locked themselves to each other magnetically and it took Grayden several precious seconds to break their limbs off enough to escape. The effort took his entire breath and as he escaped, he purposely backed away, facing the enforcers. He made a stand as he exhaled and time returned to normal.

The enforcers continued attacking Grayden with their firearms, but Grayden never felt the shells. As soon as they made contact, each missile fell uselessly to the ground. Grayden tried to grab another deep breath, but it was too soon and stabs of black began to enter his peripheral vision.

During the moment, he counted his attackers.

Seven.

Somehow he had destroyed all but seven. For a moment, Grayden considered leaving, but for some reason that neither he nor the enforcers could have predicted, he leapt into the midst of them.

Without the added protection of Speed, he tried to manually counter each blow while making attacks of his own. Closing his eyes, Grayden thrashed out as hard and as fast as he could. Several times he heard the clang of metal and felt his fist penetrate the thick agium armor that the enforcers were coated with. When he opened his eyes, only one enforcer remained.

Grayden walked over to it and struck his hand inside the chest cavity of the android until he was wrist deep in machine blood. His other hand joined the new hole and then he tore the enforcer down the seams.

Grayden took one last look around the scene and then fell to a sitting position, sucking in air. It was not often that a Witness felt pain or faint, much less both.

Within minutes, his men had returned to the fortress in their tanks, celebrating. They had captured a major stronghold, which held multiple weapon systems.

The men came inside the fortress, forcing the men they had captured into the hanger. There were fourteen men from his father's army and they stared at Grayden's men with disgust.

"We're too close to the palace," Malthus said. "We can't risk involving Maugaine."

"Pack all of the arms you can into the carriers and destroy this fortress."

"What about the prisoners?" Malthus asked.

Grayden paused for a moment, thinking about the bloody piece of robe that was in his pocket.

"Execute them," he said before launching into the cold sky.

His shame hung heavy, like thick iron chains. Each of the six thousand people seated in the Court of Reconciliation was a link in that chain, binding Eythan Mashal with their merciless stares. Each was aware of the sin that he, the Witness Imperium, their King, had committed with his lie. Even those seated in the back stared judgmentally at his three-dimensional projection, their faces warped in disappointment and anger.

The look was mimicked on millions of faces worldwide as satellites carried the holographic signal across the planet and to the off world colonies. This was not the same man who appeared as a symbol of hope after the fall of his father Rawshah's horrific reign. His dark beard still carried the bound curls he favored as a regent, but his face had begun to surrender to the weight of age and strain of office. His vestments and mantle branded him a man of greatness, but his expression revealed a man of sorrow, and in that manner, Eythan identified with his people. The person he betrayed, more than anyone assembled before him, was himself.

Despite their apprehensions, the people filled the chamber, each awaiting an audience with the Witness Imperium. Some came for healing, some for justice; each coveted a piece of Eythan's most precious asset: his time.

Eythan's expanded senses could see each and every face and hear every whisper, from the front of the throne room to the seats near the exits.

"Why don't we hear from the Creator Himself?" an old woman toward the back whispered to her husband. "He once spoke directly to us."

"That's their gimmick," the man huffed. "They call themselves Witnesses to prevent us from asking about the Creator. That way, we have to go to them for all the answers."

Eythan wished it was that simple. As he grew older, he realized just how few answers he really had, but their comments didn't disturb him. He had long ago learned to ignore remarks which could land their speaker in prison.

Eythan ordered a recess as military scouts entered the court. The projections above the baldachino switched from a live view of the Witness Imperium to a rotating three-dimensional symbol of the House of Arter: a column separating two small circles. The platform curtains pulled together separating the throne from the rest of the court.

Eythan's large frame seemed to shrink in his throne as each scout gave their report: The rebellion had reached the edge of Throne City. Military squads and small mobile armament freely roamed the suburbs, smashing smaller structures to the east while larger units of armored infantry attacked from the south. Each report added yet another link to the shame that bound him. It was his son that led the rebellion, just as he in his earlier years had led a rebellion against his own father. It was not the way of things in Arterra.

It was just the way of things lately.

Eythan turned to the throne on his right, suppressing a frown as he took a quick glance at his heir, Shiloh. At eight, the prince was far too young to claim the Emerald Throne, but everything had changed once his elder brother Grayden was banished. Shiloh was advancing well in the training centers for his age, but he still had so far to go. Shiloh squirmed in the large throne. It was obvious that he had inherited his mother's short stature as well as her bronze colored hair.

Eythan held up one hand and the scout immediately ceased reading his report. Eythan waved them away as a group, and after a quick bow, the scouts removed themselves from the throne.

"Do you have any questions about today's schedule?" Eythan asked, his eyes searching Shiloh's face.

No response.

"This is too much for a child," Eythan thought. "The healing ceremony will be next. Then each Assemblyman will meet with you to publicly recognize your ascension to the Regency and your mother will be teaching you the braids later this evening."

Shiloh's eyes went to the floor for only a second before his training made him return his father's gaze.

"The boy is too young," Eythan caught himself thinking.

"Shiloh?"

The expression on Shiloh's face revealed many questions, but one came quickly.

"Why must I meet with General Maugaine?"

"Gerah is a member of the Assembly. Shiloh, there's nothing to be frightened of."

"He killed grandfather Rawshah," Shiloh said.

Eythan winced.

"My father...your grandfather...committed sins, Shiloh; sins far too great to ignore. And no man...not even a Witness is beyond the judgment of the Creator."

"Will he kill me?"

"Of course not."

"He wants to kill Grayden," Shiloh said, weak with fear.

"He wants to stop your brother," Eythan corrected, trying also to convince himself. "Shiloh, Gerah's mission is to protect the line of Witnesses, not destroy us."

Eythan struggled for the right words. He had two wives and eight children, but his schedule left little time for family. He had rarely taken the time to talk with Shiloh before this, but he would not fail Shiloh the way he had failed Grayden.

"The Helmet he wears was given to him by the Angel of Death, who also looked very frightening. Angels are God's servants and they would not choose a bad man for the Call."

"Is he an angel?"

"No, he's a man, like me."

"Why doesn't he ever take off his helmet?"

"That is his agreement with the Creator. His Call is a lifelong one, like ours. Is it his Helmet that makes you so afraid of him?"

Shiloh's face lowered in thought as he considered the question. His eyes returned with the answer.

"Nana says never look at his eyes, but he's always staring at me, like the palace painting of Father Arter. No matter where I stand in the room, it stares at me."

"And yet wasn't Arter the greatest of us all? Shiloh, I trust Gerah Maugaine more than any man in the empire."

"Why?" Shiloh asked.

"He was sent by the Creator, and there is no better judge of character."

Eythan could see that his words weren't reaching Shiloh. He would have to find a way to explain so Shiloh could understand, but that would take time.

"It's time for the healing ceremony," Eythan said, motioning to the sentries at the edge of the platform.

As the curtains opened, a small group of people in various stages of disease and injury were led by a priest toward the base of the throne. Eythan and Shiloh walked down to greet them.

"His Will is that none should perish," the priest said, giving the traditional greeting.

"His Will shall be done," Eythan answered with the traditional response. "Let those present today share as witnesses that His Will is inviolate."

Shiloh stepped forward to get a better view. Although he had heard stories of miracles, he had never actually seen one. He had always been too young to enter the great court. Technically, he still was.

The first person to approach Eythan was a young woman with a slight limp, clutching her side. Shiloh couldn't tell what was wrong with her, but as Eythan laid his hands on her head, the pained look drained from her face. Her eyes searched around in disbelief. She nimbly fell to one knee, kissing his hand and then ran toward the back of the group as the crowd erupted in cheers.

Shiloh was disappointed. There were no lights or winged angels like he'd seen in the paintings. His father had just placed his hands on the woman's forehead, said a short prayer and then she ran away.

The next man looked normal as well. Shiloh couldn't see

anything wrong with him, but again, when his father placed his hands on the man's forehead and prayed, the man ran away.

Then Shiloh noticed an elderly man on a stretcher at the end of the line. The only movement was in the spasming fingers of his right hand, flinching as if they were trying to escape the body's pain. An elderly woman (*his wife*, Shiloh assumed) held the hand as if to touch the only spark of life remaining in his body.

Shiloh watched as the people were healed of their invisible sicknesses. Then they brought the stretcher to the front. Eythan opened the man's eyes, but there was no response. As he laid his hands on the man's head, Eythan bowed his own head and began praying. The man's fingers stopped shaking and his hand fell to the bedside. There was no other movement. Shiloh couldn't even tell if the man was still breathing.

As Eythan removed his hands, the man's back arched and his lungs took in a sharp, desperate breath. The sudden movement startled Shiloh and he took a step back. The old man twisted in his stretcher and sat up, panting. He looked at the priest and then Eythan, unaware of where he was. Upon seeing the Witness Imperium, he quickly scuttled from the stretcher to kneel before Eythan, grabbing his outstretched hand and pressing it to his forehead in thanks. His wife began crying and ran forward, quickly pulling him back, her eyes thanking Eythan as she left.

The priest nodded toward Eythan and bowed as he walked away. Eythan walked back toward the throne. As he did so, he saw Shiloh, whose face still captured the wonder of seeing his first miracle.

"How does that work?" Shiloh asked as he neared.

Eythan smiled. The ceremonies had been routine for so long, he had forgotten how incredible they actually were.

"It's not like a machine that you can turn on and off, Shiloh. It's one of the many blessings that Witnesses are given to spread the message of His existence."

Shiloh thought for a moment. This was the first time he had ever spent a day with his father.

"Can you heal animals?"

"Well, yes, though it's not normally done."

"What about plants?"

"I...uh, I don't know. I've never heard of a Witness healing a plant. Why would..."

"How strong are you?"

"As strong as I need to be."

"Could you move the world?"

"It's not like that, Shiloh. We weren't given these abilities for vanity or to do foolish things," he said.

Shiloh's eyes turned to the floor. Seeing the disappointed look on his son's face, Eythan leaned toward him as if to divulge a great secret and whispered, "But between you and me, if I needed to move a small mountain, I'm sure that I could."

Shiloh dropped back into his throne as the vision of his father moving a mountain played in his mind's eye. Eythan braced for another question when the conversation was interrupted by the fanfare of the chamber sentries, quieting the still cheering crowd.

Eythan and Shiloh both turned to recognize the entrance of the new guest. The smooth sounds of the main chamber doors echoed through the chamber and dutiful, heavy footfalls introduced the visitor. The sentries scrambled out of the way as Arterra's newly appointed Minister of War, Gerah Maugaine, entered the court. Eythan glanced over to see Shiloh's response. His eyes were darting from the floor to General Maugaine and back to the floor.

Maugaine approached the throne, moving with the same confident and fluid manner of a nightmare. Two gnarled wings protruded from the sides of the coarse gray helmet given to him by the Angel of Death. Shiny razor-like feathers shot from the sides, with bony claws seemingly growing into the faceplate. The only evidence of humanity was two eyes, the color of tempered iron, visible through an opening slit in the front of the faceplate. Eyes, Eythan often thought, of a man raised in harsh surroundings.

Eythan felt an involuntary shiver in Shiloh's hand as Gerah approached. He could tell that Shiloh's training was the only thing keeping his feet firmly planted.

People turned their gaze from Gerah as he approached the throne, some blatantly covering their eyes as he walked by. Gerah didn't seem to notice or care. He was staring at one of the many cameras stationed in the throne room. He slowed his pace until he reached the throne, and only then did his eyes leave the camera.

Eythan stepped off the walkway and guided Shiloh down to where Gerah stood. He could feel Shiloh's tight grip on his mantle as he followed closely behind.

"Welcome, General Maugaine."

"My Witness," Gerah responded. Though the ancient metal faceplate covered his nose and mouth, his austere baritone voice could be clearly heard.

"Gerah, I want to formally introduce you to Prince Shiloh."

Gerah turned toward Shiloh. Shiloh froze.

"My Prince," Gerah acknowledged.

"Shiloh's been approved for the regency studies," Eythan said with a modicum of pride, forcefully moving Shiloh to the fore. "Today, we officially recognize the appointment of his regency."

"Fair well, but our business is best not heard by children."

"Yes," Eythan warily agreed. "Shiloh, you can return for your meeting with Minister Ahmahl in one hour. Caretaker?"

Eythan had to ask only once. The small woman who was Shiloh's nanny moved quickly to Eythan's side, careful to avert her eyes from General Maugaine as she walked to the platform.

"We'll talk later," Eythan told Shiloh.

The caretaker quickly and quietly led the eight year old from the throne room through the side door.

"He fears you," Eythan said, grinning at Gerah.

"If he fears the Creator, he has nothing to fear from me, unlike your elder son. His troops have breached the inner gates."

"What?" Eythan asked, clearly surprised.

"They launched an offensive with the weapons stolen from Mibtsar. Didn't the scouts tell you?"

"Assign security to the city perimeter," Eythan said, ignoring Gerah's question. "And clear the throne room. We'll continue the ceremonies tomorrow."

A command into his headset caused the throne room lights to brighten. The sentries started at the rear, escorting the people out while the platform curtains closed. Eythan returned his attention to Gerah.

"As long as he remains free, these people will never be safe."

"Our troops can isolate him," Eythan insisted.

"And then what? Grayden possesses the power of the Witness Regent. You're losing hundreds of men every day."

"Once he's been isolated, then I can apprehend him. You know I can't be an active participant in military strikes."

"No, I don't. I only know that Grayden is using your suicidal handicap to his advantage. Men who have sworn allegiance to the throne of Arter are dying, and they don't know why. It is all I can do, not to enter the fray and stop this lunacy myself."

"Gerah, if you were to kill another Witness..."

"I was not Called to watch."

"Have you been Called to stop Grayden?"

Gerah paused in angry silence.

"I stopped your father because he was committing murder while hiding behind the Mantle as your son is even now doing."

"I won't bring back the death laws to destroy one mad dog."

"One mad dog who has the strength of a thousand men and is responsible for the deaths of ten times that number."

Gerah expressed his anger in the way he spit each word.

"Even for him. My father abused the death laws; I will see proper justice for my son."

"Justice? I tally the lives he has taken, Witness, and the time will come when you have to answer to the families of those who have fallen. What will you tell them?"

Eythan's pause was uncomfortable as he returned to his throne. The office of Witness had changed drastically since the time of Arter. The personal intervention of the Witness was declared improper when their rule spanned the globe. The role of Witness had been reduced to that of judicial and social decision-maker. The power that once toppled governments was reduced to a dormant reminder of its former greatness.

Thus sat impotent the most powerful man in the world.

"His little war is nearly over," Eythan mused. "After he is isolated, I will personally bring him in...but not before."

"But I can stop him. Right now. He came within two hundred miles of the temple last week and you did nothing! You ignore the obvious danger here," Gerah asserted, shaking his head. "If you had listened to the reports, you would know that Grayden has left the front. His personal craft was last reported heading north. And if he has access to Ventura, then you must realize that you're leaving the citizenry open to massive destruction."

"He's had access to Ventura since he was banished; why would he leave the front when he is so close to what he thinks is victory?"

"Surely you don't believe that he thinks he can defeat you, even if I were not at your side? Ask yourself this question, Witness: what would be so appealing as to draw him away from the front at this time?"

"But you said yourself that the prisM was not at Ventura when you searched for it."

"No, I only said that I couldn't find it."

"It doesn't matter. Even I can't just wander around Ventura and without the medallion, he couldn't begin to know where to start searching."

Gerah walked to the golden pedestal that housed the medallion.

"I agree," he said, opening the container.
It was empty.

Grayden had never considered himself an atheist, but rather a rebel. He had never questioned the existence of the Creator. It was His role in creation that Grayden protested, specifically His role in Grayden's life. Grayden stared out the display window of his airship. The storm was strong enough that Old Darton was barely visible below them.

If He were truly a fair God, Grayden would still be regent and living at the palace. His punishment and subsequent exile to hide his father's sins ran counter to every expression of righteousness that he had ever been taught. His prayers went unanswered, his pleas for mercy seemingly ignored. Grayden wasn't naive enough to believe that he could fight the Creator, but he could attack the Creator's representative, the Witness Imperium.

Even if that Witness was his father.

Grayden had divested himself of all the trappings associated with the House of Arter. His black hair, which had been carefully braided since taking the ring of regency, was allowed to flow savagely down his back. The covering that every Witness wore to hide their center braid in honor of his commitment was long ago discarded. No longer would he be bound by the formal vestments of the regency or the small crown given to him by his father. He wore the dark robes normally reserved for mourners, down to the plain black sandals that his father despised. The only sentimental object he allowed himself to retain was a small, burnt scrap of red cloth which he carried with him at all times.

He had spent his time in exile searching for a weapon, which was not an easy task. As he had been taught from childhood, *"No weapon that is formed against you shall prosper,"* and it was true; knives, swords, concussive explosions, poisons, radiation blasts; nothing was effective against the Witness Imperium.

Grayden found his weapon in a book, from a time when books were still printed on paper. *The History of the Elders* provided details about his ancestors that Grayden had never heard before.

The book told of a man who had never realized that he was a Witness. Another Witness had been a woman. And Grayden learned that contrary to what the histories said, it was a Witness, not the criminal Rhygus, who was the real cause of the cataclysmic vortex that withered Ehrettan life spans from five hundred years to barely two hundred. Most importantly, one Witness was killed - yes, killed – by the prisM of edraH while in possession of the full power of the Witness Imperium. Some Witnesses had betrayed their Call; the book referred to them as Dark Witnesses and described in gory detail each man's fall.

Grayden devoured the eight hundred page account four times. It took him past the naive idea of military conquest to a plan that brought him to the Ventura Ruins, the one place on Ehrets that was off-limits to everyone, especially Witnesses.

The book explained that the supernatural qualities of Holy or unholY grounD dampens the supernatural based powers of all Witnesses, which brought him to his current dilemma; Grayden was himself a Witness Regent, and he was heading directly into the Ventura Ruins.

The Ruins were doubly dangerous. Both Holy and unholY grounD, it was made Holy when the Angel of Death obliterated the armies that came against a young Arterran nation, when it was just one of many nations. The first temple had been built on the site. It was made unholY grounD when it became the site of the blasphemous Tragedy of the Ages that resulted in the misnamed Rhygus Vortex.

The book also revealed a Witness' vulnerability to curseD and, to a lesser degree, Blessed items. But to kill a Witness Imperium would take something so cursed....

That was when he knew what he had to do. He would find the second prisM oF EdraH. The first had struck down the Witness at Amagrath, and the second would be used against his father. The problem was that it had been hidden by wizards somewhere among the thousands of abandoned temples of the Ventura Ruins millennia earlier.

The storms outside weren't strong enough to harm his airship, but he could still feel the rumbling in the floor plates. They were hovering above Old Darton, in the southern area of the Ruins. The bare site of the funnel that thundered from the ground to the lower atmosphere even intimidated Grayden. A tornado old enough to be named, the Rhygus Vortex had produced violent storms in the immediate area, carving out lakes and rivers over the past thousand years. It had driven all human and most animal life from the area, leaving plants and insects to fight for survival in the barren land.

Some scientists said that in a few generations the vortex

would drain the majority of the atmospheric cover and dissipate, leaving only a scattering of clouds. Storms had been appearing further to the south in the past few years. A few of the larger storms even had to be dispelled by the Witness Imperium before they could reach Throne City.

A small, elderly man walked to Grayden's side. Malthus had a worn face, but Grayden knew he wasn't as old as he appeared.

"Its beauty is its power," Malthus said.

"You don't have to go out there."

"My time for adventuring is long past."

"Why can't we just send in troops to find it? Destroy each building if we have to?" Grayden asked.

"A normal man would succumb in minutes and destroying the buildings would defeat any chance we have of finding the prisM. You are a Regent. While the Ruins exploit your vulnerabilities, certain...protections are still afforded to you."

"How am I going to find anything in this storm?"

"You'll have to rely on your navigational suit," Malthus said and then leaned close to Grayden. "I've shown you the secret histories and prophecies. Now it is time for you to learn more."

"About what? Your religion? My father's religion? They're equally useless..."

"Your spiritual blindness weakens your impact on this world. It took fifty years for me to realize what I am trying to teach you now. Before you leave, let us again seek your center."

Grayden angrily shrugged, but sat before Malthus.

"You must first purge your mind of this notion of revenge. Vengeance is the feeble reflex of a weak mind that doesn't know how else to react."

"How many more times do we have to go through this?"

"That answer is yours, not mine."

Grayden lay on his back and his long black hair fell to both sides of the pillow. Malthus sat at the head of the cot.

"Think back; what was stolen from you?"

"My wife, my friends, the throne."

"Do you seek the power that is rightfully yours or sympathy?"

Grayden thought a moment and nodded in understanding.

"Then why do you wish to mindlessly vent instead of regaining that which was taken from you?"

Grayden quieted his breathing; sometimes Malthus made sense.

"Close your eyes and be healed."

Grayden closed his eyes and felt the faint pressure of Malthus' long nails press against his temples. Immediately he felt the sensation of his body falling into the darkness and his arms instinctively jerked up to catch himself. His senses slowly shut down and were replaced with their spiritual equivalents. When he opened his spiritual eyes, he saw the familiar scenes that always started the sessions: himself as a child, laughing with his father, momentary glimpses of his mother (*how he missed her!*) and joy.

Always joy.

"This is how it was and how it was meant to be, yes?" Malthus' disembodied voice asked.

"Yes, and that...worthless man threw it away," Grayden said.

Anger and love washed over him as he looked at his father.

"Emotions can be either power or chains; the choice is

yours," Malthus scolded. "The reason I reached my potential is because I long ago realized that the chains of damaging emotions have to be broken. Let us see the scene unfold."

While Grayden said nothing as the scene dissolved before him, he felt hollow leaving the scenes of the peaceful times of his life.

The scene changed to show his father and a few Assemblymen in the southern regions, ending their hunt for the animals to be used for the annual sacrifices. A much younger looking Malthus sat quietly toward the back of the crowd.

"The Creator has blessed us with a grand sacrifice!" one of the Assemblymen said.

"Yes, He has, "Eythan said, motioning for the Assemblymen to come closer. "Let us take a moment to give thanks."

The men gathered around the huge fire and each knelt. A few fidgeted with their robes, uncomfortable kneeling in dirt. Eythan smiled a moment before beginning his prayer.

"Almighty Creator, we give thanks for Your many blessings in our lives. In our expression of thanks, I..."

"Stop!" Grayden screamed, waving his arms, and the scene froze. He walked in front of the frozen image of his father and lowered his face until he was gazing directly into his father's eyes.

"You always talked to me about the power...and the *danger* of the spoken word, yet you never acted like you believed it. I was told that the power of the Witness was more than strength and healing. For a moment's impulsiveness, you will learn your own lesson...but I would be the one to pay the price for your failure!"

Eythan's unmoving face did not answer him, and after Grayden remained silent a moment, the scene continued.

"...I will sacrifice the first thing that I encounter on the flight back to the palace."

Grayden fell to his knees.

"It never changes, does it?"

"It is your destiny; self-pity is not," Malthus scolded. "Nothing will change until you willingly accept the fact of this moment."

Grayden ground his eyes shut to keep the tears from escaping.

The scene changed and Eythan was flying ahead of the aircraft carrying the Assemblymen. He had searched for hours on the return trip for a bird to sacrifice, but saw nothing until he reached Throne City. Then, a quickly darting figure flew towards him. A look of shock slapped Eythan's face as he saw Grayden proudly approach his father in mid-air.

"Father! I can fly!"

Eythan stopped in the middle of his flight, speechless.

"Grayden!" he choked out, grabbing the boy by the shoulders. "You weren't supposed to return from training until next week!"

The young Grayden's face drained of the joy it had shown moments before. "I just wanted to surprise you; I can fly!"

Eythan turned around to see the stares of condemnation from the Assemblymen in the craft hovering behind him. While a few dropped their heads in sorrow, most of the Assemblymen grinned.

The image swirled to view the inside of Eythan's quarters.

The entry door slid open and a young Malthus entered. Eythan sat at the end of a couch, his head resting in his hands.

Malthus waited a moment before speaking.

"My Witness, perhaps I can soothe your conscience. Yours was a rash mistake in judgment, but it is repairable."

"How can you repair a vow to the Creator? It's either honored or broken."

"That is true...and a sacrifice *will* need to be made, but isn't the regent promised to the Creator?"

"Yes, but..." Eythan replied weakly.

"Is it within your authority to take that which is the Creator's?"

"No, but I specifically..."

"Misspoke," Malthus interrupted. "And though some in the Assembly believe that Grayden should pay for that mistake, we should take the more spiritual path and realize that a sacrifice needs to be made, but Grayden is not yours to sacrifice."

"What are you saying?"

"A boy needs to be sacrificed in his place, on the Altar of the Holies to pay this sin debt."

"What?" Eythan asked, suddenly alive. "I said nothing of the Altar!"

"Forgive me for addressing such a sensitive area, but if this act is to be believed by future generations, it must occur in the one location where Witnesses are most vulnerable."

"You're skirting a fine line, Minister."

"I am trying to stop you from making a serious mistake."

Malthus leaned in closer, making sure that he looked Eythan straight in the eye.

"My Witness, Grayden need not die..."

The words hung in the air longer than Eythan wished to admit.

"And who should die in his place?"

"All we need do is find a young man who is already dead and cover him in the ceremonial vestments of the Witness Regent. No one would recognize him. This will also benefit the young man and his family, who will be given a far better burial than he would have had otherwise."

Eythan lowered his head into his crossed arms.

"Grayden...what would become of Grayden?"

"He would go into hiding, but his life will be spared."

"And his regency would be lost."

"Only on paper. He would, of course, retain the powers of the regent and would be in no real danger."

Eythan looked up to Malthus, tears still slowly finding escape.

"I can't make this decision."

"I've already made the proper arrangements. The family of the dead boy will be amply compensated."

"Don't tell me anything more!" Eythan shouted. "Do what you have to, but just leave!"

Unseen by Eythan and unnoticed by Grayden, Malthus smiled as he exited. The door closed behind him and the scene once again changed. A tall dark haired woman stood at the edge of a tower, fighting back tears. Her beautiful face was twisted in grief. Grayden waved his arms and the vision collapsed. He sat up, his eyes still not seeing the physical world around him.

"This isn't working!" he shouted, blindly stumbling off the cot.

The visuals of the ethereal state dissolved slowly and his senses returned to him in an awkward stagger. Malthus merely stared in disappointment. Grayden sat down as the memories rushed out of his direct consciousness, taking the emotional rush with them.

"I don't know what you want to accomplish with this torture!"

"I was hoping that you would conquer this weakness."

"Weakness? My mother killed herself after she thought I died! I will not watch her die again!"

"Then avenge her!" Malthus thundered. Grayden leaned back in his seat as Malthus pulled the medallion from his robe.

"Ready yourself. You'll need this."

Malthus held the medallion out to Grayden. It twinkled in the glare of the overhead lights. Grayden was amazed that the cheap-looking trinket was the only clue to the whereabouts of one of the most powerful weapons in existence.

"The true power of the medallion is not the internal map as most believe. Many have followed the map, or interpretations of the map and paid with their lives. The medallion is spiritually linked to the prisM and as Regent, you are more spiritually sensitive than most people. As you near the prisM, it will let you know."

Malthus placed the medallion around Grayden's neck while chanting an old verse that was remotely familiar. Then Malthus spoke in a frighteningly calm voice.

"The medallion protects a person only once. You must find

the prisM on this trip! In less than five hours, my protective spell will collapse and without its protection, we will die. Through my life-long studies, I have determined the last resting place of the prisM to be in one of these temples," he said, pointing to a small corner of the map on the wall display screen.

"There are terrors outside that I cannot shield you from. The Ruins are both Holy and unholY grounD, and as such, your powers are vastly diminished. You can probably feel their effects even now. You won't be able to fly; your speed will be reduced to that of a normal man. Your strength will remain, but you'll be partially vulnerable to physical attack. Most of all, beware any desecrated temples; the spirits inhabiting them are bound to the land for their sins. They can drain the life from your body."

"Don't you have control over these spirits?"

"My pacts are with...other beings. Now you must leave and be quick with your search. Speed is of the essence. We can't turn back. The prisM will be easy to see if you are looking."

Grayden donned the final protective layers of his energy suit and left the safety of the battered craft. He looked around and saw little but old buildings and the tornadic Rhygus Vortex, an atmospheric wound that filled the horizon, thundering from the ground to the sky.

"Curse his mother!" the Minister of Commerce shouted as he knocked his drink to the floor. "He won't interfere with me again!"

Although the Minister's voice bounced off the stone walls of the Assembly Chambers, the sentinels guarding the entranceway ignored the outburst. Minister Fensid's temper was legendary. A quiet figure sitting next to him watched the display of weakness with dull interest. When the fit ran its course, he leaned forward.

"Be silent and become wise, Fensid," the restraining voice said, low enough that the sentinels posted at the door could not hear.

"Your problems with Maugaine will soon be addressed."

"Ahmahl, you said his appointment as Minister of War was only symbolic!" Fensid grunted, his face showing the vein bulging strain necessary for him to keep to a whisper. "He overstepped his boundaries with his raids and he refuses to talk of being bribed."

" 'The unbending reed is easily broken'."

"Will you stop it with the religious crap? Maugaine's raids are costing me a fortune!"

Fensid stood, his large frame completely hiding Ahmahl from the sentinels. Ahmahl also stood. Twenty years younger than Fensid, he was also two hundred pounds lighter and six inches shorter, a small man by anyone's measure.

"If you can't stop him..." Fensid left the statement open to

Ahmahl's interpretation.

"A threat?" Ahmahl asked uncomfortably.

"If that's what it takes for you to act, then yes. My House will stand against you," Fensid snorted down at Ahmahl.

Ahmahl sat down.

"This session will produce the relief you beg for."

"Words. All you have ever given me are words," Fensid said, returning to his own seat.

"Be thankful for that," Ahmahl thought.

The room grew silent as the huge Assembly chamber doors swung open and the sentinels turned in salute.

"The Empire's Minister of War, General Gerah Maugaine!"

The traditional announcement rang through the chambers. Ahmahl refused to acknowledge his entrance. Gerah glanced around the table, searching the eyes of each Assembly member. Except for affable nods from the Ministers of Agriculture and Security, each man seemed to be searching the ancient ceiling tiles for new patterns.

The chamber buzzed with the Assemblymen's murmurs until the doors to the Royal Entryway swung open. The Assembly rose to its feet as the sentinels snapped to attention. The lead sentinel stepped forward, holding the banner of the House of Arter.

"The Witness Imperium, Ruler of the tribes and peoples of Arterra, Eythan Mashal!"

Eythan dismissed the sentinel with a nod and after he took his seat, the Assembly seated themselves. The Minister of Records remained standing and cleared his voice in a superficial manner.

"My Witness, this session is in order. Let each member give a quick and full account of his office to the throne of Arter."

As quickly as the Minster of Records sat down, Eythan stood.

"Ministers, due to the extreme nature of this meeting, I will only be hearing reports from the Ministers of Religion and War. General Maugaine..."

Even at a casual glance, Gerah Maugaine stood out from the other Assemblymen. Though he wore the proper tunic and mantle, his helmet and armor were clearly out of place. As Eythan sat, Gerah stood. Ahmahl quietly coughed, but Gerah ignored the obvious insult.

"My Witness, your Minister of War is pleased to inform you that the invading armies are being routed from the city. The rebels captured the armories at Mibtsar and Owtsar and it is with these new weapons they were able to launch their latest offensive. The first brigade has secured the palace grounds and is working their way toward the outer gates of the city. The air fleet has already secured the second and third perimeters, but with the populace in the streets, they are unable to launch an assault on forces within the city proper."

"General, move them out of the city as quickly as possible," Eythan said. "I'm not worried about their escape routes."

"If they attack the temple..." Gerah warned.

"The throne recognizes your Call and your right to defend the temple, but my primary concern is the citizenry."

"Of course, my Witness. God save Arterra," Gerah said and sat.

Eythan turned to his immediate right.

"Minister Ahmahl?"

With a grandiose movement, Ahmahl slid to his feet. Of all

offices, his was the most important and he knew it. He made a dramatic pause as he opened the thick book before him. He smiled as his finger slid across a certain page and he looked up to face Eythan.

"My Witness, I bring to the remembrance of the Throne the words of the Prophet Massalum, who foretold the falling of the outer gates of Arterra seventeen hundred years ago."

"I am remotely familiar with the passage. Please, read for us," Eythan instructed.

Ahmahl's voice grew quiet and controlled.

" '*Shall the gates of Arterra fall? Never, they say! But pride is not sufficient guard and the gates and peace of Arterra shall fall in the same hour. Ancient evil scatters the ones through one. The people cry, 'where is the Witness?' One dead, one soon dead, one lost. A quick return will not warrant a return to glory but signals the end. Hearken, poor, poor Arterra! Twelve days you will not see!'* " Ahmahl paused and closed the tome.

"The Quorum met this afternoon concerning these very events."

Eythan cocked his head in irritation.

"I wasn't informed of the Quorum's session," he said.

"It was an emergency session," Ahmahl explained.

Frustrated, Eythan leaned back into his seat. An organization of sixty priests whose original responsibility was to advise the throne on spiritual matters, the Quorum had instead majored in bureaucracy since its inception twelve hundred years earlier.

"The Quorum's interpretation?" Eythan asked.

"The Quorum agrees that the destruction of the outer gates of Arter signals a coming crisis to the empire and requests the throne take precautions against ignorant attitudes such as those voiced by the Minister of War. The scriptures plainly indicate that this is a time of trouble. The Quorum has issued an exclusion to allow the direct intervention of the Witness himself."

Eythan sat up. In his lifetime, he had never known the Quorum to issue an Exclusion.

"Then they interpret this as a Sign?"

"A Sign important enough to directly involve your throne, my Witness. God save Arterra."

Ahmahl seated himself slowly, watching the response. The ministers murmured amongst themselves. It had been generations since the Witness directly intervened in military affairs of state. Fensid scowled at Ahmahl, questioning the action. Gerah sat up in his seat, glaring at Ahmahl. Eythan turned toward Gerah.

"General Maugaine, you have something to add?"

Gerah was seething, but held his anger in check as he stood.

"My Witness, I believe the walls were destroyed for just this type of propaganda effect. I also remind the throne that Minister Ahmahl has in the past questioned whether the Prophet Massalum belongs in the Scriptural Compilation, which calls into question why he now suddenly believes this one prophecy."

Ahmahl bolted to his feet. "My Witness, this man isn't qualified to instruct the throne on spiritual matters!"

"Minister, you are out of order!" Eythan barked at Ahmahl, smacking the table with the flat of his hand. Sentinels stepped toward Ahmahl, holding their firearms strongly in front of them. Ahmahl slapped his robes as he returned to his seat. Eythan nodded and the sentinels returned to their posts.

"General, proceed."

"Grayden is headed to Ventura in search of the prisM."

The murmur of the Assembly made Ahmahl squirm. Gerah let his words simmer, staring a hole in Ahmahl, who was looking everywhere but at Gerah.

"God save Arterra," Gerah said and sat, continuing his glare.

"Minister Ahmahl?" Eythan called.

Ahmahl stood without glancing in Gerah's direction. His face was red with embarrassment and anger.

"My liege, the General's suggestion is...it is preposterous! He is ignorant of the situation, which is nothing to be ashamed of. I merely ask the same question as the scriptures: 'Will the Witness abandon his people?' "

Ahmahl knew he had hit a nerve. Eythan criticized himself for years for fleeing the palace to amass an army against his father. Thousands of lives were lost due to his lack of courage at that young age. Eythan leaned back in his seat, hands folded in front of his face and after a moment, a nod signaled that a decision had been made.

"Council, I'm not as familiar of these scriptures as Minister Ahmahl, and these specific scriptures puzzle me. I have not felt The Call as to what direction I should go, so I have reached a compromise; I will institute an evacuation plan. The royal family, to the third rank, will be evacuated to pre-designated off-world sites. However, since the scriptures seem to say that tragedy will follow the leaving of the Witness, I will stay until these events have run their course."

"Compromise is just another word for self-betrayal," General

Maugaine thought, lowering his head. Eythan noticed the look.

"I'm sorry, general. Minister Bachan?"

The Minister of Records stood at attention.

"My Witness?"

"You will initiate the evacuation. Stand by after the meeting for specifics." Eythan noticed Ahmahl vying for his attention.

"Minister Ahmahl?"

"My liege, one small note. Since you've been cleared to take over wartime operations, would that not conclude the temporary commission of the Minister of War?"

Fensid sat up, the smile on his face registering the fact that he finally understood what Ahmahl had planned. Noticing the favorable response, Ahmahl continued.

"General Maugaine speaks the truth. It is his sworn duty to protect the royal line, and for that reason, shouldn't the General escort the royal family for protection? If the Witness is to defend the empire once more, the home front is safe, but I fear for the perils that the royal family might encounter in their travels. God save Arterra."

Eythan's eyebrows lowered in anger.

"Perhaps the Minister is placing his personal animosity toward the Minister of War into his suggestion? But you are correct; the General's commission is hereby concluded. Does anyone else have anything?"

Fensid leaned back in his seat and gleefully crossed his arms across his stomach. The Minister of Security raised a hand.

"General Frannel?"

Khayle Frannel, a large muscular man who had seen more time in his highly decorated military uniform than out, stood.

"My Witness, fellow Assemblymen," he said, looking at each member. "I joined this Assembly as a young man full of energy and drive. Policing the land is not an easy task, but it is fulfilling seeing to the safety of Arterra. Today it is my sad duty to notify the throne of my intention to retire at the conclusion of Festivals in three months."

Ahmahl stifled a smile, trying to look as if he were going to miss the old nuisance. It would be an easy matter of intimidating the new man in the post, especially if it were his effetely delicate son Ramon. With both Frannel and Maugaine out of the way, their illegal operations could run unhindered. Ahmahl ignored Fensid's too-jubilant smile. The fool never could hide his emotions.

"As is custom, my last official act as Minister of Security will be to suggest a replacement. As many of you have known, I had considered suggesting my son Ramon to succeed me, but today's events have led me to a different conclusion. With his permission, I would like to nominate General Maugaine to the office of Minister of Security."

Fensid's smile vanished; even Ahmahl was caught off guard.

"An excellent choice, General Frannel," Eythan said, turning to look at Gerah. "General Maugaine?"

Gerah looked directly at Ahmahl. "I accept the nomination."

"So be it. I approve the nomination. Assemblymen?"

"Your suggestion is our desire," Ahmahl numbly replied.

"Let us tally the votes. Those who favor General Maugaine's appointment to the Ministry of Security?"

Eleven hands never took so long extending.

"It is unanimous. Welcome to the Assembly, Gerah. Minister

Bachan, inform the people of Minister Maugaine's appointment and tell them that the Witness will directly take over the defense of the empire this evening. No mention will be made of the evacuation plan. Assembly, you each have preparations to make."

The Assemblymen stood as Eythan escorted General Frannel out the chamber. When the doors closed behind them, all eyes turned toward Gerah and Ahmahl; some in curiosity, some in fear. Gerah walked toward Ahmahl, studying him.

"Priest, the scent of wizard's magic is strong about you."

"If you have any accusations, General, use the proper channels. But you really should run along. Don't you have things to do?"

Gerah leaned toward Ahmahl and the Minister of Justice nervously jumped between the two.

"General! If you have a grievance, you may file it with me!"

Gerah saw the Minister of Records quickly inputting data on his recording pad.

"Make sure you record this correctly," Gerah said. "A wizard can't be convicted without evidence."

The tension level dropped immediately as General Maugaine exited the chamber and even Ahmahl began to breathe normally. Fensid walked toward Ahmahl and shoved him backward into the wall. Ahmahl fell to the floor as two other Assembly members grabbed Fensid, holding him back.

"You idiot! Now he has a permanent seat!" Fensid roared, no longer worried who heard him. "And what seat? Head of all policing agencies in the empire!"

Ahmahl returned to his feet, twisting his back for relief.

"You are wrong. He has merely been *appointed* to the office. My office can overrule any trouble he can produce."

"No more words! My House stands against you!"

"Then your House falls this very day."

Fensid swung at Ahmahl, but the Minister of Justice grabbed his arm. "Fen! What are you doing?"

Fensid ignored him.

"As my mother birthed me, you won't live to see tomorrow!"

Ahmahl motioned toward his assistant and they exited the chamber. Ahmahl's assistant, stared numbly at the tapestries on the walls of the hallway as they entered Ahmahl's chambers.

"He has no one idea what he just threw away," Ahmahl said, opening the secured doors to his own chambers and shoving the assistant into the prayer rooms.

"Now, we can speak freely. You must first notify the Quorum of Fensid's withdrawal from protection. Hmmm. You'll need to supervise the fortification of my personal quarters."

"Master, your own resources are dwindled from Maugaine's raids. Fensid's House is a powerful enemy."

"What do you think you know of such things? The ways of the world are not based on weapons, but of the spirit, and despite his public proclamations, Fensid is a spiritual barbarian."

"What shall we do? His House will no doubt be readying their attacks within hours."

"Forget him, summon your guidE; I need to send a message to Grayden."

"Maugaine's not even a league away! He'll detect me!"

Ahmahl covered his assistant's mouth with his hand.

"No, he won't. He's still upset from the Assembly meeting

and I must speak with Grayden before he enters the vortex."

"*Besides,*" Ahmahl thought, "*your life is in danger, not mine.*"

The assistant sat with his legs crossed and began to chant. Ahmahl dared not use spells himself, because Maugaine could detect magical activity like a magnet detected iron ore. Ahmahl would have to be more careful in the future because Maugaine could obviously detect even minor magical traces.

How spiritually sensitive was he?

"Minister," the assistant said, looking up from the dancing flames, "It is too late. They have entered the Vortex."

The first kick of her second baby was celebrated by the entire world. The doctors had identified the baby as a healthy male.

'Healthy' satisfied Peri's motherly concerns, but 'male' satisfied her political ambitions. The first male heir in a common home meant the next patriarch of the family. The first male heir to a Witness Imperium meant the next Witness Imperium and the Queen to bear that child became the First Queen, ruler of the White Throne.

Peri was Eythan's third wife as well as his youngest. Her father had approached the representative to the throne the very day she reached the age of consent. While he was not an intelligent man, Peri's father knew two things: Peri's beauty was rare and his family had no land to call their own. Peri had taken Eythan's attention on the first day of processions. Though she was dressed in the finest apparel her father could afford, she appeared ragged next to the gold and silver adorned courtesans from the east.

None of that mattered once the women were introduced. Peri entered the throne room quietly, but once Eythan asked for her attendance, the other girls were asked to leave.

Upon receipt of Peri's hand, Eythan granted her father a large parcel of land on the populated west coast of Lieber as dowry, though if pressed, he would have granted ten times as much.

Her family left immediately after the processions. Only her mother waved goodbye, but even she had a large smile.

That was the last time Peri saw her family. She was left alone in a building that was larger than the village she came from with a man whom she had only read about.

At first the marriage was a matter of duty, but Peri began to see the man behind the crown. He was strong - frightfully so - but when he touched her, it could have been a flower petal. His words were soft and his affection pure and though she couldn't believe it, Peri fell in love with Eythan Mashal.

That was eleven years ago, and though Witnesses traditionally marry continually throughout their reign, Eythan never married again. To her knowledge, she was the only one of Eythan's wives he genuinely loved.

Perhaps her earlier lack of political ambition was because when she married Eythan, Grayden's mother sat on the White Throne, so she had never considered such a thing possible for her. But everything had changed when it was thought Grayden had been sacrificed. Upon hearing the news, his mother jumped from the high tower. While Eythan grieved, the vacuum of power started a race between Peri and Nakah, the senior Queen.

Each of the women became pregnant the next year, but when it was confirmed that Peri was bearing a son, everything changed. While she could not claim the White Throne before birthing her son, her daily status took on the air of the First Queen and Nakah found herself reluctantly yielding.

Peri's dreams then changed from the childish notions of love to the aspiration of political power. The First Queen was, without question, the most powerful woman on Arterra.

And now, eight years later, Shiloh stood before her as the culmination of those dreams. Shiloh's security retinue had left him and his personal handmaidens in the care of his mother while they stood outside the chamber. Peri's handmaidens surrounded him with brushes and combs. Shiloh seemed slightly embarrassed as they removed his cap. His hair fell to his waist and the handmaidens began combing it.

"What beautiful bronze hair," one of the girls teased.

"It's like a lion's mane!" another giggled.

"Ladies!" Peri said, shushing them behind a thinly concealed smile. "You're speaking of the future Witness Imperium!"

The girls giggled, continuing to comb his hair. It was apparent to Peri that a few of them were already taken with Shiloh. She would have to watch them in the years to come. The close bond of a handmaiden was a powerful temptation for a young man and Witnesses were no exception. With youth came temptation and a lack of good sense.

"I wish I didn't have long hair. The other boys don't," Shiloh said, his head being yanked in different directions as each of the combs pulled at him.

"Your hair is a link to the Promise," Peri said, separating Shiloh's long hair into seven locks. The three on each side were handed to the handmaidens sitting around him. The strand from the top flopped over his face. Peri bound it with a string and threw it back over his head. Shiloh sat quietly as the women each took one of the remaining locks of hair and began to brush it smoothly. Peri sat in front of him, separating the section of hair she had into six equal parts.

The handmaidens had already began to braid his hair, starting from the roots, in an intricately tight pattern of six strands; in, out and through, around twice and back through, then reversed.

The process was delicate and tedious, but resulted in a finely detailed braid.

"Father Arter had seven braids; the three on his left represented his past, the three on his right represented his future and the one in the middle represented his promise to the Creator."

"What does that mean?" Shiloh asked.

"After his hair grew back, he dedicated the center braid to the Creator. The center braid was always a special braid for him and he had several special weaves he used. He covered it as penance for revealing his sacrifice. Every month, before the High Service, your hair will be braided anew. Are you watching? You're going to have to practice this when we're done."

"Me?"

"The six braids on the sides of your head will be braided by others, but you will braid the center braid yourself. The center braid of a Witness is personal; each one is unique. It represents your dedication to the Creator. That's why it is always covered."

"If I cut my hair will I lose my power?" Shiloh asked.

"No, your long hair is only symbolic. Your sacrifice will be something different."

"Like what?"

"Well, some Witnesses chose never to wear colored clothing or jewelry...or touch a dead body."

"What will my sacrifice be?" Shiloh asked.

"That will be your decision and you are never to tell anyone what it is. But you don't have to worry about that now. During the Regency ceremonies, the High Priest will offer you the ring of Regency and ask you to present your sacrifice to the Creator."

"What if I break my sacrifice?"

The question hung in the air so thickly that no one wanted to touch it.

"You can't allow that to happen," Peri curtly replied.

Shiloh noted by the reaction that the question wasn't to be asked again. The jovial mood that had earlier permeated the chamber had been instantly extinguished. The handmaidens quietly continued braiding his hair.

"I'm sorry, mother," Shiloh said.

Peri leaned down to Shiloh and cupped his face. Shiloh had never seen her more serious; she looked like she was about to cry.

"You will learn that *nothing* is more important than your sacrifice. It is the Bond between a Witness and the Creator. We will not speak of this again. Now pay attention; you'll be weaving the seventh braid."

Shiloh had been watching, but hadn't been interested enough to really pay attention. He could see in the mirror that the braids were tightly woven from the front of his head to the back like his father, and in that one small moment, he saw a little bit of Eythan in himself.

By the time the braids were finished, Shiloh's scalp hurt.

Peri handed him an oblong blue cap with ornate white stitches, designed for covering his center braid.

"You'll get used to it," she said, stretching it over his head.

Shiloh kissed Peri on the cheek. His two handmaidens escorted Shiloh to his chambers where they would teach him to braid using their hair. Not ten feet down the hallway, they were already giggling with Shiloh. His guards followed a respectful distance behind. Peri watched the girls until they disappeared around the corner.

Eythan stood silently in his chambers, staring out the western window at the stone walls that had ceremonially protected the city for the past two thousand years. The rebels had breached them in four places. Smoke still wafted over two sections. A chime from the entranceway of his chambers announced a visitor, interrupting his ruminations.

"Enter," Eythan said and the doors slid open.

Gerah Maugaine entered slowly. The only other time he had been called to Eythan's private chambers was after Eythan's first wife – Grayden's mother - had killed herself. Eythan continued staring out the window, his arms crossed behind him. Gerah could feel the melancholy from the door.

"We've made a difference, Gerah. Haven't we?" he asked, more to himself than this man who had become his best friend.

"You serve your people well," Gerah replied.

Eythan removed himself from the window and attempted a smile.

"How's your Mattis unit performing?" he asked, referring to the two rectangular boxes mounted at Gerah's waist. "Uh, Gentry?"

"Yes, Gentry. It is amazing, although I had to adjust it to shut down unnecessary chatter."

"You'll need to calibrate it with Healey, the unit on Peri's ship before launch. The three units will be coordinating routing and security. I've put off General Frannel's retirement for the duration of this evacuation, but you will retain his Assembly seat. After you secure Shiloh, General Frannel will rendezvous with a few agents that I have sent into deep space."

"Agents?" Gerah looked puzzled. Off world travel had been achieved centuries ago, but was rare except as vacational oddities.

"Oh...right. You never met him."

"Who?"

"My elder brother Mossad. If he hadn't been banished, this would be his throne. I can't find him anywhere planet side and none of the extraterrestrial bases have recorded his presence, either."

"So you assume that he exiled himself into deep space?"

"It wouldn't be the first time someone had taken to the stars for isolation. While you're out there, I'd consider it a... personal favor if you would keep an eye out for him."

Eythan uncustomarily looked toward the floor.

"I thought he was a coward," Eythan admitted. "I couldn't understand how he could make a public stand against my father's crimes, and then quietly leave without a fight. But I quickly understood once I was in his place. A direct confrontation would have only resulted in his death. Gerah, I know Mossad's out there somewhere. I want to find out where he is, and tell him it's alright to return. This throne is rightfully his."

"Mossad relinquished any claim to the throne long before you claimed the mantle."

"Maybe he doesn't feel that way. I only became regent because of his stand, but I couldn't make the stand he did. I gathered an army."

"A foolish thing to do," Gerah said.

"I didn't know what else to do."

"It was in The Will that I stopped Rawshah, just as I should be here protecting you now."

"I understand how you feel. I've heard disturbing reports about Ahmahl. Not enough to bring him to trial, but enough to be suspicious."

Eythan stared into space as melancholy played with the time it was given. His attention slowly returned to Gerah.

"The Witness has been called to defend the empire once again. It shall be done."

It was an awkward moment frozen in time. Gerah quietly studied the Witness as Eythan's shoulders bowed to a stress that would never yield under mere physical weight. Gerah stepped forward and placed a hand on his shoulder.

"Above all on this world, you have received me as a friend. My alien ways and mannerisms could not exist in this society without your support. I was commanded to watch the line of the golden throne by the Angel of Death and I gladly serve you as a friend... and as a brother."

Eythan straightened his back and placed his hand on Gerah's arm. He looked directly into Gerah's eyes.

"I have never known a more trustworthy man than you. Even when we've disagreed, never for a moment have I thought that you had anything other than the best interests of this empire in mind. Surely there's a greater Call than that of a global caretaker. May that Call be yours."

"While I await The Call, I serve with honor and with pride. Stay well, Eythan Mashal; may the Creator light your path."

"And He yours, Gerah."

Gerah left to finish last minute preparations for evacuation. The Angel of Death had told him that his place was with the throne; his last breath would be spent defending the rightful heir to the throne.

And so it would be.

Eythan strode with hurried purpose to his ready room. Placing his command helmet on, he was instantly tied in to every audio, video and data broadcast on the planet. Only extraterrestrial and undersea computers were out of his immediate range of influence. The initial sensory input was confusing, but Eythan quickly sifted through the unnecessary information and tied himself into the main computer frame. This was the place he directed the war, yet the sounds of battle could not muffle the sound of the door behind him. Peri walked to his side and stood in somber silence. Eythan turned and mentally wiped away the information from his visor so he could look at her. Their marriage was a rarity for Witnesses, based on love, not lust or political arrangement.

Before he met Peri, Eythan already had two wives and he was expected to have many more, all of noble blood and proper birth, but his heart remained empty and longing for something that could not be provided by the title 'queen'. The call for Procession was rarely granted outside Throne City, yet Eythan not only called for it to be sent to the outer regions, he personally had a hand in the final invitations.

Peri hadn't realized it at the time, but Eythan had met her when she and the others had first arrived on the palace grounds. The man whom she and the other girls had imagined to be the grounds keeper was, in fact, Eythan in disguise. He followed them during the next two weeks of preparation in several disguises and had come to know each girl before they entered the throne room. He saw the rages of jealousy, the petty bickering and the infighting. And each time he had returned his attention to the one who held herself above it all. He had grown to love the quiet purity that Peri exuded.

She was chosen as his next queen before the procession entered the throne room. Peri was everything he had been missing and Eythan had tried to give her all she had been missing. It pained him to now take something away from her. He prayed that she would understand.

"I have received news of an evacuation?" she whispered.

"It is true."

Peri visibly winced.

"What has Grayden done that requires us to leave?"

"The Quorum has granted an exception. I'll be intervening in the hostilities. While I shut down Grayden's army, I don't want to risk your safety if he decides to attack the palace."

Eythan could not explain the apprehension he was feeling; a buzz just under the surface of his consciousness.

"You need to prepare the children," he merely said.

"Your order states that the children are to be separated."

"For security reasons."

"Is Shiloh to be without defense?" Peri sharply asked.

"General Maugaine is supervising his safety. Think of it as a holiday; you've always wanted to travel past the moons."

"Then grant him the mantle of regent."

"Peri, the mantle can't manifest until he's fifteen."

"It is written that the Witness Rigeth was given the ceremony years before he manifest the Regency. I beg you to grant him the Regency."

A chill shook Eythan's bones as his brain registered Peri's words one by one. Her request made no sense. They would only be gone a short time, and yet echoing her words was a fluid sense of deja vu; a comforting knowledge which established her words as Truth, already written somewhere as history.

It was The Call, confirming her words with its soothing reassurance. And with the revelation, Eythan also learned that he would not stop with giving Shiloh the Regency. He would also perform the ceremony of Witness Imperium.

"Bring Shiloh to the court this afternoon. It shall be done," was all Eythan could say.

Though victorious in her appeal, Peri said nothing as she suppressed her tears and left to prepare her children for the trip.

Though the sun was still in the sky, the clouds and debris from the storm drowned the sky in its twilight depths. Grayden glanced around at the dusky gray temples surrounding him. None of the buildings in the area were more than two or three stories tall, and each had window frames that had long ago surrendered even a pretension of holding glass. The few trees still living in the area were short and thick, with few leaves. The cold, howling wind blew waves of sand into his eyes, nose and mouth.

Glancing at his chronometer, Grayden calculated that he had less than twenty minutes remaining before the medallion's spell reverted. His protective suit's energies were depleted, making it merely another burden to carry in the dark wastelands.

Tearing at the snaps, Grayden removed the useless suit and leaned into the wind toward the next temple. Five temples had already been searched in this sector and they were empty, their contents ransacked by looters long before the vortex started. The small talismans outside the various temples were continually draining his life force, but he lurched forward.

Moving behind a building to get out of the wind, Grayden saw something move from the corner of his eye. He turned, but saw nothing.

"*Here*," a voice whispered, close to his head. Grayden swung quickly on the balls of his feet toward the direction of the voice, but again saw nothing. He was tiring; probably beginning to hallucinate. The sobering thought that he might just die here slapped him instantly awake.

Laughter.

To the right.

"I won't be toyed with!" Grayden yelled. "Come face a son of Arter!"

"*A shameful son,*" another voice taunted. How was he hearing whispers in this wind?

"Who are you?" Grayden asked, turning his head to see any indication of movement.

A minute of silence followed, and as he stood still, another wave of sleep washed over him. Shaking his head, he arched his back straight and grabbed a deep breath. Cursing his situation, Grayden opened the medallion and held it close to his eyes. The map inside clearly indicated that he should west on the other side of the ruins, yet he was waging his life on a theory. Malthus said that the medallion was linked to the prisM, but if there were such a link, Grayden hadn't noticed it.

A strong gust of wind and sand blew the medallion from his hand and Grayden cursed as he tried to follow the hand sized piece of jewelry but it was quickly lost in the flow of dust. Anger overcoming reason, Grayden picked up a piece of column and threw it with all his strength. It fell eighty feet away, in front of a temple that he hadn't seen before. Slightly behind two smaller buildings, it stood in ghastly contrast to the other buildings. As was the manner of Darton's ancient temples, one window stood open in front. This one, though, had something in the window.

Or was it someone?

Grayden lowered his head and ran. The regent power of Speed kicked in with his first few steps and he began to cover the ground to the temple at an incredible rate. But before he could reach the doorway, The Speed disappeared, and he tumbled face-first into the temple's stone steps. When he stood, he saw spots of blood amidst the rubble where the steps had been. Grayden reached to the side of his head where a throbbing pain originated and came back with more blood on his fingers. He yelled at Malthus, raising his face toward the bitter sky.

"Why did you bring me here?"

The powerful forces that had built inside Ventura over the past two thousand years were such that even with Malthus' protective spell, his life force was still being drained by the idols. His lips ached with numbness; not from cold but from the slowing down of his blood. Grayden had to shake his arms to keep the feeling in his fingers. If he had not retained some of the powers of the Witness Regent, he would have been dead hours ago.

This temple, like the four before it, had a carved symbol of the prisM over the entranceway, but that meant little now. The next temple was merely a dot on the horizon. The door was jammed shut, but as Grayden pushed it with his shoulder, a spark of his Regency strength flared and the entire framing collapsed inward. Grayden fell to the floor and looked around at the idols that the pagans set up and felt a cold numbness splash into his body.

"*Weak*," a voice said, no longer whispering.

Grayden felt hands reaching for his shoulders but stood to his feet defiantly. He looked around but saw no one. Too weak to fight, he fell to the floor to escape the hands. As much as it angered him, he would have to flee the temple. But as he hit the floor, he noticed a blue spark briefly illuminate the next chamber. The doorway was close enough that he could escape the temple and signal retreat, or he could go forward. Retreat would mean the end of his quest with no hope of return. Going forward could mean death.

Cursing Malthus, Grayden turned inward.

He had just one chance and he was going to take it. Hope reinvigorated his limbs as his desperate fingers clawed at the aged wooden floor, dragging him over his own spittle. Pain shot like dull needles through his leaden arms and his shoulders ached with each movement. Grayden inched forward, slowly losing control of his legs.

As he pulled his body through the side doorway, he saw a pedestal similar to the one in the palace that housed the medallion. Maybe it showed where the prisM was located. Grayden ignored the fingers that still noosed around his throat, trying to pull him down. He now used his anger as strength and moved closer to the pedestal, but before he could reach it, the dull glow of Malthus' protective spell evaporated away.

He had taken too long.

The spell dissipated with a sharp implosion of air and Grayden screamed as a vacuum of energy enveloped him. Thousands of hands now pulled at him and he surrendered to their grasp.

In the shuttle, Malthus attempted to weave further protective spells around himself, abandoning his defense of the shuttle. The walls of the craft, no longer under his protection, surrendered to the mystical energies that now sifted through them. The warlords fell to the floor, their dried husks giving up life as they dried and cracked, shattering into dust. Malthus, through his rapidly fading defenses, prepared his own body for death. The risk had been great, and they had lost.

The shrouded sun reflected off each of the palace's six towers. From a distance, there was no evidence of the previous days' battles. The inside ruling chambers had been cleared and the entire western wing was deserted. It was only in the eastern wing that any sign of life appeared, where everyone was busy initiating the royal evacuation plan.

Completely out of place was the discussion taking place in the Court of Reconciliation. Ahmahl had been taken from his duties to perform the ascension ceremony not only of Witness Regent, but also Witness Imperium. Mindful of Malthus' wrath, he walked straight to the Witness. Eythan motioned for him to approach.

"My Witness, this has never been done before!" Ahmahl lied.

"It shall be done," Eythan asserted.

Ahmahl took a nervous, but defiant stance.

"As Minister of Religion, I don't think you have the scriptural authority for this procedure!"

The tone of Ahmahl's voice slapped Eythan across the face and the temper he inherited from his father flashed to the surface. The air parted before him as he rose from the throne. He stepped into Ahmahl's face so quickly that the air crackled as it filled the void behind him, shaking the throne room like a thunderstorm.

The Minister of Religion didn't even have time to gasp.

Eythan was too angry to be surprised that he had accidentally triggered the Witness power of Speed. He leaned into Ahmahl's face to better his point.

"Minister, you'll perform both ceremonies, one after the other!"

Ahmahl quickly backed down.

"Sire, I....what I only meant to say was that even if I perform both ceremonies at this time, Master Shiloh is not old enough for the Regency, not to mention that your own power level will be reduced to that of Witness Regent and you have a war to fight! Arterra will not have a true Witness Imperium until the prince reaches adulthood. If there was ever a need for the power of the Witness Imperium it is with you and it is now."

Eythan stepped down to his heels and took a deep breath.

"Minister, proceed with both ceremonies."

"But...the Quorum needs to be consulted. If you would just give me time to consult with Assemblyman Bachan, we could..."

Eythan grabbed Ahmahl by the jaw. Ahmahl's eyes instantly watered as a grip like a steel brace held his jaw immobile. He had always been terrified by the legal power that gave the Witness Imperium power of life or death over his subjects, but that fear was nothing when compared to the terror of actually being in the physical grip of the Witness Imperium.

"If you speak another word to me before the ceremonies, I shall throw you into Peysha Island myself. Bring the first volume of the Histories. We'll use the original ceremonies that Arter did in transferring the Mantle to his firstborn, Gentry."

Fifteen minutes later, the trio took their respective places. Under normal circumstances, hundreds of thousands of people would be present to witness the ceremony and billions would remotely watch the event. This day, counting the accompanying ministers, there were forty people present.

The hectic events occurring all around him intimidated Shiloh. He had already begun training for the Regency ceremony, but he was still nervous.

Eythan saw it differently; it was to him hope in every definition of the word and a confirmation from the Creator that the Blessing of Arter had survived to another generation.

The small audience stood as Ahmahl led Shiloh past them to the platform. Shiloh tried to ignore the people staring at him by counting the steps as he climbed them. At the thirty-second step, he reached the top. Eythan and his mother were standing in front of their thrones. Shiloh looked around, but his nanny was nowhere to be seen.

"Ahem," Ahmahl coughed. Shiloh turned his attention back to Ahmahl who was now standing in front of Shiloh's throne.

"The sons of Arter welcome the twelve houses of Jusinan to witness the Promise of the Creator realized to another generation. May the blessings of the House of Arter follow this one. May the wisdom of Rigeth lead his path. May..."

Eythan interrupted with a cough and Ahmahl turned to look. Eythan lowered his head and raised an eyebrow.

"Um, yes," Ahmahl stammered, flipping to the next page.

"Now let each house witness as the ring of regency is granted to Shiloh Mashal, proving to all his future claim to the throne of his father Eythan and our father Arter."

Ahmahl took Shiloh's right hand and tried to slip the adult-sized ring onto his middle finger, but the ring was too large and it slipped off, clinking loudly on the polished marble floor. Ahmahl placed it on again and cupped Shiloh's hand, making it into a fist. The ring hung loosely from his finger, but stayed on. Shiloh stared at it. The ring was silver embedded with a large blue gem. Twelve small glyphs bordered the edge of the ring. The symbol at the top brought a smile to his face. A bold line separating two circles, it was the symbol of the House of Arter.

"Shiloh?" his father asked. Shiloh looked up. Everyone was staring at him.

Shiloh looked back to his father, who was holding the mantle before him. Handing it to Ahmahl, Eythan turned his back to Shiloh and walked to the court entrance. Ahmahl motioned for Shiloh to approach the Golden Throne. Shiloh had played with strips of cloth many times, pretending it was the mantle of Arter, but the actual mantle was now being draped over his chest.

To conclude the condensed ceremony, Ahmahl led Shiloh to the Witness' personal altar to make his sacrifice to the Creator.

"Come, Prince," Ahmahl said, motioning to the stone altar.

"I've got my sacrifice ready, minister. Mother made me think about it all afternoon."

Ahmahl turned around to see the deep stare that Peri gave him and bit his lip.

He hadn't counted on the prince understanding the sacrifice of the Witness or treating it seriously.

"Why, yes, normally at this time we bring our sacrifice to the Creator, but since we are, uh, handling both ceremonies at once, we have to do things a little differently. Don't worry; just do as I tell you."

They arrived at the altar. Ahmahl glanced back toward the

small crowd. Eythan had turned his back, as was tradition, in order to keep the Witness Imperium from being tempted to use his targeted hearing to listen in on his son's sacrifice. Peri stared, but could not tell what was happening from so far away. For the moment, Ahmahl was safe to play his deceitful hand. The pair fell to their knees before the altar.

"This day, we ask the Creator for the blessing of our empire; to beg wisdom and guidance from Him," Ahmahl began.

"When do I get to tell my sacrifice to God?" Shiloh whispered.

"Later."

"What do I say?"

"Just pray as you normally would," Ahmahl started.

Shiloh hesitated for a moment and then asked for wisdom and guidance in his life. It was much more mature than Ahmahl had expected. As they lifted themselves from the altar, Ahmahl leaned over to Shiloh.

"Remember, this part of the ceremony is between the Creator and yourself," he whispered. "You may tell no one what we have discussed in the ceremony."

"I know," Shiloh replied with a proud smile to be trusted with such a big secret. "When do I give my sacrifice?"

Ahmahl smiled.

"You already did," he said, confusion dripping from his voice.

Shiloh looked directly into Ahmahl's eyes, his face asking a dozen questions.

"It's been a long day, my regent. It will all make sense later."

Ahmahl motioned and Eythan returned, removing the tokens from his robe to place on Shiloh's. Eythan stepped back to bow before the new Witness Regent. Ahmahl and the surrounding priests bowed behind Eythan. Ahmahl forced a worried smile.

"Of course, while Shiloh has ceremonially been proclaimed Witness Imperium, he shall not manifest as such until the title is passed to him through abdication or death," Ahmahl said.

"I don't understand," Shiloh said. "You are the Imperium."

"I still hold the title, yes," Eythan explained. "But these ceremonies insure that you will rule after me."

Eythan turned to the people gathered around him. The crowd was small, he thought, much like the first crowd Arter saw at his son's coronation.

"Give the proclamation to your tribes," Eythan said to the people surrounding him. "Arterra has a new Witness Regent, and named its next Imperium and his name is Shiloh Mashal!"

The crowd erupted into cheers. Shiloh shrunk from the noise. Ahmahl closed his eyes and hoped Malthus would understand. Peri approached and bowed before her son. Shiloh came to her, and offered his hand to her. She accepted it and Shiloh violated protocol to give her a hug. Peri grabbed him tightly, forcing tears back.

"Peri, the regent is within your care this afternoon," Eythan said. "I will be personally preparing your flights."

Peri said nothing as she led Shiloh from the chamber.

Gerah sat quietly in his quarters, alone with his thoughts. A row of meditation candles lit the room, casting shadows on the bare stone wall behind him. Converted from a storage area, his residence was located near the servants' quarters in the east wing. Gerah refused the comfort of royal chambers when he agreed to move into the palace, so a storage room was cordoned into four separate rooms, though Gerah only used two: the large living area for reading and prayer, and the sleep chamber for the few times he allowed himself to sleep. The lavatory and dining areas hadn't been used since he moved in. The servants had long ago stopped filling his cabinets.

A thin window pane provided his sole contact with the outside world. Surrounded by a large but plain frame, it provided a good view of the palace market. Gerah walked to the window to look below.

Men and women rushed on their normal routes to work and home, purposely ignoring the workers repairing the damage around them. The same people who fled with their families to hide in shelters, fervently praying for deliverance the night before, had seemingly forgotten the horrors of the battle. Did any of them truly understand how fragile this society was? Were they taking the moment for granted as they appeared to be - blind to the events unfolding around them - or did they simply choose not to see?

Gerah watched as a man bumped into a woman, knocking her

to the ground. The food in her bags tumbled with her. She looked around, but the man had already disappeared into the crowd. The woman raised to her knees and for just a moment, bent her head as if to cry. No one stopped to help. Even those who noticed her ignored her, unwilling to identify with her dilemma.

Gerah turned his attention to himself. He had seen her need, why hadn't he helped? The angel who gave him the Helmet hadn't said that he was only Called for great things. Maybe the distrust the people felt toward Gerah wasn't all Ahmahl's fault. Maybe Gerah had isolated himself from the people to the point they didn't trust him.

As he glanced back down, Gerah noticed the woman was gone. The few items of food still remaining on the ground were the only reminder of her presence, but even those were being kicked and stepped on without notice or care. They would be gone within minutes, and tomorrow, no evidence would exist that she had ever been there.

Would that be Gerah's legacy? When he was gone, would he have made a difference? Or would he be forgotten, swept away by an uncaring future? After all, how much could one man really do?

How much was one man *expected* to do?

Gentry interrupted his introspection. A display hovered before him, visible only to Gerah. It was a communique from Eythan to all involved with the evacuation. It simply read:

Loading will proceed thirty minutes prior to launch.

Without a need for food, water or creature comforts, the order meant little to Gerah. What could he bring? Gerah looked around the living area. The furniture, tapestries, even the plants belonged to Eythan. Then his eyes rested on a table near the divan. Gerah picked up a small pouch, tied by a simple piece of worn string and placed it inside his tunic.

A second communique came, ordering Gerah to report to General Frannel's ship prior to launch to calibrate his Mattis unit with Peri's. The manifest for the four ships was also displayed, listing Gerah as commander of the third ship, the only battle cruiser in the group. The manifest for his ship included Shiloh, some sentinels and the regent's personal handmaidens.

When he became regent, Shiloh had fallen under Gerah's direct protection. It was his mission; the very purpose for his existence. Gerah may not have been able to help Grayden, but he would not fail Shiloh.

Three hours remained before he would report to the dock. Gerah sat beside his bed on a mat, and lowered his head toward the temple in prayer.

The few hours that remained before launch passed quickly, and the families separated into their assigned ships. Gerah entered the docking bay and reported to the second ship. General Frannel greeted him at the hatch and escorted him inside.

"I never got a chance to congratulate you on your commission to the Assembly," he said. "Eythan could not have appointed a better man."

"Most of the Assembly would disagree with you," Gerah said, looking around the ship. "I was told to report to your Mattis unit for calibration."

"Second chamber to the left, behind the medical bay. Unit's name is Healey; it's embedded in the First Queen's staff. I need to personally assign each ship its orders. Will you hold command until I return?"

"I will," Gerah said, walking down the hallway.

Eythan had been surveying the scene from the control room when he saw someone exit one of the ships. He relaxed as he recognized General Frannel walking toward Shiloh's ship.

"Is everything okay, General?" he asked over the bay speakers.

"Assigning orders and making sure Ramon does you proud."

"This will be a good first mission for him."

"I appreciate you personally appointing him to the regent's ship, my Witness. It truly is an honor."

Eythan allowed himself a brief smile. Eythan had known the

General since he was a child. Sometimes, he allowed himself to think of the General as the father he should have had.

As General Frannel entered Shiloh's ship, Eythan returned his attention to the launch schedule. Several engineers surveyed each computer bank, making last minute alignments and calculations prior to launch. As Eythan surveyed the many monitors, one of the technicians stood out. He was standing alone near the lead cruiser and security protocols demanded that technicians work in pairs at all times.

"Commander," Eythan called to him through the bay speakers, "Where is your co-worker?"

The technician wheeled about and reached into his pocket.

"Remember Grayden!" he yelled.

The hackles rose on Eythan's neck and as he involuntarily held his breath, his senses instantly widened. In one frozen moment he noticed the small blood stains on the technician's arms and chest. More importantly, he saw the detonator in the man's right hand and recognized the situation. The bulge in the man's jacket only further confirmed an explosive.

"Control!" Eythan yelled, instantly gaining command over every space, sky and water vessel in the fleet.

"Shields!" He screamed, an impossibly long instant before the technician exploded inside the forming shields of the first ship. The blast was partially contained, but the crew working in the docking bay was instantly battered lifeless.

The first ship surrendered a large chunk of its hull as the force of the blast slammed it against the retaining wall. The gravimetric shielding of the other ships held.

"No!" Eythan screamed, smashing his fist into the stone wall beside him. Marbled shrapnel shot all around him. Eythan shook in fury; he was being thwarted at every turn. Eythan calmed his breathing and looked at the console through weary eyes. Using the command helmet was so much easier, but he had given it to General Frannel to coordinate the evacuation.

"Communications: flagships."

Four images opened in the command helmet visor. The first image only displayed static instead of a signal from the vessel that had contained Nakah and their three children. Peri's startled face searched the monitor for answers. Eythan noticed the control codes for opening the hatch of her vessel being entered.

"Gerah, stay inside!" he yelled, canceling Gerah's attempt to open the hatch.

"Eythan! What happened?" Peri asked.

"Everything's under control," Eythan said, turning his face to keep his anger in check.

"I need to return to the regent's ship!" Gerah said.

"No! Under no circumstances am I going to lower shields!"

Mattis signaled Eythan through the control panel.

"The bay gates were damaged in the explosion and will need to be opened manually," Mattis said.

"I'll open them," Gerah replied, desperately seeking any excuse to return to Shiloh's ship.

"No! I'll force them open," Eythan said.

Gerah started to protest, but Eythan cut off his signal and locked the ship's hatches. Gerah would have plenty of time to worry about seating arrangements once they were safely away.

Eythan walked to the front of the bay. The blast had warped the inner seals, jamming the bay doors into the wall. Eythan could feel everyone's eyes as he grabbed the gate; he could feel their doubt as he pushed. The metal gave, but not without tremendous effort. It had been so long since he had operated under the limits of the Witness Regent that he forgot to compensate. Eythan had to twist the gate off its hinges. The smell of burnt seals attacked his nostrils as the metal screamed in his ears. After it was bent back enough, he jerked on the gate. The hinges groaned, but held. Embarrassed, Eythan took a deep breath and yanked again. This time, the gate gave way.

"Control: Bay Two, Gates: Open", he commanded and the second gate slid open on its magnetic grooves. Eythan walked to the back of the burnt husk of the first ship and pushed. The torn ship dug grooves into the floor as it skidded out the bay doors. It hovered on the edge of the ledge for a moment and then fell to the small valley below the launch deck. Eythan pushed it out of the way, both physically and mentally. The longer he took, the more danger his remaining family was in.

Returning to the control room, Eythan glanced at the monitors of his family as they were strapped in, each trying to be strong in their own way.

"Mattis, begin launch sequence and give me a status report."

Mattis opened the channel from his vantage in the third ship.

"Launch will commence in two minutes. Manifests have been modified to accommodate Generals Frannel and Maugaine. The first ship has been destroyed; there are no survivors. There are no detected injuries and no damage to the remaining vessels."

Eythan watched as Shiloh stifled a tear. Seeing the impending countdown, he opened the comm link.

"Be brave, Shiloh. I will see you soon. Always remember

that you are a son of Arter and the Creator will protect you."

Eythan punched in final instructions to Mattis and tried to tell his son that he loved him, but the ignition of the three remaining cruisers' engines drowned him out.

"Creator, grant him strength," Eythan prayed silently, "watch over him as you have me."

And in that instant, a wave of grief engulfed him. As the three spacecraft escaped Arterra's atmosphere, Eythan started to weep, but now was not the time for tears.

It was time to go to work.

Nature raged throughout the northern plains of the continent, leaving the boundaries of the Ventura Ruins. Inside a lone temple, Grayden screamed. The pedestal that symbolized his only hope rested inches away. An arm, dead but for raw will power, reached only far enough to touch the pedestal. As his arm fell to his side, a splash of anger animated the arm and with it, the last splinter strength of the Witness Regent he possessed.

Grayden's attack ruptured the foundation of the building and the entire floor collapsed. Everything - Grayden, pedestal and flooring - fell to the compartment below. His eyes locked open in agony, despite the dust that exploded from below. His body involuntarily spasmed into a fetal position, surrendering to the numbing touch of death.

As the pedestal crashed to the bottom floor, it shattered, and a blinding blue light illuminated the chamber. The prisM bounced out of its resting place, and took an arcane twist, bouncing on a corner. The rattle of crystal on ancient cut stone reverberated throughout the chamber until it touched Grayden's cold fingers.

Then there was silence.

The funnel that had been bleeding the protective atmosphere dissipated, leaving a thundering roar and clouds of falling mist in its wake. The dancing colors disappeared, each swirling into the prisM and Grayden's mind was overwhelmed with the alien thoughts of long dead priests.

A surge of power enveloped him and Grayden screamed

again, but not out from pain; this was a scream of power! He tore off his mourner's robe and thrashed around in his newly found exuberance. His anger at the buildings around him built and a blue column of light spit from the prisM, collapsing several temples in the area. In his exuberance, Grayden failed to see the small piece of cloth he had treasured, left behind in his discarded robe, burning in the smoldering rubble of his wake.

Grayden looked hungrily at the glowing prisM in his hand, gleefully grinning at the damage he had caused the temple that nearly claimed his life.

Sensing from the stillness of the surrounding idols that their owners were no longer present to vent his vengeance upon, he called upon the power of the prisM and rose high into the air, defying Ventura and gravity itself. Grayden enjoyed flaunting his newly found power rather than his inherited power of the regency. He landed beside his battered ship, which was little more than a rusty casualty in nature's fierce battle.

Entering the ship, he found Malthus, lying still in the center of the ship. Light from the prisM led his attention to various piles of ash and bone meal, which explained the crew's fate. Malthus sat up, seeing the prisM in Grayden's hand.

"So it begins..." he whispered.

Malthus limped toward Grayden. "We must go quickly. My guides are incoherent from pain. We must take the temple first."

Grasping the prisM tightly in his hand, a blue beam spat out of the crystal and encased the ship, lifting it into the air. In minutes, Grayden carried it and himself thousands of miles to Throne City.

They landed just outside the Temple of Jusinan and a wave of blue energy crushed the army that pinned his men down. Grayden levitated to his men on the ground and ordered them to take the temple first. The priests never had weapons. The fools probably wouldn't even defend themselves.

Leaving the temple, Grayden traveled to the palace. Glancing upwards, he noticed the fading ion trails of three interstellar class cruisers. The hairs on the back of his neck stood on end. How could they have known? Grayden turned toward the hangar. He would not so easily be denied his victory.

With a sickening rumble, Grayden ripped through walls until he reached the launch bay. One of the attendants saw Grayden's intrusion into the chamber, and his jaw dropped as the rebel son of Arterra peeled away the remaining battleship's hull like foil. When he noticed the glowing blue crystal in Grayden's right hand, he ran away screaming.

It was the end of the world as he knew it.

Grayden turned his attention to the scene around him. Eythan was still here. He could sense it! Grayden let the energy from the prisM swell out from him, until it collapsed the entire chamber.

Explosions were erupting to the west. Grayden raised himself into the sky and saw his father in full battle armor tearing through his army like rag dolls. As Grayden descended before him, Eythan raised a thin sword above his head. It looked familiar.

"Grayden, what have you done?" he shouted.

Grayden slowly descended, keeping an eye on the sword.

The book Malthus had given him to read came in handy again. He recognized the Sword as the one the Angel of Death used against the original prisM. As such, he dared not use the prisM directly against his father. Ordering his men to halt their attack, Grayden landed a few yards in front of his father.

"Blasphemer!" Eythan shamed his son.

"Hypocrite!" Grayden shouted back. "This is on your head! I didn't violate a vow to the Creator! What does Maugaine always say? *'Live to learn and then learn to question'*? Well, I've learned to question, father!"

Something felt wrong, but Grayden couldn't tell what it was. "My sins do not excuse your own," Eythan shot back. "Every man... every Witness must answer for his own sins!"

"Who answers for my mother's death?"

"I loved your mother, Grayden. She was my first wife!"

"She was my only mother!" Grayden yelled, grabbing a breath as he leapt forward, triggering the Witness power of Speed for both men. Grayden was prepared for the transition and was already swinging at Eythan with a piece of metal. Eythan defended with his sword, swiping toward Grayden's neck.

Grayden disappeared in a cloud of blue mist to appear behind Eythan and blue arms spat out of the prisM, causing the remains of two war machines to fall on Eythan. One machine almost instantly careened back toward Grayden. Both men fell to the ground, releasing their breath, entering normal time. Slowly, the sound of twisted and tortured metal began to fill the air. Eythan shoved the machinery off as Grayden lifted into the air.

"Odd," Grayden thought, noticing how long it took Eythan to recover. Grayden repeated the attack, hurling tons of sharp metal at his father, but Eythan dodged the barrage and launched into the air toward Grayden at the same time. Eythan led with his fist this time, striking Grayden in the side of the head, knocking him

out of the sky and onto his back. The pain was strong, but not as strong as Grayden's surprise that his head was still attached.

Then Grayden noticed what was wrong. He hadn't seen it at first because his father was wearing armor, but now that he was looking for it, it was easy to see that Eythan wasn't wearing the mantle. Anger overcoming reason, Grayden aimed a blue tendril directly at his Father. At the short range from which it was fired, it not only connected, but also knocked Eythan to the ground.

The sword was a fake! Grayden summoned a column of blue energy to smash Eythan and ordered his men to take him. They came from all sides. Although Eythan tried to defend himself, the sheer numbers of men pummeled his nearly paralyzed body into the ground and wrestled the sword from his hands.

Grayden looked at his father with rage pulsing through his veins. How could he have transferred both offices? He couldn't have had that much notice! He grabbed Eythan by the throat and roughly lifted him into the air.

"Where is my birthright, father?"

"Where it belongs," Eythan gasped.

"That mantle is mine!" Grayden roared, throwing his father to the ground. Countless stabs of blue energy attacked Eythan, each one further paralyzing him until he was immobile.

As his father lay helpless, Grayden picked up the sword Eythan had been carrying and studied it carefully. Though finely detailed in every way the human eye could detect, it lacked any kind of supernatural origin. The prisM didn't react to it in any way.

"A fake!" Grayden screamed. "It was a fake!"

Grayden snapped the sword in two. His father had obviously

been aware for quite some time of his plans. Grayden knew of only one man who had access to that information.

Loading his father over his shoulder, Grayden returned to the temple, but the battle there was already over. Grayden tossed his father to the ground and aimed the prisM at the temple. A blue spiral arm spat out from the prisM collapsing the temple's western wall. It returned with Ahmahl, hanging upside down in its eldritch grasp.

"Betrayal at this stage?" Grayden asked.

"What do you mean?" Ahmahl asked fearfully. "I did nothing!"

Malthus walked upon the scene.

"What are you doing?" he asked Grayden.

"My father knew I was coming. I wonder who could have told him?" he asked, staring at Ahmahl.

"I said nothing!" Ahmahl screamed. "During the last Assembly session he suddenly came to this insane decision to evacuate the Royal family!"

"*If Ahmahl did not tell him, who did?*" Grayden wondered.

Ahmahl fell to the ground.

"Where's Maugaine?" Malthus asked with a tinge of worry.

"He's gone!" Ahmahl bragged, standing to his feet. "I had the Witness send him with the royal family."

"Why wasn't I advised?" Malthus asked.

"You were too far into Ventura...and the prisM and Maugaine's Helmet need to stay as far away as possible."

"That was not your decision to make," Grayden snapped. "I'll roast the General's head inside that Helmet!"

"Be warned," Malthus said in an anxious but hushed tone.

"He speaks the truth. When the Angel of Death came into contact with the first prisM, it self-destructed, and while the second prisM is more powerful than the first, you want to stay as far away from the Helmet as you can. But this is a stalemate; you have nothing to fear from the General as long as you possess the prisM."

"Why do you say that?"

"When Maugaine first appeared, I was at Eythan's side. The general explained that when the Angel presented the Helmet to him, it scolded him for trying to find the prisM. It told him the prisM was a source of evil and placed a sacrifice on the general."

"Impossible. Only a Regent may receive a sacrifice."

"That is what I, too, once believed. That puzzles me. The old God is bound by His Word. There must be some passage in the scriptures that explains this, but I can only find the commandment that strictly limits sacrifices to Witnesses Regent. I suspect his sacrifice is somehow linked to the prisM. I mentioned obtaining it once. Eythan thought it was a good idea, but Maugaine refused to even discuss it."

"I'm going to the temple. Report back to me when you locate Maugaine and the Queen," Grayden said.

"As you will," Ahmahl said, breathing a sigh of relief. Malthus motioned and Ahmahl followed him to the temple, where he had already made some changes. A pair of idols were placed near the front altar; a banner over the table of bread. Ahmahl walked up to Malthus.

"Master, forgive me..." Ahmahl said to Malthus.

"You fool! Because of your blundering, the power of the

Imperium has been transferred and that alone is enough to drive Grayden mad."

"Eythan forced me to perform both ceremonies at once, but I tricked him."

Malthus stopped in his tracks. "In what way?"

"I left the sacrifice out of his regency vows."

"And the Arterran pledge? Was it included in the vows?"

"There was no time. I had to condense both ceremonies into one...I had less than an hour to prepare! I assumed the more things I left out, especially the important things...maybe it would short circuit the transfer of power."

"Aieeee!" Malthus screeched. "You simpleton!" Malthus shoved Ahmahl to the floor.

"I don't understand," Ahmahl whimpered, "Without a sacrifice, the Regency ceremony will have no effect, so I have banished the power of the Witness."

"Dolt! Haven't you read the prophecy of the last Witness? He *'carries neither sacrifice or burden of throne.'* "

"I place no credence in those ancient writings."

"Then you may have upset the balance of power and placed into motion a series of events beyond the capacity of your dull mind. Why do you think that the Quorum has personally scripted every word of every Regency and Imperium ceremony for the last twelve hundred years?"

"I don't know, Master. I'm not allowed to attend high sessions of the Quorum."

Malthus turned away and took a deep breath, attempting to regain his composure. This complicated things, but there was no reason to worry Grayden.

At least, not yet.

"What sector did Eythan send the cruisers to?"

"I wasn't allowed into the war chambers during the planning of the evacuation. One of our operatives managed to sabotage the lead cruiser, which killed Queen Nakah and her children. After the launch, Eythan emptied the computer banks, but the crafts headed into the western skies."

"That means nothing," Malthus said. "Were you able to get any operatives on the ships?"

"One, I think..." Ahmahl said, trying to remember.

Grayden saw the soldiers scouring over the Temple grounds. They had already destroyed the outer Court and had begun raiding the inner Temple itself. A flash of panic sparked in Grayden's chest and he dropped Eythan near the Altar before landing inside the inner chambers. The soldiers turned and fired, thinking they were being attacked. Each shell bounced off Grayden, stinging him as they struck. Grayden grabbed the soldiers by whatever piece of armor or clothing he could and flung them back out of the Temple.

"Heathens! Do you want the Wrath to come down on us?"

The soldiers' bodies became small missiles, crashing into homes and fields miles away.

The commander of the local squad dropped his weapon and held his hands out to his sides. He stepped over the thick veil that had concealed the innermost chamber of the Temple for thousands of years. Grayden followed, though he could feel something was wrong.

"It was empty, I swear!" he said, motioning around the small room. Grayden grabbed the man by the throat and tossed him hard, but he only landed in the outer court.

"Fools," Grayden cursed, wiping his brow. He paused as he stood inside the Holy Chamber dedicated to their annual blood sacrifices.

Only once before, when an earthquake struck the area two thousand years earlier, had the veil not covered the inner chamber. Each year, the priests added a new veil over the old one, sewing it into place. It was said to have weighed thousands of pounds and it laid on the floor a large velvety hill.

Grayden glanced inside. Surely clearing the temple wasn't part of the royal contingency plan. Had the priests known as well, or had it always been empty? He quickly exited the inner chamber and returned to the front court of the Temple and bound Eythan to the altar.

Eythan looked at his son with alien eyes.

"Grayden, fear God! He will not allow this blasphemy!"

"Yes, He will," Grayden snapped. "Don't you understand? He already has. He allowed you to make a foolish vow and then violate it by placing me in hiding and He allowed mother to kill herself! Don't speak to me of fearing your God; you defied your God on this very altar! Did you even know the name of the boy you had killed in my place? Your God either doesn't know what happens or doesn't care. I simply don't care."

Grayden placed the prisM in front of Eythan's face. Its alien gold etchings seemed to glow brighter as it moved closer.

"When I was young, you taught me that history was important. Today, you gave me a final history lesson with your fake sword. Now it's my turn, though you can be sure this is not a fake. You recognize it; this is the second incarnation of the prisM. The first was used to assassinate the Witness at Amagrath. I learned from the history of Witnesses that this story is to be read as a lesson in humility. A pity that you never heeded the wisdom of this story, because the prisM accomplishes today what it failed to do long ago. The line of Witness ends today. It is time for the House of Arter to answer for its sins."

Eythan relaxed, turning his face to face Grayden. "Son, forgive me," he said, closing his eyes. "Creator, receive me."

Grayden saw Eythan's tears and it enraged him.

"No! You don't get to do that!"

He raised the sharp blue stone over his head and plunged it into his father's chest. Eythan screamed as the prisM cracked his ribs open. The prisM burnt through, instantly clotting the blood in his heart. Grayden struck until Eythan stopped moving. The blood on the prisM disappeared into the intricate golden etchings that detailed the edge of the pyramid shaped piece of cobalt.

Grayden dropped to his knees and wept. He rested his hands in the ground. Eythan's blood pooled around his fingers.

"You did this to me, you..." Grayden choked back tears.

A slight breeze wafted through the chamber, bringing with it the scent of ancient spices.

"*The true threat lies in the Helmet...*" a chorus whispered.

Grayden stood and looked around but saw no one.

"Who's there?"

"*The power before the dawn of flesh, our pact barred from the eyes of humanity. You are now ours,*" the voices continued.

Grayden felt the prisM slowly vibrating. The words were coming from the prisM.

"*The Helmet must be destroyed.*"

"Helmet? Maugaine's helmet?" Grayden asked.

Another pause.

"*You will speak of this to no man.*"

"I don't understand." Grayden said, but there was no answer.

The cruisers began their separation from the main interstellar path and General Frannel glanced at the screen one last time at the rapidly shrinking view of his home world. The swirling tan and cottony atmospheric gases made it look so peaceful.

"*That's odd*," he thought. Ordinarily, the Rhygus Vortex was the only surface feature viewable from space, but for some reason, it wasn't there. He forced his attention back to his duties.

"Mattis, run a continual diagnostic and notify me immediately of any changes."

"Of course, General."

"Monitor all transmissions from the surface and catalog them for me; I'll want to review them later."

"It shall be done."

He then turned to address the sentinels assigned to this ship.

"Men, I'm sorry General Maugaine isn't here. Once security protocols are re-established, we'll return to our proper ships. Until then, our mission remains the same: guard the regent until we are signaled to return. We lost a crew prior to launch, and we honor their memory with this mission. Men, the Witness Regent, Shiloh Mashal."

Shiloh looked at the heavily armed men, not knowing what to say. Each one had placed his life on hold indefinitely to protect him. Their eyes seemed to carry an unspoken question that asked the young regent if he were worth that sacrifice.

"Regent, your sentinels."

Shiloh stood silently. The large group of armored men clearly intimidated him.

"Hello," he managed to say.

As one, the sentinels saluted and Shiloh flinched.

"That'll be all for now," General Frannel said, seeing Shiloh's reaction. "Man your posts. We'll go over the duty roster later."

The sentinels began to disband when General Frannel grabbed one by the arm. The sentinel jerked away until he saw who it was.

"Son, I'm glad you made the mission," General Frannel said.

"Yeah," Ramon said, his face betraying stress.

"Are you alright?" General Frannel asked. "You don't look well. If you want to..."

"Leave me alone. I'll be fine," Ramon said and walked off.

Shiloh walked to the front of the bridge to look at a sword mounted on the wall. His father's command helmet was placed on a console next to it. General Frannel walked to Shiloh and bent at the waist to talk with him.

"Your father's command helmet. He gave it to me so I could coordinate the evacuation," General Frannel said. "Try it on."

Shiloh sat down and placed the helmet on his head. It was too large for him, but the internal padding instantly resized itself to fit his head.

"Hello, Regent. I am Mattis."

"I remember you. You showed me some games."

Shiloh was nervous. He wasn't familiar with any of the men around him. His handmaidens were in the sleep chambers until they arrived at their final destination and his Nanny was nowhere to be seen. But Shiloh remembered Mattis from a demonstration given when Eythan led a tour of the command system last month. Shiloh was supposed to be using Mattis to learn the history of the first Witnesses, but he mostly played games.

"Mattis, is everything going to be alright?"

"No. Grayden has overthrown your father's government."

"Is my family okay?"

"Yes," replied Mattis, who was programmed to lie about only one thing. "They are."

A cracking sound erupted from the port side and the ship violently lurched to one side, tossing the occupants around the controlled gravity environment. One sentinel was at the control panel, but it took General Frannel only an instant to realize that he was the problem, not the solution.

"Step away from that console, sentinel!" he barked, trying to distract him long enough to get a decent shot.

The sentinel wheeled around, ignoring Frannel, firing wildly in Shiloh's direction. Several sentinels jumped between Shiloh and the attacker.

Two men fell.

With the added seconds from the distraction, the assassin began launching the life pods while they were still docked on the vessel. As the first two pods exploded, the ship violently pitched sideways, disrupting localized gravity, throwing everyone around the bridge. General Frannel could do little more than roll into a ball and attempt to cushion the impacts.

By the time Mattis partially restored gravity, the assassin had found another weapon and began firing blindly. Another sentinel fell before Ramon wrestled him to the floor. During that time, the assassin managed to aim the weapon at Shiloh.

"Remember Grayden!" he screamed as he began to pull the trigger. But before his finger could tighten, the mental impulses that sent the command to flex the finger died midway as General Frannel fired point blank to the back of his head.

General Frannel ran to Shiloh and scooped the boy up in his arms and carried him to the medi-lab. Shiloh's little body didn't take up half the space of the diagnostic table. General Frannel took the command helmet from Shiloh and put it on.

"Mattis, is the regent alright?"

"Yes; he only suffered minor bruises. However, I direct your attention to the damaged navigation and life support systems, which pose a much more immediate threat to his life."

General Frannel activated the diagnostic table's sleep function and sealed Shiloh inside.

"Attend the regent's wounds and seal the medi-lab. Open only by my authorization."

"Access lock confirmed."

General Frannel returned to his sentinels who had assembled on the bridge. "I'm sorry to treat such a cadre of fine professionals like this, but until I can verify every one of you for dedication to the throne, I will have to claim all of your firearms. Ramon, you will assume command of the sentinels, placing them through Mattis' scanner systems."

"We don't have time for that," Mattis said.

"What?"

"This ship is off course and is being pulled into spacial anomaly 4191. I am unable to compensate."

"Ramon, steer us clear of that anomaly!"

Ramon sat behind the comm panel.

"It's not responding!" he yelled.

"Mattis, send out a distress signal and notify the flagships of our situation."

"I already have; the other Mattis units have responded. Their vessels are on their way."

General Frannel watched as his ship tilted out of control. The ghostly moan of stressed metal gave an eerie feeling to the crew, as if the ship itself was protesting the strain.

"Incoming message from General Maugaine!" Ramon yelled.

Gerah's face replaced the view of space on the view screen. Everyone but General Frannel turned their heads.

"General, what happened?" Gerah asked.

"You've got to pull us free of this anomaly!"

The bow of the ship was now just a hundred thousand miles from the event horizon. The other ships activated their graviton systems, but the ship still continued to inch toward the glowing funnel.

Gerah Maugaine leaned into the face of his technician.

"What can we do?"

"General, this is a force of nature; we can only slow it down."

"Enough that I could rescue the regent?"

"Sir, if anyone opens a hatch on that ship while it is under that much stress, it'll implode. Its hull is only secure as long as they can maintain structural integrity."

"I will not stand by uselessly!" Gerah shouted. "Add more power to the graviton emitters!"

"We're already stressing the system past safety levels."

"I need options...right now!" Gerah demanded.

There was silence as the technicians looked at each other. One technician looked up at Gerah, clearly troubled by the situation.

"We can pray," he said.

"Then start praying," Gerah replied and left the room.

Even if he wasn't on the regent's ship, he was still responsible for the regent's safety. Gerah entered the docking bay, sealing the door behind him and entered the codes to open the hatch directly into space. The airlock alarm sounded; air hissed out as precious seconds ticked by and Gerah tried not to think about what he was doing. Flying in an atmosphere was unnerving enough, but at least there were visible perimeters; the ground below, clouds above. Throwing himself into something without boundaries or air caused Gerah to hesitate. The hatch opened and the last wisps of oxygen emptied into the vacuum of space.

Gerah instinctively took in a deep breath, and his lungs filled with air that didn't exist. Again, he breathed, and again, air filled his lungs. He leaned out the hatch like a paratrooper, as the cold of space brushed across his exposed eyes, reminding him that it was not a realm meant for mortals.

Gerah leapt, tumbling for a few seconds as he compensated for the lack of gravity.

There was no up.

There was no down.

"The vessel," Gerah thought. *"Focus on the ship."*

Gentry had already displayed a directional beacon toward Shiloh's vessel, but it was unnecessary. He was close enough that the anomaly was easily visible. Gerah proceeded toward

Shiloh's ship as fast as he could muster, but was unable to calculate his rate of speed. A speed reading of 75,904 MPH shimmered at the edge of his vision.

"The ability of the Mattis units to read mental intent can be annoying at times," Gerah thought, and the display immediately disappeared.

Still, in the infinite area of space, it didn't seem fast at all. In fact, reminding himself of the regent's predicament, it was slow. He concentrated on Shiloh's ship and his speed increased.

No, he was *not* curious as to how fast he was moving.

It took Gerah four minutes to reach the ship and by that time, the anomaly wasn't a part of the horizon: it was the horizon. Even light was stretched into small streaks as it entered the anomaly. While Gerah could feel its pull, the anomaly had no effect on him. Flying to the back of Shiloh's vessel, Gerah grabbed the rear tail fin, but it tore off in metal slivers. He needed something sturdier if he were going to succeed. The accelerated gravity was already tearing the ship apart.

As Gerah moved to get a better grip, he noticed a shadow cast over the back of the ship was moving toward the front. Gerah followed it, flying directly in front of the ship, but it disappeared. He grabbed the nosecone and pushed. The ship continued to move slowly into the anomaly, and Gerah willed himself to a complete stop. The metal of the nosecone began collapsing into his hands.

Gerah hovered dangerously near the interface, close enough that his peripheral vision was filled with blinding streams of light photons as they were drug into the anomaly.

The shadow appeared at the back of the ship and the ship's

momentum increased beyond Gerah's capacity to safely stop it.

His only hope was to use forward momentum to twist the ship and angle it back out. Gerah moved out of the way and the ship began to plummet toward the anomaly. Gerah grabbed a piece of the wing as it passed by and twisted with the momentum of the ship. It turned a few degrees, but the wing mount crumbled to pieces and the ship slid from his grasp. Although he tried to grab the side of the ship as it entered the anomaly, Gerah was left holding slices of metal trimming from the starboard wing mount.

"No!" he yelled as the last of the ship disappeared into the anomaly. Gerah hovered in place for a moment, still holding the trimming tight.

Both Witness Imperium and Regent lost on the same day.

Gerah activated his communication screen to Peri's ship. He saw Peri in the background, her hunched shoulders betraying a loss that could not be communicated any other way.

"I'm...sorry," Gerah said, staring numbly into the anomaly.

"Mattis, I need a full maintenance sweep!" General Frannel yelled, surprised to still be alive.

"Internal sensors are offline," Mattis replied.

The ship moaned as it careened through the anomaly. Artificial gravity and internal compression were malfunctioning, throwing the occupants around the ship. General Frannel grabbed a console to steady himself and looked at the view screen.

It displayed what appeared to be static, but instead of white and gray sparks, this was more fluid; an almost liquid static.

"Ramon!" He called for his son.

No response.

"Ramon is in the weapons locker," Mattis replied.

"What? Get him to the bridge, right now!"

"No response," Mattis replied.

"Mattis, get us out of here!" General Frannel ordered.

"Navigation is offline, General."

Several small explosions rattled the ship. Control panels shook and sparks flew as internal power supplies ruptured.

"Report!" General Frannel ordered.

"Deck two has been breached. Force fields are maintaining structural integrity, but total collapse is imminent."

"Seal off the lower decks!" General Frannel barked.

Mattis isolated the affected areas and sealed off access to the four damaged compartments. A hum filled the air and General

Frannel searched for the source. The hum became whispers and then words which formed into curses hurled at the ship, hurled at him, hurled at everything. The ship shuddered, as if breaking to an abrupt stop, and everything was quiet. Glancing at the view screen, he noticed stars. They had exited the anomaly.

"Where are we?" General Frannel asked, walking to his office. He had never seen star systems like this before.

"Triangulating from our records, we're located at the edge of the rim of a neighboring galaxy."

"Life support?"

"Online, but damaged."

"I need a full maintenance sweep."

"I have run a partial sweep. The primary energy core has been ruptured and will need to be ejected. Communications are mostly operational, but functionally useless due to the distance from our own galaxy. Using auxiliary systems, we are in no immediate danger, but our mission is in danger if we are attacked. Defensive systems are offline and in need of extensive repairs."

"The   escape   pods?"

"Of the eight standard pods, six are missing and assumed lost in the anomaly and the remaining two are not functional. They are repairable, but again, due to the distance from our own system, escape pods are irrelevant."

"Mattis, I need as many solutions as you can feed me."

"Is the primary objective the protection of the regent?"

"It is the *only* objective. Any solutions that hinder that mission are to be ignored."

"I am able to set aside all mission parameters but one."

"What?" Frannel asked.

"Eythan's mission to search for his brother Mossad."

"Delete it. It can't get in the way of our mission."

"I can't. It has the same priority as the regent's mission."

"Fine. Accept it, but do everything you can to place a priority on the regent's protection."

"The Mossad mission can run concurrently with the regent's. The most workable solution to include your parameters is this: find a local planet, repair what we can and return home."

"Is that possible? Can we return through the same manner?"

"No, the anomaly is not open on this side of the interface. We would have to return using conventional means."

General Frannel rotated his wrists in frustration. He needed more options.

"How long would a signal from our ship take?"

"At least eight years, but I note that it would violate our direct orders for communications silence."

"Those orders are for when we reach our destination. Send an emergency signal on the prearranged frequency, but keep it brief. Mention the regent, our location, a request for supplies and a warning about the anomaly."

"Do you wish the signal to be coded? The other ships no doubt believe that we were destroyed; they won't be looking for a message on our frequency."

"What about using one of the other ship's frequencies?"

"It would most likely be interpreted as a ruse."

"But if we ask them to verify the signal's origin, they'd have to acknowledge it. Our most remote probes have not come this far."

"Revealing our location is a violation of our specified orders."

"Understood. Broadcast using the Mattis protocol."

"Internal calibration complete; sensors are partially online."

"We need to find a planet or meteor with materials that we can use to synthesize repairs. Catalog this system and find the most hospitable planetoid."

"The third planet is not only hospitable, but inhabited."

"What?" General Frannel asked, leaning over the monitor banks seeking information on the planet. "It supports life..." His voice was a whisper of disbelief.

"Indeed," Mattis continued, "with very similar forms of life as on our own world. I have been absorbing cultural information from their broadcasts. The planet is approximately six hundred years behind our technology."

"Is it advanced enough to pose a threat?"

"No. Their most sophisticated weaponry is primarily atomic based. They have no real defensive capabilities other than using their offensive stores, but even in our current state, we are safe."

"Is stealth mode available?"

"Available but objectionable, due to its massive power drain," Mattis replied.

"Plot a spot to land and just as soon as we are within their detection range, go to stealth mode."

"Their detection does not extend beyond the atmosphere."

"Good. How long until we reach...what is it called?"

"By the predominant nation it is called 'Earth'. At cruising speed it will take three weeks. Note that most of the raw materials needed to synthesize repairs are not available on this world."

"Then I need some options, Mattis."

"Our mission is to securely hide the regent. There is no reason why the mission can't continue."

"Hide on this world?"

"That is our mission."

"How do we get back?"

"We do not. We have no way to repair the sleeping chambers and the technology present is not sufficient to aid our systems."

The words sank in: *WE DO NOT.*

"I won't accept that as a solution. Start work on another."

"I will continue to seek another solution, but unless new information provides for more possibilities, we are restricted to the current solution. General, the message has been coded."

"Let me hear it."

Regent Shiloh and crew have survived passage through the anomaly. However, the craft is severely damaged and we cannot return. Warning: the anomaly is a one-way conduit that exits into a neighboring galaxy. Verify broadcast protocols and send new ship for component and supply replacement.

"Good; repeat the signal until we receive a reply. I need some information on this world's culture."

"Which one? There are over two hundred separate nations."

Frannel shook his head in disbelief. Life on another world; it was already difficult enough to believe.

"The predominant one."

"That nation is called 'The United States of America'. It is a democratically-elected, constitutionally-restrictive republic. I am gathering information for that nation now."

"All those nations... where is this world's Witness?"

"Although many of their visual and text based entertainment describes fictional Witness-like scenarios, there is no evidence of the presence of a Witness on this world."

"Are they a computerized culture yet?"

"Not at any level that we would consider computerized."

"Are you able to interface with the technology they have?"

"Their primitive bandwidths reduce our interfacing speed, but compatibility has been matched."

"Good; what can you tell us?"

"I will be able to program their customs into your minds, but the difficulty comes in the dietary and environmental limitations you will face. These people are primarily carnivores; meat eaters. It also appears that this world suffered a major cataclysm several thousand years ago that tilted the planet on its axis, shattering the mother continent into smaller fragments. This event produced regions of extreme instability in the crust, resulting in seismic and thermologically damaging events. The level of radiation that reaches the surface is over thirty times that of Ehrets; atmospheric pressure is forty percent lower than Ehrets. Breathing should be manageable unless you exert yourself."

"What is the danger to this crew in staying on this world?"

"The radiation is enough to eventually cause varying types of cancer. The diet, if controlled, would suit the crew's nutritional needs. The breathing difficulties can be managed."

"What are the inherent dangers to the regent?"

"Until his powers manifest, the same as any of you."

The door to General Frannel's office opened. It was Ramon.

"Where have you…"

Ramon lunged forward and stabbed his father in the chest. General Frannel, caught off guard, fell back and Ramon came at him again. Frannel raised his arm to protect himself, but Ramon slapped it aside and stabbed his father in the left shoulder. The blade stuck in the shoulder bone and General Frannel pushed his son backwards. Ramon pulled out another knife.

"You should have joined us."

General Frannel cursed himself. He took a step back to protect his weak shoulder and pulled the blade out. The feeling of metal going into bone was nothing compared to feeling it come out. He went into shock and his left arm fell numb to his side. Ramon stepped back. He knew time was on his side. He just had to keep his father at bay and the loss of blood would finish the job.

The world began spinning and General Frannel fell backward. Ramon swung the knife at him again, but Frannel managed to turn around. Ramon struck his father in the back and kicked him into the console.

"Don't worry, I'll take command."

General Frannel watched his son leave through squinted eyes. He was right; his son would take command control when he died. Even more foolishly, he had trusted Ramon with the command codes. The deep draw in taking a breath indicated that his lung had been punctured. The warm shock surging through the left side of his body told him he didn't have much time.

He was going to fail his mission.

Even if there was a loyal sentinel onboard, what would stop the next attack? The traitors seemed to reveal themselves in stages. Frannel closed his eyes as he understood what he must do.

"Mattis...." He gasped, pacing his words. His strength was quickly fading and he didn't want to waste any words. Mattis must be able to understand what was said to carry out the order.

"Yes, general?"

"Change command protocols...flush the system," he said.

Grab another breath, he told himself; a big one. The command must be repeated.

"Confirm system flush," Mattis said.

Blinking his eyes, Frannel used the pain to focus and scream the confirmation. "Flush the system...confirm!" he yelled, holding on long enough to hear the verification.

"System flush confirmed."

He would snatch victory out of his shameful defeat. Ramon's betrayal only made the decision easier. He would not fail Eythan. He would gladly sacrifice his own traitorous son to protect the son of Arter. Frannel fought for another breath.

"Protect...regent," he groaned, and collapsed.

"It shall be done," Mattis said, importing the new codes to his programming. "You have served your Witness well."

But General Frannel could no longer hear Mattis.

Ramon stood before the medi-lab door. Through the window he could see Shiloh lying unconscious inside.

"Mattis, priority one; confirm voice print and ID. Command - One. I'm taking charge of this vessel."

"I am unable to comply."

"Uh uh; I know all about your protocols. My father's dead; I'm in charge and I just gave you a direct order."

"Command protocols have been changed."

"How? By whose authority?"

"A man you could never be," Mattis said.

Ramon could have sworn he heard anger in Mattis' voice.

Mattis sealed the medi-lab from the rest of the ship and dropped the force field over the starboard side. A soft hiss behind Ramon became a breeze, and the breeze became a gale as the oxygen rushed out into space. Ramon fell to the floor gasping. The two remaining sentinels also fell. After a few minutes, they stopped moving. Mattis allowed the ship's gravity to move the bodies toward the starboard side, then he lowered the fields covering the hull breaches and the bodies tumbled into space.

Only the two handmaidens remained, sealed in their sleeping chambers. Though it was not human, Mattis felt compassion for these two, but it had no way to determine their loyalty and the command had been given to flush the system. The safety of the regent could not be risked.

Mattis pumped oxygen into their chambers at such a strength that it caused immediate suffocation. After a few minutes, their bodies were also emptied into space.

Mattis disengaged itself from General Frannel and activated low gravity. General Frannel's body slowly tumbled out of the office and Mattis sealed the door, trapping the helmet inside. General Frannel's body was the last to exit the ship. Mattis fired the ship's thrusters, incinerating the bodies.

Only Shiloh remained. Mattis manipulated a few controls and pumped a fine yellow mist into the sleeping chamber. For the regent to survive on this world, he would need to be treated as a native. To do that, he must believe that he was one of them. Small probes attached to the side of Shiloh's head and Mattis began the mind cap process.

Three weeks later, the craft entered the orbit of Earth's moon. Mattis increased the amount of data that he was receiving to get a more accurate view of the world they approached. Their most advanced civilization was still at the primitive stages of planetary travel. Interstellar travel was still over a century away. The craft landed in a forest. By scanning conventional land maps, Mattis determined that the place was in a province called Texas.

Mattis returned his attention to Shiloh. The medi-lab chamber could keep him stable for another few months, but the only real solution was to get the regent housing on this new world. Mattis found several agencies that handled abandoned children. After an exhaustive yet almost instantaneous research, Mattis guided the ship toward a small building in Texas. At the last minute, just as its hull would have become visible to those on the ground, the ship entered stealth mode and shed its visibility to the dawn sky.

Mattis removed the probes and Shiloh's eyes blinked opened. Still in the hypnotic throes of Mattis' psychological procedure, Shiloh dressed himself in a simple white technician robe and walked down the ramp of his ship. Without looking back, Shiloh knocked on the front door of the building and waited for someone to answer.

He never noticed the small breeze behind him as his ship left the area.

SHILOH'S TALE IS CONTINUED IN

THE PRESENT

Gerah stood in the quiet shadows of the observatory at the front of the ship, far from the others. A lifeless gray landscape lit by a distant sun stretched out beyond the port window. He had seen so many planetoids over the past eight years that they all looked the same. Mountains, valleys, asteroid impacts, every single one of them were as cold and lethargic as he had become.

Safety protocols had tightened over the years so that both his ship and Peri's had to move deeper into the galaxy to avoid the detection of Grayden's men. Each movement placed them slightly outside Grayden's ever-expanding influence, and further from the world of their birth.

The bitter husks of regret had long ago made a home in his thoughts, neighbor only to the self-hatred of failure. Gerah had come to understand that his name would forever be attached to that word. If he were a weaker man, he would have taken his own life or drowned his shame in vices, but his pride wouldn't allow such an escape. No, he couldn't fail himself.

Just everyone else.

Given just one more chance, he wouldn't fail, regardless of the cost. But how much of an advantage did he already have when he failed? Still, when the time came and it would; there was no other reason why he was still alive, *no one* would separate him from his charge. Gerah had allowed himself to rest too comfortably within Eythan's laws and paid for his negligence. His Call was a solitary one, outside the comfort and jurisdiction of man. It hadn't stopped with the deaths of the Regent and Witness. With no male heirs, he would guard the daughters of Eythan until one bore a son who would carry the mantle. But that would be many years, if their mother had her way. None of the sentinels on either ship were of Mashal lineage and Peri was determined that the lineage would not be broken.

Gerah noticed that he was no longer looking at the landscape, but at his own reflection. Even though poorly lit, the Helmet gleaned just as brightly as it had the first day he had seen it. Too bad the man inside hadn't fared as well over the years. The eyes hadn't aged, of course; a side effect of the Helmet prevented him from physically aging.

But he still felt it.

The door chimed before opening to reveal a sentinel. He came to attention even though he couldn't see Gerah in the dark.

"General, we're receiving a distress signal from the Queen."

Gerah shelved his self-pity and raced to the bridge. Radio silence was imperative between pre-scheduled communication windows, yet the Queen had from time to time ignored protocol.

As he reached the bridge, Gerah was shocked to see the visibly shaken face of Queen Peri. Her eyes were puffy from crying, but wandering the screen as she looked for Gerah. She could only see the bridge of the ship and the sentinel that escorted him in. As Gerah touched the console, his image appeared on her view screen. Her eyes immediately sought his.

"Milady, wh..." Gerah asked.

"General!" she yelled, cutting Gerah off. "It's Shiloh!"

"Milady, there are strict rules concerning communi..."

"We're receiving a message from Shiloh!"

"Impossible," Gerah said, embarrassed as the wounds of his second failure were publicly re-opened.

"The signal is real! It...it's coming from another galaxy!" she stammered.

"It's a trick. Grayden wants us to reveal our location, and your communication is not helping."

"Please..." Peri pleaded, all sense of royalty gone. Only the mother of a lost child stood before him now.

"Can we receive the signal?" Gerah asked Gentry.

Gentry matched the radio frequency supplied by Peri's ship and Gerah heard the distinctively clipped baritone of the Mattis unit.

Regent Shiloh and crew have survived passage through the anomaly. However, the craft is severely damaged and we cannot return. Warning: the anomaly is a one-way conduit that exits into a neighboring galaxy. Verify broadcast protocols and send new ship for component and supply replacement.

The signal repeated itself.

"Verify the origin of the signal," Gerah commanded.

The view screen map zoomed out, with lines scanning all areas on the map. Several lines converged on a single spot until they stabbed a blinking light toward the edge of a neighboring galaxy.

"Gentry, could this be a result of an echo or other deviation?"

Gerah asked his own Mattis unit.

"No. The signal would take many more years to travel to and then echo from that location. Also, we see no other signals which would be the result of such an echo. Triangulations from both this ship and the First Queen's authenticate the signal as coming from the designated area."

"Verify Mattis protocol," Gerah said.

"Verified. This signal originated from a Mattis unit."

"One of the Mattis units remained on Arterra. Grayden could duplicate the protocol."

"Yes, that is possible," Gentry admitted. "But the signal clearly originates from another galaxy."

"General, please," Peri pleaded, seeing the argument going against her. "If he survived the anomaly with a damaged ship, we should also be able to pass through!"

"This is clearly a plot to lure us into the open," Gerah said. "Gentry, is there any chance the Regent survived the anomaly?"

"None," Gentry replied, its answer carrying through to Peri's ship. "Even light is crushed inside such an anomaly."

"Besides, Milady," Gerah said. "Even if we were to believe it, the message said that there was no way to return."

"We've got to do something! The message was sent years ago! Anything could have happened by now!"

"I'm sorry, Milady, but my mission is..."

"Your mission is to protect Shiloh! General, you made a vow to the Creator Himself to protect the rightful heir to the Throne and that is Shiloh!" she said, starting to cry.

Gerah looked off into the distance. Her words struck home, not just with the pain of his failure, but with the implied promise of redemption. Did he dare to hope? He looked back at Peri.

"My duty is with the Regent...if he lives," he conceded. "But I will not pilot you through the anomaly."

"What?"

"I will not pilot you through the anomaly. I will enter alone. If this is an authentic signal, then Grayden will have also received it. If there is any chance of safely returning, it will be with me alone. I will take one of the smaller ships back to our system and then commandeer a larger vessel to rescue the regent and his sentinels. I do, however, worry about your safety should I not be able to return."

"We'll move deeper into the galaxy if we have to!"

"Then we'll rendezvous to make the transfer," Gerah said, entering new coordinates. "At that time, Captain Tobiah, you will assume command of both vessels."

"Thank you, General! Blessings upon you!" Peri said and the screen went blank.

The men on the bridge stared numbly ahead but Gerah ignored their doubt.

"Rendezvous with Captain Tobiah."

The scientists stood in the Court of Reconciliation fidgeting in their green laboratory smocks. They looked out of place, but no more so than the man who sat on the throne. Grayden had tried to continue the ceremonies and trials when he took over, but the prisM frightened the people away, so he spent a considerable amount of his time in the courtroom absorbing the praises of an imaginary populace.

Standing to his left and right were Malthus, who had reclaimed the office of Minister of Religion, and Ahmahl, who had become Minister of Commerce. Malthus motioned them forward.

The scientists uneasily climbed the steps toward the throne, unsure of the proper ceremonial protocol. As low as the lights had been dimmed, they couldn't even tell if Grayden was awake. He hadn't been seen or heard in public for quite some time. For all they knew, he had died years ago and Malthus had propped his corpse on the throne. The blue luster of the prisM cast waving shadows across his face, highlighting his strong cheekbones, resulting in an almost skull-like shadow draped across his face.

"Speak," a voice commanded from the throne.

It startled them. One of the scientists walked forward, avoiding a direct glance at the throne.

"Lord Grayden, we have been receiving a coded signal, but we don't know what to think of it."

He looked nervously to his comrades who ignored him.

"Continue," the voice said, clearly identifiable as Grayden's. "If it's important enough to bring to my attention, it's important enough to report."

"We're receiving a rather odd signal that claims to be from Regent Shiloh's ship."

"What?" Grayden asked, sitting forward, suddenly attentive.

The scientists muffled their response at seeing Grayden. His face was an emaciated gray, a pale shade normally reserved for the dead. As he stood, his hair strung out lazily past his shoulders. His robe was torn and stained with dark patches of dried blood. The slackness of his movements reminded the lead scientist of a puppet who was trying to control his own strings.

"We don't know what to think, since his ship was destroyed in the anomaly."

"What does it say?" Grayden asked.

"Only that the anomaly transported their vessel to another galaxy. The source of the signal is indeed from a neighboring galaxy and authentication codes are accurate for a Mattis unit, but no message was received from the Regent himself. The message loops every few minutes."

"Leave," Grayden commanded.

The scientists all but ran, not once looking back. Grayden's eyes followed them all the way out the chamber doors. As the doors slid shut, Ahmahl turned to face Grayden.

"It's a propaganda ploy by the rebels!" he said. "They want to stir the people up by making them believe the Regent is still alive!"

"I don't care what they think," Grayden said. "Malthus?"

Malthus stood in silent contemplation, concentrating on the words that had been spoken. He had a hollow look on his face.

"It is odd," he said after a moment. "There is a truth to what he said, but I can't detect the regent's life force."

"He's dead!" Ahmahl said. "Nothing can escape the anomaly!"

"Perhaps not," Grayden replied. "Send in a scout ship with our most expendable man. If he lives, he can report back."

Malthus started to reply, but Grayden had already turned his back and reclaimed his seated position. Malthus wheeled around and exited without a word.

At one time, Malthus thought he had taken into account every possibility when scheming for the prisM, but he hadn't taken into account the changes in Grayden's personality.

It had changed everything.

Malthus would assign someone to enter the anomaly, but it would not be the most expendable man. It would be the man who was most expendable – and dangerous - to Malthus.

Malthus entered the general quarters, ignoring the stares of the troops until he reached the command barracks. Walking down the hallway until he saw the nameplate he was looking for, Malthus entered the room.

"Don't tell me that knocking is now beneath you?" a rough voice said upon seeing Malthus enter.

Malthus turned to his left and saw his seemingly younger twin brother Mosh sitting behind a desk, monitoring reports.

"I come directly from Lord Grayden with a task for you."

"Oh, he's calling himself Lord now, is he? I'm kind of busy right now," Mosh said, moving his hand before several monitors full of information.

"I tire of your attitude," Malthus said.

"Good," Mosh responded. "That makes it worth whatever it is you're about to do."

Malthus waved his arms. The monitors exploded and the items on his desk shattered against the walls. Mosh sat back to avoid the shrapnel.

"Haven't seen you lose your temper like that in a while," he said with a laugh. "I know how to push your buttons, don't I, big brother?"

Malthus leaned into his face, his chin quivering with rage.

"After tomorrow, you'll have no claim to my blood."

"We've done this before. You threaten me and then I threaten to start talking about things I know...things you don't want some people to hear."

"You will threaten me no more after today!"

Mosh stood. No one would have suspected that the two were twins. While Mosh was bulky and naturally tall, Malthus was thin and short, and looked unusually old for his age.

"We both fell far from the tree, didn't we?" Mosh said. "Who'd have thought that? I grew up with the mechanics and the toad squad, but you got your cushy spot in the priest's house. Now look at you; put on some fancy robes and you think you're better than me."

Mosh leaned down into Malthus' face and watched his rage silently boil. "But you're not and your magic doesn't work against first blood, does it? Hmm, who was our father again?" he asked pretentiously. "It'd be bad if you lost your high position with Grayden because…"

"Silence!" Malthus yelled. "I'm sealing your quarters. You won't leave here until you report for your assignment tomorrow."

"What is this dangerous mission? Does 'Lord Grayden' even know about it?"

"Check your mission logs and find out...oh, your terminals have been destroyed. You'll find out tomorrow, toad," Malthus said, leaving the quarters.

As soon the doors closed behind him, they began to open at Mosh's approach, but Malthus began weaving intricate patterns in the air with his hands. The metal walls poured over the front of the door until there was no indication that a door had ever existed. The sound of muffled pounding came from the other side of the wall. Malthus allowed himself a vengeful smile.

"Toad," he spat.

Returning to the general barracks, Malthus motioned to two nearby soldiers. They followed him back to where Mosh's door had been. They stared at the nameplate on the blank wall, not knowing what happened to the door.

"Mosh has been placed under house arrest and his quarters sealed. You will guard his quarters until I return. No one will communicate with him in any way!"

"Yes, Minister!" they responded, though one of the soldiers looked worried. Malthus walked over to him.

"Do you have a problem with my order?"

"I'm due on the command deck in fifteen minutes, Minister."

"That is not my concern," Malthus said and walked away.

In route to rendezvous with the First Queen, Gerah's ship had taken several detours to hide from the path of Grayden's patrol scans. The ship had come to rest on one of the planetoids in the Euraphygus Belt. It was almost perfect cover. The layout of the planetoids almost defied detection.

That worked both ways, Gerah found out, when a graviton beam was suddenly trained on his ship from an angle rendering their external weaponry useless.

"Lower your shields and surrender your Helmet, General! Grayden wants you alive!" a voice demanded over the monitor. Gerah recognized the voice as belonging to Commander Eno, even before the vocal scan displayed the information. Eno had been an assistant Minister of War prior to Eythan's fall. Gerah shook with rage as he monitored the view screens. Warlords had taken positions around the forward hatch area, too close to be fired upon. They were ready to attack anyone leaving the ship.

Gerah wasn't going to disappoint them. He programmed the force field to drop at his approach and then reseal. Before leaving the craft, Gerah passed the children's quarters. They were huddled in a corner behind their handmaidens, who were equally nervous.

"Minister, let us leave this place," one of the girls said.

Gerah turned to look each of them in the eye.

"Our ship is immobilized at an angle that prevents us from using any of our weapons. The ship can't fight back, but I can."

Gerah walked toward the hatch as Eno's voice blared over the intercom.

"General, we repeat: lower your shields and surrender. You can't leave as long as our graviton beam's on you. Grayden wants you alive."

"Then pray to Grayden!" Gerah shouted as the field dropped.

A warlord tried to block the shield from reforming, but Gerah grabbed the man's console and pulverized it a moment before pulverizing the man.

"You threaten children?" Gerah put his armored fist through a supposedly impervious agium chest plate and backhanded another over the horizon. "And you have betrayed the Witness!"

Gerah's movements began to slow. The flagship-level graviton beam that had been used to hold the ship was now aimed at him and Gerah soon found himself immobilized. Eno walked casually to face his new prisoner.

"Your witness is *dead*," Eno said. "Mine's still alive."

Gerah said nothing but his eyes never left Eno's, though he knew better than look back. Eno walked behind Gerah.

"We knew you wouldn't stay inside. We blatantly displayed the means to incapacitate you and you walked right into it. A real general would never have spent his greatest weapon so foolishly."

Gerah ignored Eno's babbling and glanced over to his ship. A few warlords were trying to decode the force field. It was only a matter of time before they broke the code, but though he was suspended in electronic amber, Gerah Maugaine was not helpless.

"Gentry," he whispered to the Mattis unit attached to his

belt.

"Yes?" Gentry answered inside his Helmet.

"How many adversarial vessels are in this system?"

"Twelve. Only four are of any considerable size or speed. One is located over the ridge; two small battle cruisers are approaching this direction. The largest is orbiting the planet."

"Class of the orbiting ship?" Gerah whispered.

"Devashil, but it includes recent upgrades not registered with my records. Its energy signature reads over two hundred percent of what a normal ship of this class should produce."

Gerah paused just long enough to call it a pause.

"Order the ship to leave orbit now, using evasive maneuvers. Do not leave a beacon...rendezvous at our previously selected emergency site. Fire defensively only."

Gerah expected a disagreement, but the ship's ignition coils suddenly came to life, blasting the nearby warlords into paste as it lifted toward the sky. The other warlords rushed to their cruisers, but they would never catch up. And if they turned their beam from him to the ship, then he would be free to move. Eno cursed loudly, screaming orders into a commlink. He hadn't counted on the ship leaving without Gerah.

Gerah allowed himself a rare smile. *"So much for being a 'real general',"* he thought.

Eno raced toward his ship, ordering a few of his men to remain with the graviton beam. Gerah struggled to no avail; the beam didn't hold him motionless, merely with no leverage to escape.

Gerah concentrated on the various frequencies emitted by the graviton beam. Gentry identified them and cataloged them, but

Gerah needed more. As great as their technology was, the Divine nature of his Helmet augmented it past anything Arterra's greatest scientists could conceive.

When he opened his eyes, Gerah saw each frequency in fluid, electric colors. Then he concentrated and each frequency was separated until he isolated the power signature of the graviton beam. He encoded the frequency into his broadcast system and overloaded the beam, causing a mechanical feedback. The blast created a fifty foot energy plume, scattering warlords across the plains.

Gerah began to plummet. As he landed, the warlords guarding him began firing their weapons. Gerah ignored the attack on him and leapt toward Eno, who had reached his cruiser.

Gerah grabbed him by the throat and Eno looked directly into Gerah's merciless eyes. In that searing moment of judgment, he understood that nothing of any value in the universe would delay his fate. The impotent ping of small arms fire surrounded him.

"Eno Mashal, I judge you a traitor to the golden throne," Gerah began, pronouncing formal sentence.

"Wait! No! Look, I can help you! I know what Grayden's planning!"

"The sentence is death."

"No! Wait! No!" Eno pleaded, hopelessly grasping for just one more second of life.

His pleas were ignored. Gerah grabbed Eno by the back of his neck and slammed him headfirst into the ground so hard that his body embedded up to the knees. Gerah turned and collared the remaining four warlords with a pulse beam. At full intensity, the ion-charge from his chest diadem provided enough concussive energy to puncture the hull of a cargo ship. With a slight change in frequency, it provided minimal concussive force, but scrambled any electronics in its wake, including the advanced technology used in the warlords' armature.

The blast escaped with the roar of a freight train as it caught the warlords in its electronic fury. Instantly, their armor began locking up, leaving the warlords to struggle against the nearly two hundred pounds of dead metal they were encased in. It took most of their strength just to remain standing.

Gerah tried to conceal his rage as he walked to them.

"You will deliver a message to Grayden," he began.

"Dog of Gehennah!" one of the warlords cursed. He spit at Gerah and though the spittle was aimed correctly, it missed. The warlord raised his chin defiantly.

"You...you don't scare me, demon!"

"Demon?" Gerah asked, his eyes narrowing to angry slits.

"*Enough!*" The ground quaked as Gerah's voice boomed across the landscape of the cold, gray planetoid.

Gerah grabbed the offending warlord by his armor. The front of the metal chest plate twisted like warm taffy beneath his steely fingers. As their eyes locked, the warlord's face distorted into a mask of terror, his mouth frozen open in an unending scream.

Even after all breath escaped his lungs, his body involuntarily fought to wail, above even its natural instinct to breathe.

He only managed a strained gurgle.

The remaining warlords stood transfixed by the scene as a creeping awareness of dread and emptiness surrounded them.

The feeling swamped them until even the horizon was swallowed in its caustic darkness.

And as their mortal vision was abandoned, a sound – at first thin and fleeting - swelled to a crescendo, filling the shallow atmosphere of the planetoid with its supernatural fanfare; a series of notes, sung with impossible perfection by a million invisible voices. The warlords frantically looked around, seeking any mortal anchor to ground themselves against the unreality of it all and immediately wished they hadn't.

The man they knew as Gerah Maugaine no longer stood before them. The being they now looked upon was more a projection of force than mortal. Their human minds instantly rejected the existence of such a being.

Such things were not possible.

Such things *could not* be possible.

"Do you realize how easy it would be to desiccate every single one of you?" Gerah thundered, looking at each man.

He pulled the first warlord back to his face.

"I am Called by the Almighty - the firstborn Exacter of Blood! You profane His Holy Office!"

As Gerah spoke, the warlord's skin began to blanch, pulling so tight around his skull that his eyes appeared to bulge. The other warlords, unable to avert their gaze, were impaled by the wrath emanating from the vindictive gray eyes looking out from behind the Angel of Death's faceplate.

Judgment flowed from those eyes, encasing the warlord before him and then spilled to the ground, flowing toward the rest. One warlord fell to his knees in lament and the flow instantly abated around him. The remaining warlords became lost in its inky depths, and their screams drowned like razors down their throats.

Then Gerah turned his glance away.

The horizon reappeared and the three warlords who had remained standing collapsed lifelessly to the ground. Gerah was breathing hard as he looked long and hard at the remaining man. "You...," Gerah said, his voice returning to its normal stern baritone. "You will tell Grayden that if he interferes with us again that I will personally come for him, regardless of the cost."

The warlord audibly sighed; he was going to live. Gerah stared directly into his eyes and the man cowered.

"I shall not fail you!" the man said, openly weeping.

"Go!" Gerah commanded and the man went.

Gerah desperately tried to control his rage as he boarded Eno's vessel. The misty afterglow of spiritual rage still surrounded him as he entered the bridge, causing the pilots to involuntarily sink back in their seats.

"Follow your lead vessel. Ahead, full speed!" Gerah ordered.

The pilots relayed backup energy to full thrusters. The ship lifted from the surface and began pursuit of the larger vessel. The cruiser was designed for speed, but the ships had been augmented since he was general and even pushing the engines, it was a half hour before he recognized the local area energy dispersal pattern of a warship at maximum thrust.

"Decelerate and match the speed of that ship!" he ordered.

Instantly, the gravimetric engines disengaged and as the low rumble of the engines shook the floor plating, Gerah saw the swarm of assault drones heading his way. The crew did their best, but several of the drones got through, damaging the hull. Then the real assault began.

Two orbs that neither Gerah nor the ship's sensors could identify jettisoned lazily from the weapon ports just as the ship headed to deep space at maximum acceleration. The orbs were much larger than conventional warheads, but fitted with simple directional rockets. The eyes of the pilot in front of Gerah opened wide as he recognized them.

"We've got to leave!" he said, turning the ship around without asking. Before the ship could finish the turn, the engines came to life taking it quickly away from the scene. Gerah kept his view screen trained on the orbs. They had finished their slow arc and began flying toward each other.

"What are they?" Gerah asked. The orbs' rockets weren't fast enough to catch them, much less present an authentic danger.

"Bad, bad, very bad," one pilot said, obviously worried more about the orbs than Gerah.

Visual display followed the orbs in their pathetically slow pursuit. The ship easily pulled away from them, and the orbs, while heading in the general direction of Gerah's ship, seemed more intent on finishing their arc than catching the ship.

The pilots continued to feverishly push the ship, ignoring all safety protocols. Gerah watched as the monitors showed the temperature of the engines sailing past safety levels. When he returned his attention to the orbs, they were flying side by side. Their ship was safely out of range of any weapon he knew of, but the pilots continued to accelerate. Gerah didn't understand why they were still pushing the ship, but he understood that the pilots' fear was based on something real.

Then, the orbs collided.

The explosion generated no light, occurring at a sub-molecular level, smashing even light particles. At the center of the collision the two cylinders vaporized, revealing for a nano-instant what appeared to be a spark. Time slowed as the spark grew, hungrily expanding exponentially in Gerah's direction. The edge of the explosion reached Gerah's ship so quickly that it didn't even have time to be pushed back by the concussive forces.

The shock waves generated by the newly converted chemicals and radiation rolled broiling through the local system, instantly sub-atomizing everything from the fourth to the eighth planet's orbit.

The attack ship had headed the opposite direction the weapon was aimed, and while it was outside the primary radius of the weapon, was still pounded by a wave of energy powerful enough to disable most systems, bringing it to a halt.

Detailed scans of the system showed no survivors within the primary blast radius.

"What just happened?" Gerah asked the pilots.

The orbs had struck each other, but instead of an explosion, only a small flash of light escaped followed by a growing circle of black from the detonation area. Sensor scans of the area returned with negative readings.

"It's too late!" one of the pilots cried, and his arms dropped from the controls in surrender. He stared ahead at the blossoming darkness on the screen.

The other pilot abandoned his controls and fell to his knees.

"General, save me!" he pleaded.

Gerah glanced down at the instruments. He had never trained to pilot a full-sized warship. Gentry began diagramming the controls, but Gerah mentally wiped the diagram away. The pilot was right. It was too late to do anything. The shock waves were approaching far too quickly.

Gerah looked up just in time to see the first wave collide with the ship. He could do nothing but look in stunned silence as the energy wave instantly dissolved the shields, and the ship vanished beneath his feet. The men who were with him were reduced to inanimate particles and then, even those particles were destroyed as the next wave smashed through them.

Yet Gerah Maugaine did not move.

Matter and energy raged like an angry river toward him, parting as it neared, flowing around him. Helpless at the center of a cosmic maelstrom, Gerah could only watch as wave after wave of destructive energy passed around him.

The largest of the shock waves took eighty minutes to pass. Gerah recovered, and stopped Gentry's ongoing sensor studies of the new weapon, training it to self-diagnostic. As always, it read 101%, but Gerah questioned the results since it always read 101%. At the hint of mental doubt, Gentry ran diagnostics again and again, it read 101%. Gerah launched himself toward the attack ship, wondering what kind of weapon was used against him. He had never heard of any device that could generate that much destructive power.

"It is a multi-signature gamma weapon, first theorized seventy years ago, but never fully researched," Gentry explained. "It uses the gravitational field of a miniature white star to fuel its own stasis field, similar to the gravitational engines used by our larger space vessels, but held outside the time/space continuum and allowed to re-enter the time stream with the power surges of an entire year or more to explode in one specific moment. The result is destruction unparalleled until now even by Arterran science."

"Defenses?" Gerah wondered.

"None" came the answer. "Only the Divine protection of your Helmet prevented us from being destroyed at a sub-atomic level."

"Prevention?"

"Prevent the white star from re-entering the time stream."

"Probability of damage to Peri's ship?"

"Unless they delayed their escape, her ship should be safely outside of the primary and secondary destruction zones."

"What about the ship firing this weapon?"

"To any ship within primary range, the result would be total annihilation. Records show that the ship firing this particular weapon would be at the edge of that range. It is likely intact, but heavily damaged."

"Possibility of having more of these weapons?"

"Unknown. Technology at this level is beyond even current projections of Arterran science."

"Intercept time to the attack vessel?"

"Dependent upon the condition of the ship."

It took Gerah four days before he saw the sketchy outline of the ship on his display and, as soon as he approached, he was attacked by dozens of fighter drones. Once more, two orbs were launched, but this time they headed directly toward him.

Perhaps there was some reason they were fired together? "Correct; initialization fields are looped between the two."

"Separate them and what happens?"

"The weapon will not arm."

Gerah fired his chest diadem at the orb to his left, causing it to miss the other orb by meters. Gerah grabbed the second orb and shredded the maneuvering thrusters into metallic confetti and hurled it in the direction of the sun. Gerah launched toward the attack ship and ripped through the hull, causing as much internal damage as his path would allow. But passing through deck after deck, Gerah didn't notice any personnel.

"Life signs?"

"Accessing onboard sensors...there are no measurable life signs on this entire vessel."

Gerah temporarily stopped his rampage.

"Bridge?"

"Thirty meters at 340 mark 64," Gentry replied, displaying a visual beacon in the exact direction Gerah needed to go. Gerah turned and as he plowed into the bridge through the floor plating, he immediately became aware that something was terribly wrong.

As he looked around, he found out what it was. Though the bridge's air was escaping through the hole he had made in the floor plating, the men on the bridge continued to man their posts, as if they didn't notice him.

Gerah walked to one of the helmsmen who stared numbly ahead at the screen, plotting in coordinates for an attack that would never occur. The light pallor of the man's skin was lit by the view screen enough that Gerah recognized him as one of his former pilots.

He wasn't breathing.

"This man is not alive," Gentry observed almost reverently. "None of these men are alive."

The nine men stood at their posts, continuing to perform their mortal duties as Gerah noticed the long settled smell of death. It was everywhere.

"They've been dead for quite some time," Gentry said.

Gerah touched the helmsman's shoulder to shake him and the man took in a deep, painful breath. He screamed as a small blue wisp exited his body and he collapsed to the ground. His eyes, open and fully conscious, locked onto Gerah's, no hint of the fear that men normally had in looking into his eyes. He had already seen – and experienced - the judgment behind Gerah's eyes.

"Please, help me!" he screamed, reaching out, but as his

breath left his body, his carcass gave up its pretense of life.

The blue mist that left the man swirled around the bridge and the others stood back from their posts. As one, they turned toward Gerah. He wheeled around just in time to see the same blue haze materialize from the rest of the bodies. The men fell screaming to the floor as the ghostly mist of prisM power coalesced into the image of Grayden.

"General," he greeted, careful himself not to look directly into Gerah's eyes. "Welcome to my ghost ship." "What you have done?" Gerah asked.

"We're all dead, we just don't know it yet," Grayden said.

"You're not dead. Your father spared your life."

"My father banished me for a mistake that he made."

"You have no idea what that mistake cost him...or what it's going to cost you. Animating the dead is blasphemy."

"Yes, punishable by death," Grayden admitted. "But that would require someone with enough power to punish me."

"There is One."

"Who doesn't care. You can't threaten me from the other side of the galaxy, Maugaine. Do you know what I've been through?"

"Yes, I do; but you ruined your life."

"Life, Maugaine? This isn't life! As God is my witness..."

"He is your Witness...and so am I!"

Grayden looked down, calming himself.

"We're at a stalemate. You can't come to me and still protect the Queen and I don't have time to come to you. But I'm still here and I can kill everyone you ever loved."

"Everyone I ever loved is already dead," Gerah said. "Even you. I have seen your death."

"Since when did you claim to be a prophet?"

"I make no such claim. I merely state that I have already seen your death. Why do you think that I've always kept careful watch over you?"

Grayden stared into space. The voices began to buzz. *"He lies! It's confusion! Listen not to the lies!"*

Gerah leaned forward sensing the spiritual activity. Grayden shook his head as if to clear it.

"Your confusing words mean nothing to me. I'm..."

"Listen!" Gerah interrupted, leaning toward Grayden. Even though he wasn't physically there, Grayden involuntarily took a half-step back.

"In your father's name, I offer you one last chance for the mercy of imprisonment. If you value your life, stand down."

The offer simultaneously offended and appealed to Grayden. He looked to the floor only quick enough to look back up.

"I will see you dead, Maugaine." The image dissipated into blue smoke, leaving Gerah alone on the bridge of the ghost ship.

"A fool and a coward," Gerah muttered. *"I need a scouting ship,"* he thought.

Immediately, a small display directed Gerah to the hanger. He studied each ship, ignoring Gentry's attempt to catalog them.

"Which is the fastest vessel?"

One of the ships glowed in outline as Gentry detailed the ship Gerah was seeking. It was a small ship, built for four. Gerah opened the hatch and stepped inside.

"Is there any way for Grayden to monitor this ship?"

"Not if I re-sequence the ship's identity codes; and the residual radiation from his gamma weapon will hide any such activity for months and by then, our trail will have dissipated."

"Restrict communications to the modified Mattis frequencies."

"Done. The ship is fully fueled, but has no weaponry. It is a scout ship per your request, but it has been heavily modified from the model in our records."

"Signal ahead an emergency rendezvous with our ship and the First Queen at our pre-established coordinates. If he has found me, he may have found Peri."

"The next signal window opens tomorrow."

"Then head toward the regrouping system so I can secure it before her arrival."

Gerah met Peri on one of the larger planetoids of the Deltor System. As soon as Gerah established security perimeters, the crews began their bi-monthly transferal of parts and supplies. The children gathered together to play in the large atrium on Peri's ship. Captain Tobiah and Peri met with Gerah on his ship.

"This plan risks your lives," Gerah warned.

"No," Peri insisted. "We can make it."

"I agree with General Maugaine," Tobiah said, clearly upset. "We would have to double security without a fallback position."

"Do you doubt the signal is real?" Gerah asked.

"Do I have a question about its authenticity? No, sir. The signal couldn't be faked, but that's not the point."

"If the signal is authentic, then my mission is clear."

"Pardon me, general, but you're wrong," Tobiah asserted.

"How?" Peri asked. "His mission is to protect the regent."

"But not necessarily Shiloh," Tobiah explained. "If the general leaves to protect Shiloh, he can't return. He would be protecting a regent, but at what cost? If he can wait five to ten years, I'm sure that one of your daughters will find someone to marry."

"How?" Peri asked. "There is not a single member of the Mashal line on either ship."

"Then, with all due respect, you're wasting the general's time."

"Excuse me?" Peri asked indignantly.

"Your policies insuring that no regent will ever be born. The Mashal line is, of course the favored line, but members of the Bachan, Lawmahd and Hilool tribes all have roots in royalty."

"We've had this discussion before, Captain. I'm not letting any of my daughters marry a sentinel!"

"Then they will never bear a son and the general will never have a regent to protect. Well, not one that will matter to anyone."

"The captain speaks truth," Gerah interrupted. "Witnesses are not exclusively of the Mashal line. If it were, the line would have died at Amagrath. How old is Audra?"

"Fourteen, but..."

"If she were on Ehrets, she would be married by now. Captain, I release any prohibition on marrying."

"You can't override the First Queen!" Peri's face knotted into an angry fist. She started to sputter.

"General, I..."

Before they left Ehrets, Peri had heard stories about General Maugaine. Many whispered of the feeling of a person's soul being laid bare for judgment before those impenetrable gray eyes. She had seen and talked with Gerah so many times over the years that she dismissed the stories as superstitious nonsense.

But when Gerah leaned down to her eye level, she came face to face with an inescapable fear. The universe wasn't large enough to separate her from that fear. No, she thought as the feeling became more familiar, it wasn't fear; it was the rejection of the things she had wrongfully been clinging to. Feelings of conviction began churning inside and came uncontrollably pouring out her mouth.

"I... I have been wrongfully holding on to power, even when it hurts those close to me. I've made decisions based on what's good for me, not my children. I'm overprotective of my daughters..." Peri began to cry. "...because I'm jealous of the attention the sentinels show them."

Peri buried her face in her hands. After a few moments, Gerah spoke, and she trembled.

"Milady, we each have sacrifices to make," he said somberly and stepped back. "It shall be done," he said to Captain Tobiah.

Peri nodded in agreement and ran from the bridge. Tobiah averted his eyes as she passed. There was a short pause as both men allowed the tension to drain. Gerah was the first to speak.

"Captain, I need you to perform a maintenance sweep on the scout ship I appropriated," Gerah said, changing the subject. "Traveling through the gamma radiation has damaged the sensors. I will be leaving in the morning."

"We'll take a look at it, General, but from what I've seen, we'll need every bit of that time," Tobiah said, saluting as he left.

The next morning, Gentry finished reprogramming the access codes for Gerah's return in time for Captain Tobiah to report back to Gerah.

"General, you took more than just a little damage. The engines are about gone. We fixed them, but you've got limited cruising speeds. We replaced every component in your sensor array, but the superstructure took quite a bit of damage. External sensors are going to be spotty," Tobiah said, acknowledging the new access codes into his own ship.

"Understood. Thank you, Captain," Gerah said.

"Godspeed, General," Tobiah said.

"Pray for a swift return," Gerah replied, entering the ship.

The engines of the slender scout came to life and as he lifted off, Gerah took one last look at the two ships he had spent the last eight years of his life protecting.

"Godspeed," Gerah said as he gave one last thought to Eythan.

And then he was gone, leaving nothing but an ion trail.

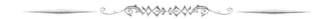

Six months later, Gerah welcomed the sight of Ehrets' solar system. He was still in the outer regions, among the orbit of the furthest planets, but it felt good to be even this close. It was the nearest he had been to Ehrets since the loss of the Witness and Regent nine years earlier.

The closer he got, the less lethargic he felt.

Gerah noticed a sentry ship stationed outside the edge of the solar system. Gerah briefly wondered if he should just plot a course around the system or risk detection. Then a thought came to him: why not just stop at Arterra and do whatever it took to end this travesty? There would be casualties, but surely he could...

Then Gerah remembered the price his pride had taken earlier and scuttled the idea. Regardless, he would not be reduced to sneaking into his home system. He didn't know how much Grayden knew, but the same reason Gerah had to stay away from Grayden would keep Grayden away from him.

He opened a channel to the sentry ship.

"Sentry, this is General Maugaine. Stand down."

The reply took over a minute. Gerah was about to signal again when the sentry replied.

"Look, Annod, stop playing around. You got me busted last week. Keep it up and they'll have my head!"

Gerah opened up a direct video channel to the ship and leaned into the camera.

"Stand down!" Gerah repeated. "Let your superiors know that the first attack on this vessel will signal an invitation for war that I will not refuse."

The ship immediately lurched out of the way to clear Gerah's path and attempted to contact Gerah again, but he ignored the request.

Gerah noticed a frenzy of message activity over the next hour.

"They know I'm coming," Gerah said.

"The fleet is heading on an intercept course," Gentry explained.

"How many ships?"

"All of them."

"Good."

Slightly outside of Ehrettan orbit, Gerah's small scout ship stared directly into the weapons of over fifty war cruisers, twelve destroyers and two hundred smaller ships; an obvious mismatch.

And Gerah wasn't going to let them think otherwise.

His view screen signaled an incoming transmission. Gerah accepted it with a quick stab of a button. A young man fidgeted on the screen.

"G-General," he stammered, glancing away from the camera. "You are ordered to stand down and prepare to be boarded."

Gerah leaned into the camera. "By whose authority?"

The Captain looked back down at his script.

"By the authority of His Majesty Grayden Mashal, you are to be taken..."

"The same man who murdered his father to gain the throne?"

"Um, taken to Peysha Island. You are under arrest for..."

"I asked you a question," Gerah interrupted. "The same man who murdered his father to illegally assume the throne?"

The captain squirmed for a moment, looked off-camera and then replied.

"Yes, sir."

"If he wishes to call for my arrest, let the coward call himself."

Gerah cut off the signal. After a few minutes, the board lit with just one signal. Gerah answered and Grayden's image filled the screen. He didn't look anything like the proud phantom image that he had projected earlier. His face was haggard; veins showed through the thin veil of flesh that covered his emaciated cheeks. His once proudly styled hair was stringy and unkempt.

He looked diseased.

Gerah noticed the cause of the disease as it cast a pale blue glow on one side of his face.

"General, I thought we had it worked out; I chase, you run. What could possibly cause you to come all the way back here? You left everyone unguarded so... what? So you could kill me?"

"Your death does not come at my hands," Gerah said. "But it does come."

"Right, you already saw me die," Grayden mocked. "Yet here I stand and here I remain. You're here about that signal, aren't you? We received it, too, but while I sent in a pawn to investigate, you are going to send your most powerful piece?"

"I will be taking a larger ship."

"You're really going into the anomaly? Fine. Take mine."

"I will choose the ship."

"They're right in front of you."

"The ships have been modified. I need to see their schematics."

"Do it," Grayden ordered to someone off-camera.

Gentry began downloading and sorting through the data.

"It makes no difference to me whether my brother's alive or not, Maugaine. I've already got what's mine. But if he is; if the signal is real and my brother is alive, tell him to stay where he is. Everyone's happy, except you. You're never happy, are you?"

"Grayden, always remember that you removed yourself from

my protection."

"Rot in Hell!" Grayden snapped. "I don't need your protection or your pity! Take a ship; throw yourself into the anomaly...I hope you die a slow and painful death!"

Grayden closed the signal.

Gerah sat back, amazed at the lack of anger he felt during the exchange. At one point, he even felt a spark of compassion for his former regent. Grayden did speak truth in one area. What *could* Gerah truly hope to achieve? Did he truly believe that the regent had survived or was the anomaly a way to forever silence his guilt in pursuit of redemption?

Gerah had hovered in front of the anomaly while trying to save the regent, but he hadn't allowed himself to be pulled in. Once he allowed it to take him in its grasp, once he surrendered to the laws of physics, Gerah had no idea what would happen. It would be out of his hands.

"Encode the latest fleet schematics and send them to Tobiah. That will give him an advantage if he is attacked."

Gentry began transmitting the data in multiple directions.

"Transmission complete," Gentry said.

"Good work. Gentry, of all the ships present, locate the one best suited for a return trip with the regent and his crew."

The images of a large black ship appeared on the view screen.

"The Desteen is designed for long trips and large enough to grow its own food and recycle water. It also has sleep chambers."

"Fine. Tell the crew to abandon ship."

Gerah left his ship after setting it to self-destruct. He guided it to the maw of the anomaly. He wasn't going to let Grayden pick through its memory banks after he left. Everyone but Gerah watched as the ship entered the event horizon and was grabbed by the anomaly, disappearing into nothing. Gerah entered the new ship as the six man crew crowded into an escape pod. He looked into the launch chamber.

"Godspeed, general," one of the men said, saluting sharply.

The fleet followed Gerah's craft, abandoning their defense of Ehrets, forming a crescent pattern around the ship's perimeter. After securing the hatches, Gerah walked to the Desteen's bridge.

"Gentry, verify we are the only ones onboard."

"Verified."

"Store current records for later study, but erase the computers and reload the banks with their primary templates. I don't want Grayden to have any access to this vessel. Recalibrate all primary communications to the modified Mattis protocol."

"System templates reloading," Gentry replied.

The ship stopped all forward momentum and the lights blinked out, to be replaced by the emergency running board lights at the bottom of the walls. Gerah walked to the bridge, but the hatch wouldn't open.

"Security is still offline," Gentry explained.

Gerah peeled the hatch off its hinges and dumped it in the hall. The view screen was still displaying computer gobbledygook. After a few minutes, the lights came on and the view screen returned to the primary display.

"Systems online," Gentry said. "Communications have been recalibrated to the modified Mattis protocol."

Gerah noted the positions of the other ships. They had moved in closer, no doubt puzzled by the odd activity on his ship.

"Grayden is watching very carefully," Gentry pointed out.

"Then he will be watching me leave. Set course for the anomaly."

The engines came to life and the Desteen steered out of orbit. It only took an hour to reach the anomaly that had taken the regent's ship almost a decade earlier. The fleet followed the entire way, albeit at a safe distance.

"Halt at the edge of the event horizon," Gerah ordered.

The ship stopped a few hundred miles short of the point of no return. Even so, the engines were straining to remain in place.

"Have you stored the original records for the Desteen?"

"Yes," Gentry replied.

"How far back do their logs go?"

"Since the computers were installed four years ago."

"Send them to Captain Tobiah. Perhaps there is something in the logs he might find useful."

Gentry broadcast the records in multiple directions and though the other ships attempted to jam the signal, it was too late; Tobiah would get the records. Gerah imagined the fleet commanders' fury at their inability to stop their most classified secrets from being given to the enemy.

Gerah paused, looking at the Arterran fleet on one screen and the anomaly in another. After this, there was no turning back. He bowed his head and after a short prayer took a seat in the command center.

"Take us in. Let them see what a true son of Arter is made of!"

Gentry turned the ship slowly toward the anomaly, its polished black hull reflecting the light discharge of the ships behind it.

The Desteen entered the event horizon and accelerated forward, disappearing into a dot of nothingness.

Fourteen men were executed after Grayden's last inspection of the flagship Nakuum, including the captain and commander. The new captain had worked around the clock for the next inspection and had personally insured that his crew was ready.

As the craft carrying Grayden and his entourage approached the dock, Captain Amil considered - for a moment - blasting the ship out of existence.

"It'd solve a bunch of problems, even if it just killed just one of them," he reasoned, but abandoned the idea as soon as he thought of the prisM. Instead, he reported to the hatch to stand at attention as if the people boarding his ship had a right to be saluted.

Grayden hovered through the hatch first. He had long ago ceased walking. He was followed by Malthus and a number of others the captain didn't recognize. But this time, instead of coming straight to the captain to begin the inspection, Grayden drifted past him as if he weren't there. Malthus, however, did stop. The captain crisply saluted the aged figure.

"Lord Grayden isn't in the mood for an inspection," and walked away. Once outside visual range of the troops, Malthus rushed his pace to catch up with Grayden.

"What happened to the inspection?"

"I don't care about inspections," Grayden snapped. "Why do we even pretend to need a military?"

"It keeps the people occupied."

"It wastes my time."

"The captain actually considered destroying our ship."

"Then kill him and appoint another one, I don't care," Grayden said, rubbing his temples.

"What's wrong?" Malthus asked.

"Voices. When I'm out in space, they stop."

"What do these voices say?"

Grayden merely replied with an irritated look. Malthus had been pressing Grayden to talk about the voices so many times it was becoming irritating. If only he didn't need Malthus to help run the empire... Grayden reached his private chambers.

"I'm not to be disturbed for any reason!" he growled.

"Your will is mine," Malthus conceded.

Grayden entered his chambers and felt relief for the first time in weeks. Perhaps he needed to station himself here. He could still travel to Ehrets when he wanted to. Grayden fell back on the bed, his body aching with exhaustion. He tried to drop the prisM on the floor, but it remained attached to his open hand even as he collapsed into sleep.

But instead of dreaming, he saw a vision of his own body lying on the bed. He walked out to the hall and saw the guards posted outside his door. Down the hallway, he heard someone familiar. It almost sounded like...

It was Maugaine's voice.

Impossible! The idiot had just thrown himself into the anomaly. If he had found a way to return... and with the regent? Grayden raced toward Maugaine's voice, refusing to acknowledge the fear that rushed through his veins. His atrophied legs ached for just a moment before the Regent power of Speed kicked in and the strength he had spiritually inherited flooded his body once again.

He ran down the corridors chasing Maugaine's voice until the halls turned dark and he could no longer see. He stumbled around until he saw a sliver of light beneath a doorway. Grayden smashed through the door.

Upon entering the room, Grayden noticed that he was no longer on the ship. He was planet-side again, but didn't recognize the area. Ancient wooden buildings were in the middle of fields of some unusual grain. As he looked around, he saw a man flying through the air wearing the Mattis helmet and an odd uniform.

Shiloh? No, this man was too old to be Shiloh, yet somehow he knew that it was. The brief moment of curiosity dissolved into rage as he saw that Shiloh was wearing the mantle, though in a strange manner: around his shoulders instead of over his chest.

Grayden sat up in the bed, a cold pain tightening in his chest. The now-familiar feeling of his senses returning shocked him. He had spiritually entranced himself, but what had he seen?

Was it a dream?

Or a possible future?

The anomaly was an eternal universe of white static, rendering the pride of Arterran science useless. Gerah had tried to study the flow and ebb of energy to counter the force which held his ship, but no discernible pattern appeared.

"Gentry, there has to be a way out of here."

"The definition of 'out' does not exist in the anomaly."

"Then send us forward; if the regent got through, we can too."

"There is no guarantee we will end up at the same location or the same time."

"You should have mentioned that earlier," Gerah said.

"There are over three hundred pieces of pertinent information concerning space folds. Do you wish for them to be explained?"

Gerah's stern mental response cut off any further discussion of space folds. Through the clouds of energy, external monitors had detected several inky blotches attached to his ship, writhing on the exterior. They reminded Gerah of the shadow that attached to Shiloh's ship just before it entered the anomaly.

"Gentry, identify those black patches on the ship."

"Except for visual display, other sensors do not verify their existence."

As one, they moved from one side of the ship to the other, and the ship began spinning. Without the accompanying sense of gravitational movement, it seemed unreal.

"The movement of the shadows correlates with changes in our course."

"Keep the sensors online, but shut off the display," Gerah said.

As he turned away from the screen, Gerah paused. He had heard a whisper.

"Forgotten son," it said.

"Forgotten sins," another said.

Gerah turned around, but saw no one.

"We know your secret," said a whisper close to his ear.

A staccato chorus of voices stabbed accusations into the air.

"Liar!"

"You lied to your brother!"

"Murderer!"

"You killed your own father!"

Gerah stepped back to the console.

"Gentry; identify the source of those voices!"

"No voice has been detected other than yours."

"Your mechanical devices cannot help you."

"Who are you?" Gerah asked, stepping away from the console.

"We know who you are..." the voices taunted.

"Hiding behind a Helmet not yours, hiding behind a name not yours...," another raspy voice taunted.

Gerah remained silent.

"And now, forever hidden in the White Hell," a voice said, followed by raspy laughter.

NEXT!

Shiloh awakes on a new world with no memories of his former life and unaware of the destiny that awaits him!

AUTHOR INTERVIEW
by Donna Courtois

Jerry will proudly tell you that he's an adopted son of Texas. He moved there in 1989. A man of many talents and interests - writing, music, art – and an avid reader, Jerry began writing soon after becoming a fan of *The Destroyer* book series in 1985. I sat down with him to get the scoop on *The Last Witness*.

Hi, Jerry. First, tell us something about yourself.

Sure. Father of three boys, living in Texas. I've been a Christian most of my life. I'm honored to be one of only four people on Earth to have ever been granted the title "Honorary Master of Sinanju". Oh, and I've created the world's first sixteen player chess game.

When did you first get the idea for *The Last Witness*?

In 1987, when I wrote my first book, a 125 page thing entitled *"Born a Warrior"*. It featured a beach bum looking guy named Thor Wagner who had magical powers. I soon realized that I wasn't writing a novel - I was writing a comic book - and a bad one at that. Shiloh was called "Magicman" back then and wore a stereotypical super-hero costume, complete with fancy boots and gloves with lightning bolts on them. Needless to say, very little survived the following purge. That's when the series changed from a story about a magical superhero to a supernatural adventure. Once I started coming up with stories, I soon had enough for a series.

How and when did religion begin to influence the plot?

When I decided I wanted *Witness* to be more than just an action/adventure series. I wanted something with depth and purpose, but I didn't want *cliché* as I've seen in some Christian fiction, with bad guys always turning good by the end of the story, complete with singing angels and Heavenly lights. I wanted it to be a bit more dark and realistic, where the good guys aren't always perfect and sometimes even make the wrong decision. And that means sometimes the bad guy wins.

Did you know from the beginning it was going to be a series, or did you only think of the plot of the first book?

Oh, I was definitely aiming for a series, but I didn't have any of the tools to build one at first. Of course, I didn't know that, so I kept tweaking and deleting and adding and deleting and proofing and deleting. After I established the basic foundation for the overall series, I broke it up into "acts" which are the basis for each book. Then I broke each of the books down into chapters and started writing. The cool thing on working on all of the books at once is that I can (and have!) written things in one book that won't be fully revealed until another book. I love Easter eggs. I've really had a lot of fun with some of the Arterran names, but there are far more Easter eggs than just the names.

What kinds of books and movies do you enjoy?

Comic books are still a guilty pleasure of mine and I still read *The Destroyer* novels on a regular basis. Currently, I'm in a political research frenzy, so I read a lot of books that most people would find as thrilling as an encyclopedia. Movies? Anything that can *move me*. I don't want to spend my money and time to see an actor. I want to see characters I care about in situations that slap me across the face.

Did you read much as a child? What were your favorite books?

Oh yeah, I read everything from the *Frog and Toad* books to the *Boxcar Children* series. I grew into reading *The Outsiders* and *Lord of the Rings*, but my favorite book during that period really has to be Madeleine L'Engle's *Wrinkle in Time*. It was the first book that made me feel like I was in the character's shoes. I haven't read that book in over thirty years and I can still feel the body-numbing electric jolt from one of the scenes.

Which authors influenced you the most?

L'Engle first taught me what it was to *feel* a book. Later influences include Frank Peretti and Warren Murphy and Dick Sapir. In fact, if they'd never written *The Destroyer*, *The Last Witness* would never have been written. The reason I started writing is because I loved reading them; I wanted to duplicate that feeling for others; it was like I became a book pusher. I could give them books to read, but I wanted to do more, so I began writing my own. See, if I can cause just one person to stay up all night and skip sleep to read one of my books and they are so excited after reading it that they can still go through work the next day living off the rush from that book, then I will have accomplished my goal.

Which characters in The Last Witness do you identify with? Who comes closest to yourself? Your ideal self?

That's the cool thing about writing; you get to identify with your entire cast! I don't believe you can be a good writer if you don't. So I get to feel noble like Gerah and bad like Legion and scared like Shiloh; as cocky as Brad and as sad as Maria. When I was first determining who they were as people, I started with a basic premise: Gerah would act like I probably *should* act in a given situation and Shiloh would act like I probably *would* act, so I guess by definition, Shiloh would be the character that is most like me, but Gerah was definitely the first character to "come alive". He almost writes his own scenes now! Sometimes I write Gerah chapters that have nothing to do with any of the books, just to see what he does!

Which character do you see as the opposite of yourself?

Probably Brad. I can't see myself sitting around doing nothing. I'm always busy with *something*. If I were Brad, I'd be working on all kinds of things, either art or my music or something else. No wonder he's always so depressed; he has no ambition.

Are there any characters drawn from real people?

The legally and politically correct answer would be "No!", but the truth is that just as any author places himself in his characters, he places those people he knows - or aspects of them - into his characters as well. Now, I don't know a guy named Shiloh who has asthma, but yeah, pieces of my friends and family get in there, though I bet they wouldn't recognize it.

Why are the last letters of some words capitalized?

The last letter of certain words is capitalized to represent that the object is unholY. The first letter of Holy things is always capitalized. It's a cool way I can tell a reader that something is unholY without going, "Hey, see that? It's unholy!"

Where do you see yourself and your writing in ten years?

While developing *The Last Witness*, I've written enough content for over a dozen novels as well as a few spin-offs, so maybe one or two of them will see the light of day, who knows? If nothing else, they've allowed me to add some depth to the world I'm creating. It's my hope that ten years from now you'll be asking me what is coming next for Shiloh.

Any last words?

As Gerah says, "Live to learn and then learn to question". You can't go wrong with that.

Sometimes Jerry can be reached at <u>jerry@jerrywelch.com</u>

CHARACTER INDEX

AHMAHL

HEIGHT	5' 4"
WEIGHT	142 lb.
BUILD	Medium
HAIR	None
EYES	Brown
RACE	Arterran
SKIN	Light
AGE	53
GENDER	Male
I.Q.	118

TRIVIA

Ahmahl is naturally bald, which is rare on Ehrets.

BIRTH NAME	Ahmahl Nefesh Dawth
BIRTH	June 16 - Khram-Doth, Jusinan
LEGAL STATUS	Arterran citizen, no criminal record
MARITAL STATUS	Single
EDUCATION	Temple of Jusinan Holiness Studies
MILITARY STATUS	Exempt
OCCUPATION	High Priest, Assembly of Ministries
FAMILY	Two sisters, whereabouts unknown
AFFILIATIONS	Assembly of Ministries

AHMAHL

Ahmahl and his two sisters were orphaned when their parents died in a pandemic outbreak. His family and tribal names were removed and he was sent to the Temple of Jusinan, where he studied for sixteen years. Shortly after ordination, Ahmahl was assigned to a remote temple in Roosh, serving without distinction.

During a visit to the Temple at Jusinan, he met Malthus, in whom he considered a kindred spirit, and for a time, something that he thought he would never find on the world of his birth – a friend.

That all changed once Malthus became Chief Priest. While he assigned Ahmahl the coveted position of personal assistant, Malthus' ambition and lust for power shattered the friendship, and Ahmahl found himself an underling.

He was placed back into the ministry that he lethargically served, but it was just a cover for something far more interesting. Ahmahl became immersed in a world that he did not know existed. All pretenses toward fulfilling his priestly duties fell to the wayside as he absorbed himself in study of the dark arts. After many years of developing his newfound power, Ahmahl decided to return to his friend Malthus and kill him. Unbeknownst to Ahmahl, Malthus had far surpassed his abilities and easily defeated Ahmahl. But rather than execute his former friend, Malthus cast a spell on him, placing him under Malthus' control.

After Malthus was banished to Peysha Island for sacrificing a boy on the Altar of Holies, Ahmahl was elevated to the position of High Priest, where he serves to this day, still under Malthus' invisible thumb.

ANDRASTE

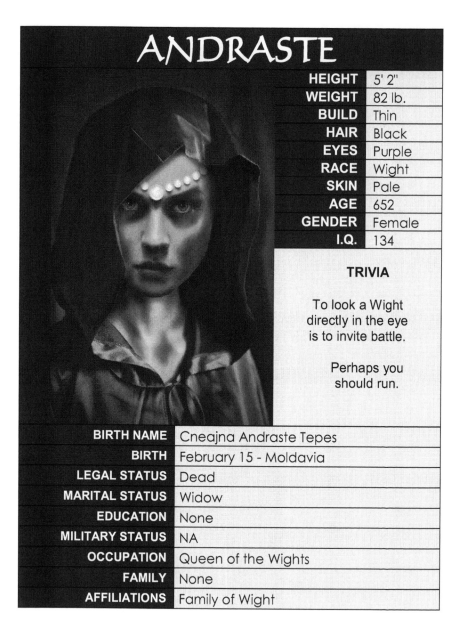

HEIGHT	5' 2"
WEIGHT	82 lb.
BUILD	Thin
HAIR	Black
EYES	Purple
RACE	Wight
SKIN	Pale
AGE	652
GENDER	Female
I.Q.	134

TRIVIA

To look a Wight
directly in the eye
is to invite battle.

Perhaps you
should run.

BIRTH NAME	Cneajna Andraste Tepes
BIRTH	February 15 - Moldavia
LEGAL STATUS	Dead
MARITAL STATUS	Widow
EDUCATION	None
MILITARY STATUS	NA
OCCUPATION	Queen of the Wights
FAMILY	None
AFFILIATIONS	Family of Wight

ANDRASTE

Andraste was born in late 14th-century Moldavia, a princess of the House of Tepes. After several miscarriages, Andraste was desperate and went to a local gypsy to assist her in becoming pregnant. Unknown to her, the gypsy's only child had been executed by Andraste's husband a year earlier for stealing food. So the gypsy placed a curse on her, stating that the fruit of her womb would be a monster whose birth would kill her. She would be the first of many brutal murders that would be laid at her cursed child's feet.

As prophesied, Andraste died giving birth to Vlad Tepes, but he left enough supernaturally charged blood in her system to resurrect Andraste several weeks later. After she dug out of her grave, she saw the damage her body had incurred while she was decomposing.

Unable to return to her home, Andraste wandered the cemeteries of Eastern Europe, calling the newly dead from their earthen mounds. Like her, those she raised were in a constant state of pain and displayed superhuman strength and near-invulnerability, though their intellects rarely survived the process. Eventually, Andraste commanded an army of twenty thousand Wights, and they infected many countries with the Black Plague.

Nimue, the guardian of the Great Sword Caliburnus, met Andraste as she and her horde set foot on the shores of England. Caliburnus drew blood, the first damage Andraste had suffered since her resurrection. Unwilling to plunge England into a war, Nimue made a pact with Andraste. The Wights would be allowed to live as long as she confined them to the caves at Eisriesenwelt and Altamira, and Andraste would be allowed to travel the world of men on the condition that no more Wights were created.

ARGUS

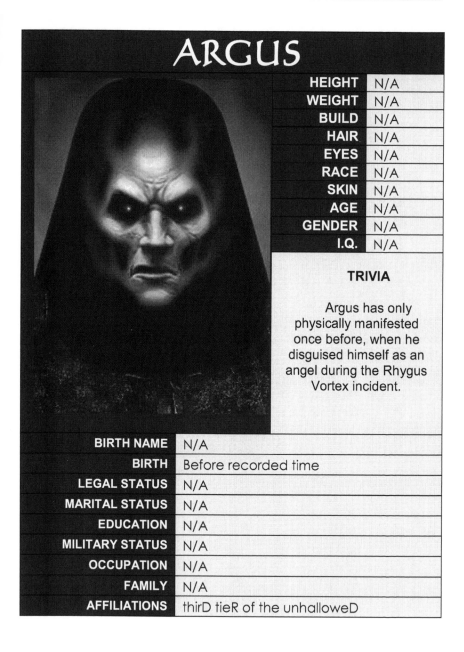

HEIGHT	N/A
WEIGHT	N/A
BUILD	N/A
HAIR	N/A
EYES	N/A
RACE	N/A
SKIN	N/A
AGE	N/A
GENDER	N/A
I.Q.	N/A

TRIVIA

Argus has only physically manifested once before, when he disguised himself as an angel during the Rhygus Vortex incident.

BIRTH NAME	N/A
BIRTH	Before recorded time
LEGAL STATUS	N/A
MARITAL STATUS	N/A
EDUCATION	N/A
MILITARY STATUS	N/A
OCCUPATION	N/A
FAMILY	N/A
AFFILIATIONS	thirD tieR of the unhalloweD

ARGUS

Even Hell has its own form of order. Consisting of one third of the former angelic host, Lucifer organized its eidolons into thirteen tierS, each with six lieutenantS, each with sixty centurionS, each with six hundred demons and each with six thousand licheN.

Argus was the third tieR lieutenant responsible for the fate of Jusinan, the so-called "Chosen Empire". Its failure to defeat Arter, who established the line of Witnesses led to its punishment. Argus' rule was taken and it was bound to the House of Arter. Its new mission: to bring about their downfall.

Being forced to tally lives of individuals instead of nations was at first thought to be a demotion, but as the Jusinan Empire covered the world, Argus recognized the power of the Witnesses was greater than that of any nation. While its charge remained the destruction of the Witnesses, it covertly aided their hold on world power, thereby maintaining its own.

At Amagrath, though the Witness Imperium had been killed, Argus assisted the continuation of the line by using the Witness' daughter as a temporary vessel of the power. At Ventura, Argus revealed the secret plans of the Witness Ahvoan who attempted to augment the power of Witnesses by polluting it with magicks, thus foiling his plans.

Argus' intentions were always suspected, but weren't revealed until it was discovered directly barring Grayden from obtaining the Prism of Edrah. Argus was stripped of authority and assigned to the thirteenth tieR. Instead of accepting its demotion, Argus hatched a plan to send the Witness Regent through the Void in an attempt to establish a new dominion on Earth.

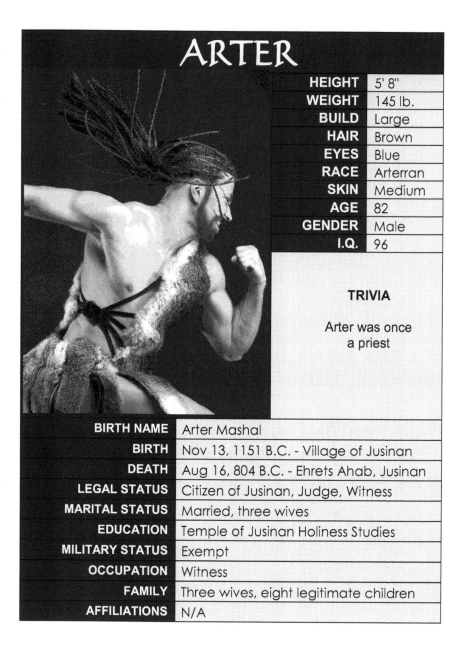

ARTER

HEIGHT	5' 8"
WEIGHT	145 lb.
BUILD	Large
HAIR	Brown
EYES	Blue
RACE	Arterran
SKIN	Medium
AGE	82
GENDER	Male
I.Q.	96

TRIVIA

Arter was once
a priest

BIRTH NAME	Arter Mashal
BIRTH	Nov 13, 1151 B.C. - Village of Jusinan
DEATH	Aug 16, 804 B.C. - Ehrets Ahab, Jusinan
LEGAL STATUS	Citizen of Jusinan, Judge, Witness
MARITAL STATUS	Married, three wives
EDUCATION	Temple of Jusinan Holiness Studies
MILITARY STATUS	Exempt
OCCUPATION	Witness
FAMILY	Three wives, eight legitimate children
AFFILIATIONS	N/A

ARTER

The first miracle of Arter's life was his birth. Born to a woman far past the age of childbirth, he was dedicated at birth. After his parents died two years later, Arter was raised by priests in the Temple of the One God. Arter aimlessly wandered through his religious studies, and left the priesthood at twenty. Temple superiors appointed him judge over a small village and he ruled without incident until his fiancée was killed in a Dagonite raid.

Arter and a group of his friends ambushed the Dagonites, who were still camped near the city. The Dagonite leader sent for reinforcements and they overwhelmed Arter's small band. Arter watched as each of his friends fell, but though he was attacked multiple times, Arter would not fall. Rage fueling vengeance, Arter killed them all. Returning to the Temple, Arter told the priest what happened and the priest bowed before him, declaring Arter the deliverer of Jusinan. Though he knew something was different, Arter refused to believe the priest's stories until his hand was forced by further Dagonite attacks.

Through arrogance he revealed the secret of his strength to a Dagonite prostitute. Arter was carried to the temple of Dagon as a human sacrifice. Only a last-minute repentance returned his strength and he destroyed the entire Dagonite government in one attack, fulfilling the promise given to his mother to deliver Jusinan.

At the time of Arter's death, the rule of the Chosen Empire had spanned most of Ehrets. When it was united under one throne, the empire was renamed to honor the man who had united the world: Arter.

His exploits were carried by vision to Earth, where they were watered down into what we now know as tales of King Arthur.

ARIEL BLOCH

HEIGHT	5' 8"
WEIGHT	124 lb.
BUILD	Thin
HAIR	Brown
EYES	Green
RACE	White
SKIN	Medium
AGE	15
GENDER	Female
I.Q.	127

TRIVIA

Before she ran away, Ariel won the lead role in her school's version of *Romeo and Juliet*

BIRTH NAME	Ariel Nacole Bloch
BIRTH	April 28, Philadelphia, Pennsylvania
LEGAL STATUS	US Citizen, no criminal record
MARITAL STATUS	Single
EDUCATION	High School student
MILITARY STATUS	N/A
OCCUPATION	Runaway
FAMILY	Parents, Aric and Shonda
AFFILIATIONS	N/A

ARIEL BLOCH

Ariel Bloch has always been on the move. In the first twelve years of her life, her family moved sixteen times in nine different states, leaving no time for making friends.

When her family settled in Salt Lake City, Ariel was twelve and she was told there would be no more moving. So for the first time in her life, Ariel allowed herself to relax.

But it was not meant to be.

On her fifteenth birthday, something stirred inside Ariel, and despite the new found security and friends she had made, Ariel found herself on the road heading east. Hitchhiking from car to car, Ariel made it to Central Illinois when she encountered her first bad ride. The man attacked her and Ariel ran from his car, but a blue bolt of lightning blasted her off her feet and the something inside awoke.

Ariel's transformation wasn't without cost. Not counting the man she escaped from, Ariel accidentally killed six people that day. In a panic and with nowhere to go, Ariel took the hand of the tall man who appeared out of thin air. She later regretted that decision. The man transported her to Mount Olympus where she was inducted into the Superiors program by Zeus himself. No longer able to speak her own name, Thanastasia became the last hope for the Superiors when Zeus turned on them.

She was able to save two people as Mount Olympus crumbled to the ground.

Thanastasia is now on the run with her friends Brine and Spectrum, trying to find their place in this world.

LISA CURTIS

HEIGHT	5' 4"
WEIGHT	137 lb.
BUILD	Medium
HAIR	Auburn
EYES	Green
RACE	White
SKIN	Medium
AGE	36
GENDER	Female
I.Q.	138

TRIVIA

Lisa has two
pugs named
"Yin" and "Yang"

BIRTH NAME	Melissa Dawn Williams
BIRTH	November 5 - Cambridge, Mass
LEGAL STATUS	US Citizen, no criminal record
MARITAL STATUS	Widowed (Thomas Edward Curtis)
EDUCATION	Constitutional Law - University of Illinois
MILITARY STATUS	N/A
OCCUPATION	Alderman, Chicago City Council
FAMILY	Two daughters: Jennifer and Megan
AFFILIATIONS	City Council, Chicago, Illinois

LISA CURTIS

Lisa Williams was the first member of her family to go to college. She majored in constitutional law at the University of Chicago, graduating fourth in her class, becoming a junior partner in one of Chicago's most prestigious law firms. There she met and fell in love with Thomas Curtis, a senior law partner. They married and continued to work in the law firm. Thomas was a devout Catholic but Lisa attended church more because of tradition than a deep spiritual commitment.

Thomas quit the law firm to run for city council. He easily won, becoming Chicago's sole conservative voice, but died of a heart attack midway through his second term. Lisa was approached to fill out the remainder of his term. She reluctantly accepted, but quickly found out that she had a flair for politics, and developed a reputation for being fair.

Despite her public successes, Lisa is in the midst of a private crisis. Her faith had always been shaky, but now she's angry with God for taking away her husband and leaving her children fatherless.

Lisa's world is turned upside down when her daughters are carjacked and are rescued by some kid who can fly and doesn't seem to be affected by bullets. She feels drawn to find out more about him and what his purpose is, but her campaign manager warns her about being publicly identified with a vigilante.

She doesn't know what she will do, but knows that she is now connected with this new vigilante and Lisa wants some answers.

ADRIANA DESPAIN

HEIGHT	5' 4"
WEIGHT	137 lb.
BUILD	Medium
HAIR	Auburn
EYES	Green
RACE	White
SKIN	Medium
AGE	36
GENDER	Female
I.Q.	138

TRIVIA

Adriana risked it all when's transformation changed her from a matronly 52 to her current age, 19

BIRTH NAME	Adriana Despain
BIRTH	March 1 – Lyon, France
LEGAL STATUS	French citizen, no criminal record
MARITAL STATUS	Single
EDUCATION	Minimal
MILITARY STATUS	N/A
OCCUPATION	Grandmistress, World Council
FAMILY	Three sons, all dead
AFFILIATIONS	Wiccan World Council

ADRIANA DESPAIN

Adriana Despain got to be nineteen years old twice in her lifetime; once during her normal life cycle and the second time when she risked everything in a blind transformational spell designed to keep her safe. In hours, she changed from a fifty-two year old woman to a nineteen year old girl.

But, as with any gain from magic, there is always a cost and Adriana Despain knew about costs.

When she was twelve, her father had been appointed Grandmaster over his local coven. During his initiation, he was told to bring his most precious possession.

Unfortunately, that was Adriana.

The twelve-year old was in the hospital for six weeks after the ritual and fortunately could never quite remember what had happened. All she knew was that her father had been killed and her mother was missing.

Adriana was taken in by witches and raised as one of their own. Her emotions, stretched raw by her trauma, boosted her natural mystical abilities and like her father, Adriana started moving up the ranks.

She was given the role of Mother at the House of Masson and began grooming the next heir. She grew in power, so when the Grandmistress Nicole asked her to bring her most precious possession, Adriana was ready.

In the resulting battle, Nicole lay dead at Adriana's feet. The ritual of ascension was a battle to the death. She took the throne of the world coven and has ruled ever since.

Her father had been weak, but Adriana was a survivor.

KHAYLE FRANNEL

HEIGHT	5' 11"
WEIGHT	229 lb.
BUILD	Large
HAIR	Gray
EYES	Green
RACE	Arterran
SKIN	Medium
AGE	115
GENDER	Male
I.Q.	127

TRIVIA

General Frannel
was a slave until
he was 28

BIRTH NAME	Khayle Shawmar Frannel
BIRTH	August 29 - Mawkohm, Lawmahd
LEGAL STATUS	Arterran Citizen, no criminal record
MARITAL STATUS	Widower, (Salla)
EDUCATION	Arterran Royal Military Academy
MILITARY STATUS	Active, Rank: General
OCCUPATION	General, Minister of Defense
FAMILY	One son: Ramon
AFFILIATIONS	Minister, Assembly of Ministers

KHAYLE FRANNEL

Born into a family of slaves, Khayle was granted his freedom when he saved the life of a Valiant. Though free, Khayle found himself without food, money or even a place to stay, and enlisted in the Royal Military Academy.

He graduated without honors, but the genius that was invisible in the classroom became apparent on the battlefield when he orchestrated the defeat of an insurrection from the tribal leaders of Abidawn, who had tried to secede from the Empire.

Promoted to General by then Witness Imperium Rawshah Mashal, Khayle served faithfully for many years, to the detriment of his family and his personal life.

His real test came during the fourth civil war, when his support was called for by both the Witness Imperium and then Witness Regent Eythan Mashal. Choosing to stand on principle, Khayle sided with Eythan in an admittedly futile attack. Eythan quickly befriended Frannel, and Khayle became one of his closest confidants.

After Rawshah was overthrown by the sudden appearance of Gerah Maugaine, Frannel was officially given the security seat on the Ministries of Assembly.

His personal life was forever put on hold as duties to the Empire took front seat. His wife died a few years ago, leaving Ramon as his only surviving family member. Before he could retire, he was called for one last mission; protect Eythan's son, Shiloh Mataran, by any means necessary. Khayle didn't know his own son would have to die to accomplish the mission. In the end, Khayle sacrificed the life of everyone onboard his ship to save Shiloh's life.

RAMON FRANNEL

HEIGHT	5' 11"
WEIGHT	165 lb.
BUILD	Light
HAIR	Brown
EYES	Brown
RACE	Arterran
SKIN	Medium
AGE	26
GENDER	Male
I.Q.	108

TRIVIA

Ramon was best known
for his exotic garden

BIRTH NAME	Ramon Shawmar Frannel
BIRTH	February 1 – Thronecity, Jusinan
LEGAL STATUS	Arterran citizen with no criminal record
MARITAL STATUS	Married (Feysha)
EDUCATION	Arterran Royal Military Academy
MILITARY STATUS	Active, Arterran Diplomatic Corps.
OCCUPATION	Lieutenant
FAMILY	Wife – Feysha, no children
AFFILIATIONS	Royal Military Diplomatic Corps

RAMON FRANNEL

Ramon Frannel was twelve years old before he ever met his father. Ramon's mother died shortly after Ramon graduated from the Academy, leaving him alone, except for the obligatory monthly visits from his father.

During this time, Ramon's anger was noted by several of his friends, one of whom was a loyalist to Grayden. When the time came for saboteurs to be chosen, Ramon was placed at the top of the recruitment list. It didn't take much coaxing to get Ramon to join. His wife Feysha noted the change in Ramon and their marriage became a burden to them both. She moved back with her people and Ramon took this as further evidence that the system needed to be overthrown by any means possible.

He placed himself on call for suicide duty, but was instead called to the High Priests' chamber. Ramon worried that the High Priest had, through his contacts, discovered Ramon's betrayal. He was right, but Ahmahl wasn't going to punish Ramon; he wanted Ramon for a specific task. The Witness Imperium had ordered the first tier of royal family off-world. Ahmahl wanted Ramon onboard the Regent's ship to assassinate him. Despite General Maugaine commanding the ship, Ramon eagerly agreed and petitioned his father for duty.

His father, trying to heal the rift between them, obliged, even though Ramon was neither active military or had taken a mental exam within the preceding year, mandatory for all personnel who work on royal grounds.

Ramon was almost successful with his assassination attempt. He managed to kill his father and almost took control of the ship, which would have led to Shiloh's death. He was suffocated by Mattis and his body dumped in deep space.

HABIDEH

HEIGHT	5' 6"
WEIGHT	177 lb.
BUILD	Medium
HAIR	Black
EYES	Green
RACE	Arterran
SKIN	Dark
AGE	127
GENDER	Male
I.Q.	127

TRIVIA

Habideh was
left handed.

BIRTH NAME	Habideh
BIRTH	October 4, 1197 B.C. – Eastern District
LEGAL STATUS	First Citizen of Dagon
MARITAL STATUS	Married
EDUCATION	No formal education
MILITARY STATUS	Ruling General of the Dagonite Army
OCCUPATION	Premiere for the House of Dagon
FAMILY	Two wives, nine children
AFFILIATIONS	Royal Council of Dagon

HABIDEH

Habideh was born to a poor tribe in the dry plains of Dagon's eastern district. Frustrated by his family's poverty, he and his slaves stole the bulk of his father's gold and moved to the more prosperous northern district, where he began learning everything he could about trading. After establishing himself as one of the chief northern businessmen, Habideh established Dawshane - a new port city - with himself as City Lord. While low tariffs attracted the honest, bribes attracted the dishonest. Dawshane outpaced the economies of other local city ports.

During this time, unrest in the royal cities erupted into a civil war. Random bloodshed was common until Habideh amassed a coalition of eight factions to crush the holdout eastern districts. Habideh established a new government with himself as Premiere and after order was restored, things prospered.

Habideh's territorial eye then turned toward the small cities that surrounded Dagon; specifically the small city-state Jusinan. A port city like Dawshane, Jusinan had prospered while other city ports surrounding Dagon had failed.

Habideh made it his personal goal to crush Jusinan and add its riches to his own. After a series of battles, Habideh replaced the head of the Jusinan city-state with a puppet leader. A relative peace ensued until the advent of Arter, who destroyed the Dagonite army at every turn, inspiring rebellion.

After tricking Arter into revealing his weakness, Habideh defeated the Jue and planned on using Arter as a human sacrifice. However, Arter regained his strength and destroyed the Temple of Dagon. Habideh died with all the royals, bringing an end to the Dagonite Empire. It is said that Habideh's bones were interred in a secret chamber beneath Arter's tomb to insure that the Dagonite Empire would never rise again.

ANDRIS LAIMA

HEIGHT	6' 1"
WEIGHT	202 lb.
BUILD	Strong
HAIR	Black
EYES	Blue
RACE	White
SKIN	Medium
AGE	48
GENDER	Male
I.Q.	112

TRIVIA

Andris Laima is an accomplished pianist.

BIRTH NAME	Andris Laima
BIRTH	April 13 – Rye, New York
LEGAL STATUS	Citizen of Nornswain, no criminal record
MARITAL STATUS	Widower
EDUCATION	Philosophy, University of Dublin
MILITARY STATUS	None
OCCUPATION	High Priest
FAMILY	None
AFFILIATIONS	Greater Worship Worldwide Temple

ANDRIS LAIMA

Andris Laima was born into the lap of luxury, living the shallow life of an aristocrat until a car collided into his limousine, running him off the road. Only the skill of Andris' driver kept it from rolling over. Andris' door was fused shut, preventing him from escaping. Glancing at the fiery wreck of the smaller car that had struck his, Andris saw the female passenger futilely trying to pull the driver out. The woman began waving her hands over the car and it began shaking and then opened like a sardine can, allowing the driver to levitate away. When she saw that Andris was watching, she ran away with her friend.

Andris found that an invisible world existed alongside the one he saw every day and in that world, he was less than a pawn. Andris soon found that his wealth was not the proper coin for the spiritual realm and for the first time in his life, Andris began to work. He researched every topic that was remotely associated with magicks and those who claimed to have magical powers.

After weeding out the charlatans, Andris found a real witch and married her. Together, as Brother and Sister Eternity, they created the "Worldwide Order of Worship," dedicated to the celebration of all religions. They gained worldwide attention as Hollywood's most popular actors started converting. Andris' power extended to the point that he virtually controls the small European country of Nornswain.

His wife was murdered and sacrificed by Andris after she left the cult to become a Christian. The increase in supernatural status placed him on the world stage of those who tread both worlds.

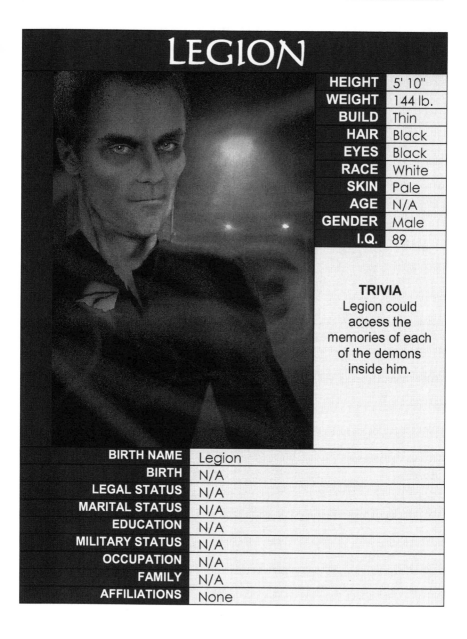

LEGION

HEIGHT	5' 10"
WEIGHT	144 lb.
BUILD	Thin
HAIR	Black
EYES	Black
RACE	White
SKIN	Pale
AGE	N/A
GENDER	Male
I.Q.	89

TRIVIA
Legion could access the memories of each of the demons inside him.

BIRTH NAME	Legion
BIRTH	N/A
LEGAL STATUS	N/A
MARITAL STATUS	N/A
EDUCATION	N/A
MILITARY STATUS	N/A
OCCUPATION	N/A
FAMILY	N/A
AFFILIATIONS	None

LEGION

Legion is to the supernatural realm what a category five tornado is to the physical realm. Neither occurrence is common, but when they occur, they bring death and destruction.

The first Arterran Legion manifestation was recorded by Gentry, the son of Arter and first heir to the powers of Witness Imperium. During the ceremony that turned authority of the empire over to Gentry, a man toward the back of the crowd began screaming. He jumped into the crowd and began savagely killing people.

Gentry, overconfident with his newfound powers, leapt toward the man, who merely backhanded him, sending him into the crowd. The man jumped on Gentry, beating him mercilessly. Though not as powerful as Gentry, Arter was a more experienced fighter and together, the two Witnesses were able to subdue Legion. Before it was exorcised, Legion warned that the spiritual wake that had been created by the Witness' new powers would open the gates for its brothers... and sisters.

Forty-six known appearances of Legion have occurred on Ehrets and two on Earth. The first Earth appearance occurred during the ministry of Christ and was easily dispelled. The second known Legion appearance was caused by the spiritual turbulence surrounding the build-up prior to the manifestation of the powers of the Witness Regent.

This manifestation of Legion was birthed in the fires of Hell and delivered on an autopsy gurney, hosted in the body of Shiloh's best friend, Brad Murray. Its life was fueled by vengeance and hatred toward Shiloh. Thanks to the direct intervention of the Regent, Legion only killed two people during its short four day life.

MALTHUS

HEIGHT	5' 6"
WEIGHT	145 lb.
BUILD	Thin
HAIR	Silver
EYES	Blue
RACE	Arterran
SKIN	Pale
AGE	70
GENDER	Male
I.Q.	152

TRIVIA

Malthus secretly cast spells on Rawshah's wives, hastening his lapse into madness.

BIRTH NAME	Illegitimate Birth – No birth name
BIRTH	April 3 – Throne City, Jusinan
LEGAL STATUS	Arterran criminal, escaped convict.
MARITAL STATUS	Single
EDUCATION	Temple of Jusinan Holiness Studies
MILITARY STATUS	Exempt
OCCUPATION	Escaped prisoner of Peysha
FAMILY	Brother: Mosh
AFFILIATIONS	Prior High Priest, Assembly of Ministers

MALTHUS

Born of royal blood, but illegitimate stock, Malthus was not given a name until he was sent, with his non-identical twin brother Mosh, to the House of Priests after being weaned at age two. Like other children at the orphanage, he was only given one name, having no need for family or tribal affiliations.

At four, Malthus fell ill during the rawmas plague, and like other young survivors, his growth was dramatically stunted. Like the orphans he lived with, Malthus wondered who his parents were. A sympathetic servant revealed to Malthus that his father was then Witness Imperium Rawshah. Knowing both his own age as well as that of then Witness Regent Mossad, Malthus realized that if his birth had been recognized, the throne would have been his.

Malthus threw himself in his studies, quickly rising to the top of his order. An older student in his order planned to attack him, but was thwarted by Malthus' much larger brother Mosh. One of the would-be attackers died in the fight and Mosh was sentenced to the Toad Squad. Rising in the ranks of the Priests was difficult until he began studying the dark arts. It was at this point that he met Ahmahl, a studious priest with a great imagination. When Ahmahl found out that Malthus betrayed him, he left to study the dark arts himself.

Malthus manipulated events so the Witness Imperium had to sacrifice his own son. Sacrificing a boy on the Altar of the Holies gave Malthus great power. Eythan found out later that he had been tricked and banished Malthus for his deception. Malthus in return, later revealed Eythan's deception with the faked death of his son Grayden to the public. Malthus became Grayden's mentor, turning his rebellion into a weapon powerful enough to kill the Witness Imperium.

EYTHAN MASHAL

HEIGHT	6' 3"
WEIGHT	235 lb.
BUILD	Large
HAIR	Brown
EYES	Blue
RACE	Arterran
SKIN	Medium
AGE	51
GENDER	Male
I.Q.	112

TRIVIA

Eythan was originally groomed to be governor of Roosh

BIRTH NAME	Eythan Pawlol Mashal
BIRTH	June 19 – Throne City, Jusinan
LEGAL STATUS	Citizen of Arterra, no criminal record
MARITAL STATUS	Married (Pesec, Nakah & Peri)
EDUCATION	Witness Education Academy of Jusinan
MILITARY STATUS	Commander of all Arterran Armies
OCCUPATION	Witness Imperium
FAMILY	Three wives, eight children
AFFILIATIONS	Ruling Council, Assembly of Ministers

EYTHAN MASHAL

As second born male to the house of Arter, Eythan Mashal grew up in the Mlechaw palace with no realistic chance of ascending to the golden throne. Like all princes, he would govern one of the territories and was assigned the governorship of Roosh.

When his father began his decline into madness, Eythan's elder brother, was banished, leaving Eythan as the Regent. Eythan reluctantly accepted and showed a natural aptitude for leadership.

His father had tortured and killed hundreds of people. One day during prayers, a mother of a family who was murdered by Rawshah approached Eythan, begging for mercy from his father's abuse. Rawshah killed her on the spot, but her words would not leave Eythan's thoughts.

Though futile, Eythan began raising an army, declaring war on Rawshah the following year. Rawshah ignored his son's ragtag army until they destroyed his favorite palace.

Rawshah took a personal hand in retaliation, killing thousands of members of the impromptu army and Eythan lost all hope. He sent a message for his father to meet him at the Temple of the Holies. That's when Gerah Maugaine entered the scene. He killed Rawshah with the sword of the Angel of Death and handed the weapon to Eythan for safekeeping.

Eythan took a personal hand in reorganizing the empire so that this abuse of power couldn't happen again. He abolished the death penalty, retrying every case his father had judged.

GRAYDEN MASHAL

HEIGHT	6' 3"
WEIGHT	203 lb.
BUILD	Medium
HAIR	Black
EYES	Blue
RACE	Arterran
SKIN	Medium
AGE	26
GENDER	Male
I.Q.	117

TRIVIA

Grayden married prior to becoming Regent.

BIRTH NAME	Grayden Mashal Mashal
BIRTH	December 9 – Throne City, Jusinan
LEGAL STATUS	Arterran citizen, no criminal record
MARITAL STATUS	Widowed
EDUCATION	Witness Education Academy of Jusinan
MILITARY STATUS	Commander of all Arterran Armies
OCCUPATION	Usurper, Arterran Throne
FAMILY	Wife, deceased, brothers and sisters
AFFILIATIONS	Ruling Council, Assembly of Ministers

GRAYDEN MASHAL

Grayden Mashal was born with the ultimate promise; rule of his world and powers unknown to most mortal men. His youth was paved on the road of that promise. His mother, First Queen Pesec had a smooth reign as governess of Abidawn. While a scandal erupted when he married prior to becoming Regent, everything else was perfect until a sacrificial hunt the year after he had obtained the ring of regency.

As in most areas, Grayden had excelled in his regency studies, including mastering the regent ability of flight. Eager to show off to his father (as well as the ministers), Grayden intercepted the return flight home. He thought that his father would be riding in the sky ship, but was excited to see him flying ahead. Grayden didn't know that his father had promised to sacrifice the first thing he encountered on his return trip.

Devastated, Eythan tried to cover his sin by sending Grayden to hide in a remote palace in Hilool and allowing then High Priest Malthus to sacrifice another boy in Grayden's place, a boy that Eythan was told was already dead. The ruse worked and no one suspected anything until Malthus was arrested for witchcraft, a crime normally punishable by death. Eythan revoked the death penalty after his father had abused the death laws, so Malthus was instead sent to Peysha Island.

Escaping Peysha, Malthus found Grayden and showed him the secret histories of the Witnesses, promising him the return of his throne. It worked and Grayden pledged allegiance to Malthus and agreed to raise an army.

Grayden renounced the heritage of the Witnesses, though he retains the power of the Witness Regent. He has recently obtained far greater, though darker, power with the possession of the prisM of edraH.

PERI MASHAL

HEIGHT	5' 1"
WEIGHT	115 lb.
BUILD	Thin
HAIR	Bronze
EYES	Green
RACE	Arterran
SKIN	Light
AGE	27
GENDER	Female
I.Q.	106

TRIVIA

This is Peri's official marriage portrait. She was 14 at the time.

BIRTH NAME	Peri Sheffer Roosh
BIRTH	October 13 - Hawdarah, Roosh
LEGAL STATUS	Governess of Roosh
MARITAL STATUS	Married (Eythan Mashal)
EDUCATION	No formal schooling
MILITARY STATUS	Exempt
OCCUPATION	First Queen
FAMILY	Four children: Paige, Lira, Audra, Shiloh
AFFILIATIONS	Governor's Council (Roosh)

PERI MASHAL

The Lieber Wastelands are so named because of the harsh living conditions there. Peri was the youngest girl in a family that belonged to Roosh, the poorest of all tribes. Her family moved to the Lieber Wastelands to help mine mineral rich areas, but a deceitful overseer tricked her father into signing away his rights and they returned penniless to their homeland.

News of the Witness' call for Procession reached Roosh and her father immediately knew what to do. Peri was to reach the age of consent a few days before Procession, so he petitioned to place Peri in the roster. He was surprised days later when a royal courier announced that Peri had been accepted and escorted her family to Jusinan.

They were overjoyed when Peri was chosen as queen. As part of the dowry, Peri's father was officially awarded land in the mineral rich eastern sector of Lieber he had mined. Her family immediately left to begin building on their new land. Peri stood alone on the platform in front of the cheering crowd as the only people she had ever known left her. A brief wave from her mother was the only goodbye she received. She never saw them again.

Peri quickly settled into the system as the youngest of Eythan's queens. Things quickly changed when Grayden's mother killed herself. Peri gave birth to Shiloh, promoting her to the rank of First Queen, placing her as Governess of her home territory of Roosh.

When she believed that she lost both Eythan and Shiloh in the same day, sentinels on her ship, mindful of the suicidal response Grayden's mother had, determined to watch Peri very carefully.

RAWSHAH MASHAL

HEIGHT	6' 4"
WEIGHT	246 lb.
BUILD	Large
HAIR	Bronze
EYES	Blue
RACE	Arterran
SKIN	Medium
AGE	76
GENDER	Male
I.Q.	121

TRIVIA

Rawshah was an
only child

BIRTH NAME	Rawshah Mashal
BIRTH	February 24 – Throne City, Jusinan
LEGAL STATUS	Citizen of Arterra, no criminal record
MARITAL STATUS	Married
EDUCATION	Witness Education Academy of Jusinan
MILITARY STATUS	Commander of all Arterran Armies
OCCUPATION	Witness Imperium
FAMILY	Seven wives, twelve children
AFFILIATIONS	Ruling Council, Assembly of Ministers

RAWSHAH MASHAL

When he became Witness Imperium, Rawshah inherited a planet experiencing a golden age. Exploration had already begun outside their solar system; science and religion had become a technological powerhouse that had eradicated hunger and disease.

To Rawshah, who pined for the adventures of his forefathers, he had become Witness on a world that no longer needed one, so he tried to ease his boredom by hunting sorcerers. Finding no worthy adversaries, Rawshah crossed the line.

Ignoring centuries of warnings, Rawshah tortured several witches until he found a coven leader and forced her to create a monster for him to fight. The beast was simply no match for Rawshah, so he let the witches reclaim their ancestral castle. He gave them three months to create a beast that would be worthy of battle.

When an army of beasts appeared on the streets of Throne City two months later, they slaughtered over ten thousand people. Instead of granting power to one beast, the witches had created hundreds of smaller beasts that Rawshah found impossible to catch.

Faced with the blood of thousands of innocents on his hands, Rawshah snapped. He fled the city to avenge the deaths he had inadvertently caused. When he reached the castle, the witches were gone, but left something behind: the broken and tortured body of his firstborn son Awgum.

He was the sacrifice they used to conjure the beasts.

It took Rawshah over a month to find and kill the beasts. He returned to his throne a broken man who slowly lost connection with his sanity.

MATTIS

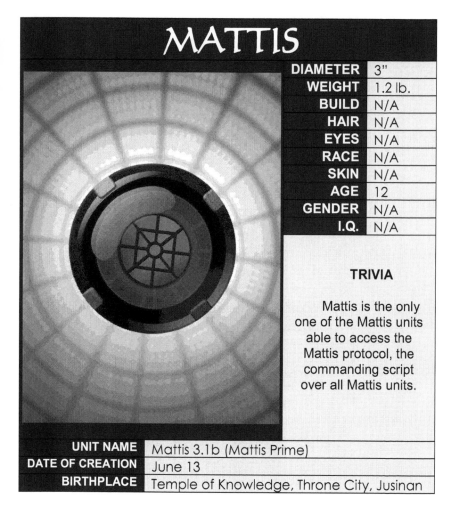

DIAMETER	3"
WEIGHT	1.2 lb.
BUILD	N/A
HAIR	N/A
EYES	N/A
RACE	N/A
SKIN	N/A
AGE	12
GENDER	N/A
I.Q.	N/A

TRIVIA

Mattis is the only one of the Mattis units able to access the Mattis protocol, the commanding script over all Mattis units.

UNIT NAME	Mattis 3.1b (Mattis Prime)
DATE OF CREATION	June 13
BIRTHPLACE	Temple of Knowledge, Throne City, Jusinan

MATTIS

Every aspect of Arterran society is regulated by computers. Directly integrated into homes, vehicles and devices of all kinds, computers manage the more mundane tasks for the average Arterran such as temperature and humidity control, food preparation, medical attention and transportation.

After a brief dalliance with robots and visible technology, Arterran society grew tired of the intrusion of "the tech look". Ever since, all technology was designed to blend in with their surroundings. Attendant programs that monitor conditions within the home are the only computer interface a family normally has. Even Arterran police androids are created to look human.

The Mattis units are the newest type of technology, which is based on biogenetic material instead of traditional circuitry. Matter has been reconstructed to behave as neurons in the brain does, providing a dramatic increase in processing efficiency. The Mattis units were literally painted into the objects they were assigned to; Mattis in a cavity specially designed for it inside Eythan's helmet; Gentry in the two boxes on Gerah's belt; Healey in the head of Peri's staff and Sumac in a chamber on the back of the throne.

The photo in this entry is of the credit card sized units that Shiloh used to contact Mattis before using the helmet.

It is no coincidence that it resembles the relic chamber that housed a lock of the prophet Mattis' hair. One of the hairs was placed in the Mattis unit, which, mixed with the biogenetic material, basically make it an electronic clone of the prophet.

GERAH MAUGAINE

HEIGHT	6' 5"
WEIGHT	265 lb.
BUILD	Large
HAIR	Unknown
EYES	Slate gray
RACE	Arterran
SKIN	Medium
AGE	Unknown
GENDER	Male
I.Q.	Unknown

TRIVIA

Gerah's voice can be heard clearly, as if he wasn't wearing a faceplate

BIRTH NAME	Unknown
BIRTH	Unknown
LEGAL STATUS	Citizen of Arterra, no criminal record
MARITAL STATUS	Single
EDUCATION	Unknown
MILITARY STATUS	General, Arterran Provincial Armies
OCCUPATION	General, Minister of War
FAMILY	Unknown
AFFILIATIONS	Assembly of Ministers

GERAH MAUGAINE

Very little is known about Gerah Maugaine prior to his appearance at a critical moment during the Fourth Civil War. Then-Regent Eythan Mashal was leading a rebellion against his father, then-Witness Imperium Rawshah. Eythan led the fight to the Temple of Jusinan, praying for Intervention. His prayers were answered with the arrival of Maugaine. Rawshah immediately dropped the defeated Eythan and fell to the ground on one knee, believing Gerah to be the Angel of Death. When Gerah revealed that he wasn't, Rawshah attacked. Gerah instantly killed him.

Eythan awoke to find Gerah standing over him. Eythan asked him to rescue the Temple of Holies. Gerah destroyed everyone who stood against him and saved the priests who were being held hostage. Gerah left and wasn't seen again for several months. When he returned, Eythan convinced him to move onto the palace grounds, granting him the commission of general in the security forces.

Gerah exists outside the jurisdiction of man, including the Witness Imperium's rule, which sometimes places him at odds with Eythan. Gerah is also known to have had a sacrifice placed on him, something normally reserved for Witnesses when they take their vows as Regent. His sacrifice, like regency sacrifices, isn't publicly known, but has been rumored to deal with either the Temple or the Prism of Edrah.

Gerah claims lineage through the Maugaine tribe through his last name, though the Maugaine tribe was wiped out two thousand years ago. His very name is an affront to Malthus and Ahmahl, a constant reminder that he has tribal and spiritual claim to the ministry they occupy.

MOSH

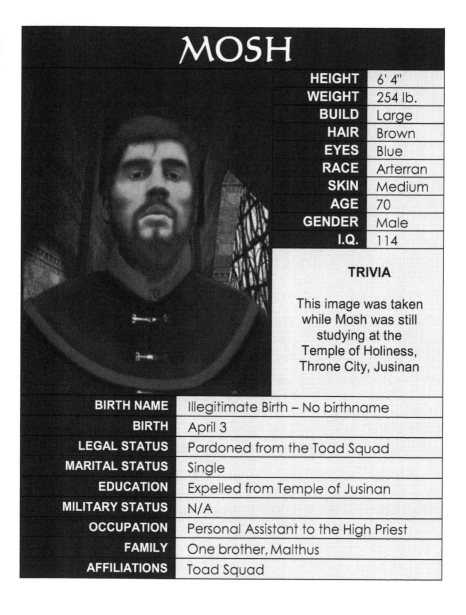

HEIGHT	6' 4"
WEIGHT	254 lb.
BUILD	Large
HAIR	Brown
EYES	Blue
RACE	Arterran
SKIN	Medium
AGE	70
GENDER	Male
I.Q.	114

TRIVIA

This image was taken while Mosh was still studying at the Temple of Holiness, Throne City, Jusinan

BIRTH NAME	Illegitimate Birth – No birthname
BIRTH	April 3
LEGAL STATUS	Pardoned from the Toad Squad
MARITAL STATUS	Single
EDUCATION	Expelled from Temple of Jusinan
MILITARY STATUS	N/A
OCCUPATION	Personal Assistant to the High Priest
FAMILY	One brother, Malthus
AFFILIATIONS	Toad Squad

MOSH

Life in the "Toad Squads" is rough. They do the dirty work – sewage and mechanical tasks - that computers can't and people won't. As illegitimate children of the throne, both Mosh and his younger twin brother Malthus were placed in the House of Priests. Non-identical twins, Mosh was much larger and stronger than Malthus and was constantly protecting him.

Mosh caught wind of a plan to harm Malthus and attacked the boys before they could reach Malthus. One of the boys died in the attack and Mosh was taken to the Tribunal. His punishment? Seventy years in Peysha or fifty years in the Toad Squad. Mosh chose the Toad Squad.

Malthus continued to advance in rank and when he was assigned to the Temple, he used his influence to visit Mosh. After twenty years in servitude, Mosh had become bitter. Mosh was angry that his life was ruined indirectly because of Malthus while Malthus was embarrassed to owe Mosh such a great debt.

Malthus grew higher in the ranks of the Temple priests and used his rank to prematurely release Mosh from the Toad Squads as his personal house slave. Animosity between the brothers deepened.

Eventually, Mosh pushed Malthus too far and in a moment of rage, Malthus tried to cast a powerful curse on Mosh, which didn't work because of the blood ties of a twin. The act exposed to Mosh that Malthus had been training in the dark arts. That and the knowledge that their father was Rawshah has kept Mosh safe from Malthus.

BRAD MURRAY

HEIGHT	6' 1"
WEIGHT	228 lb.
BUILD	Large
HAIR	Brown
EYES	Brown
RACE	White
SKIN	Medium
AGE	18
GENDER	Male
I.Q.	107

TRIVIA

Brad's first car was a red Mustang, which he received for his tenth birthday.

BIRTH NAME	Bradley Newton Murray
BIRTH	May 3 - Chang Mai, Thailand
LEGAL STATUS	US Citizen with a criminal record
MARITAL STATUS	Single
EDUCATION	High School diploma
MILITARY STATUS	N/A
OCCUPATION	N/A
FAMILY	Father – Phillip, Mother – Angeles
AFFILIATIONS	None

BRAD MURRAY

Brad Murray's parents had always been wealthy. They had everything they ever wanted, but when Brad came along, they found out that he was the one thing they had they didn't want.

Though they went through the motions, took all the right family pictures and spent ridiculous amounts of money on him, Brad never felt at home in the house of his parents. The only moment of familial feeling for Brad was when his aunt Camilla came to live with them after her divorce. Brad met his cousin Maria for the first time and she became the sister he never had. While they soon moved to their own home in Champaign, they still both attended the same school. Brad has kept close ties with her, and she has been the one constant in his life.

Brad was held back in sixth grade when he was out of country most of the year. When his family returned from France and moved to Champaign, Illinois, he had just broken his leg and placed in a class with disabled students. He was made fun of by everyone but one; a new kid named Shiloh Wagner. Brad quickly attached to Shiloh and even after his cast came off, they remained best friends.

Later, Brad began drinking and using drugs to escape his family problems. Shiloh tried to help him, but Brad fell off the wagon time and time again. When he met Kristi Thomas, everything changed. Though she was clearly not in the same social circles that Brad belonged to, there was something about her that drained all of the self-hate out of him and Brad was drug and alcohol free for the first time in years. When Kristi rejected Brad, he instantly returned to the daily ritual of despair that eventually claimed his life and set in motion events that would threaten the life of his friend Shiloh.

MARIA PHILLIPS

HEIGHT	5' 9"
WEIGHT	132 lb.
BUILD	Thin
HAIR	Black
EYES	Brown
RACE	Latino
SKIN	Medium
AGE	18
GENDER	Female
I.Q.	116

TRIVIA

Maria was Girls' Varsity MVP last year

BIRTH NAME	Daniella Marie Phillips
BIRTH	December 4 – Chicago, Illinois
LEGAL STATUS	US citizen, no criminal record
MARITAL STATUS	Single
EDUCATION	High School graduate
MILITARY STATUS	N/A
OCCUPATION	N/A
FAMILY	Father – Mark, Mother - Camilla
AFFILIATIONS	Varsity Basketball, Cheerleader,

MARIA PHILLIPS

Maria Phillips is the only child of Hall of Fame quarterback Mark Phillips and clothing designer Camilla Guadalupe. Maria moved to Champaign during her sophomore year of high school after her mother divorced Mark for having multiple affairs.

Her father visits once a month, but while Maria looks forward to his visits, her mother is still stinging from the divorce and the visits usually result in arguments.

Maria is a senior at Champaign High School. She's a forward on the girls' varsity basketball team and has been a varsity cheerleader for the past two years.

The weekly allowance from her father allows Maria to purchase whatever clothing she wants and though she doesn't purposely try to maintain the latest fashions, she is considered one of the school's "fashionistas."

Maria's major quirk is that she loves the "Trek Wars" movies. Her bedroom is a mixture of Trek Wars posters, books and action figures. She still sleeps with her "Vulkie" bear and on every Halloween dresses up like one of her favorite characters.

As a favor to her cousin Brad Murray, she goes on a Trek Wars movie date with his friend Shiloh. After a wreck takes Brad's life, Maria bonds to Shiloh. Then she discovers that the nice kid that has an eternal crush on her is more than he appears! Drawn to Shiloh for his fame, Maria is now having strange and terrifying dreams.

MARCUS TAYLOR

HEIGHT	5' 8"
WEIGHT	190 lb.
BUILD	Medium
HAIR	Bald
EYES	Brown
RACE	African
SKIN	Medium
AGE	42
GENDER	Male
I.Q.	186

TRIVIA

Marcus' father was an accomplished general.

BIRTH NAME	Marcus Alan Taylor
BIRTH	May 21 – Berlin, Germany
LEGAL STATUS	US Citizen with no criminal record
MARITAL STATUS	Single
EDUCATION	Multiple Masters Degrees
MILITARY STATUS	N/A
OCCUPATION	Unofficial Senior Analyst for the CIA
FAMILY	Parents deceased, sister Arimentha
AFFILIATIONS	National Security Agency, CIA

MARCUS TAYLOR

Marcus Taylor was born to an Army family and moved several times before his family settled in Houston. His life would have been uneventful had it not been for a retired CIA analyst turned second grade teacher who noted that Marcus possessed off the chart intelligence.

After testing Marcus with advanced materials ranging from algebra to quantitative theory, she made a call to her former superiors at the CIA. Though he never saw his benefactors, Marcus' family was quietly moved to Maryland so he could attend a government school for extremely gifted children.

Marcus graduated from their equivalent of high school at ten and their campus college at twelve. He earned his first master's degree in computer programming at thirteen. His graduation gift was one of the first personal computers on the market. The rest is geek history as he invented the first virus and then became the electronic fist for the federal government.

At first, Marcus refused to play the DC political game and quickly made serious enemies, most notably a senator from New York. Marcus struck first, hacking the Senator's bank accounts, revealing several illegal transactions. The Senator was removed from office and served seventeen years in federal prison.

Subsequent enemies found the price for crossing Marcus too expensive. Some of the old-timers even claim that Marcus possesses more power than J. Edgar Hoover.

But they would never make such a claim in public.

KRISTI THOMAS

HEIGHT	5' 1"
WEIGHT	109 lb.
BUILD	Thin
HAIR	Blonde
EYES	Hazel
RACE	White
SKIN	Light
AGE	17
GENDER	Female
I.Q.	134

TRIVIA

Kristi could probably beat you at chess.

BIRTH NAME	Christiana Michelle Thomas
BIRTH	October 4 – Clinton, Illinois
LEGAL STATUS	US Citizen with no criminal record
MARITAL STATUS	Single
EDUCATION	High School diploma
MILITARY STATUS	N/A
OCCUPATION	N/A
FAMILY	Mother – Shelly, Stepfather – Joe
AFFILIATIONS	Yearbook Committee

KRISTI THOMAS

Kristi Thomas wasn't supposed to be born. Doctors told her mother she was infertile, but Shelly Thomas was surprised to discover that she was pregnant less than six months after her wedding. Kristi never met her father, though.

He died in a training accident before she was born.

Her mother was devastated and became overprotective of Kristi even before she almost died of pneumonia at three. As a result, Kristi grew up an inside kid, never playing outside with her school friends. This gave her plenty of time to read and draw and her natural talent for art bloomed early.

Kristi's mother remarried later and her step-father Joe adopted her as his own. Her mother's protectiveness lightened up as Kristi's health improved, but her artistic skills had already replaced most of her social skills. She began painting at eight and sculpting at ten. By the time she entered high school, she already had an extensive portfolio highlighting three mediums.

Kristi's favorite subject is the sky, and her sculpture "Lazy Dawn" won first place at the state art show her junior year. She has already been granted scholarships at three colleges, including the University of Illinois, where she plans on graduating with an art design major.

YAWSHAH TOBIAH

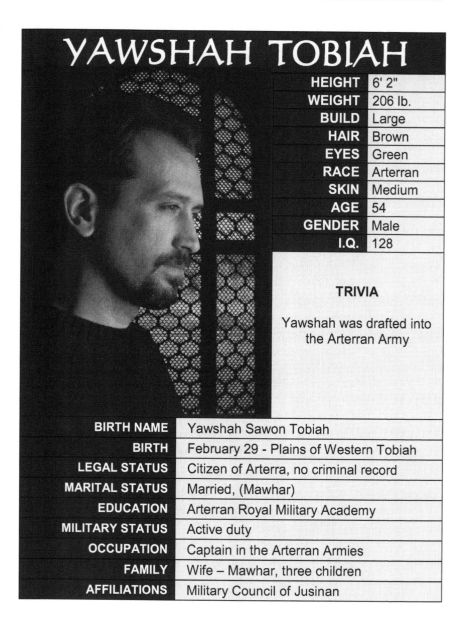

HEIGHT	6' 2"
WEIGHT	206 lb.
BUILD	Large
HAIR	Brown
EYES	Green
RACE	Arterran
SKIN	Medium
AGE	54
GENDER	Male
I.Q.	128

TRIVIA

Yawshah was drafted into the Arterran Army

BIRTH NAME	Yawshah Sawon Tobiah
BIRTH	February 29 - Plains of Western Tobiah
LEGAL STATUS	Citizen of Arterra, no criminal record
MARITAL STATUS	Married, (Mawhar)
EDUCATION	Arterran Royal Military Academy
MILITARY STATUS	Active duty
OCCUPATION	Captain in the Arterran Armies
FAMILY	Wife – Mawhar, three children
AFFILIATIONS	Military Council of Jusinan

YAWSHAH TOBIAH

The Sawon family of the Tobiah tribe had a long heritage of military service, but Yawshah never saw himself carrying on the tradition. There was a huge world that existed beyond servitude. He began investing in lucrative industrial plants and lived his own life until one day when he received a summons to Throne City.

He threw it away, as well as the next four. When one of his plants shut down for a day, Yawshah was furious. He travelled to the plant and when he arrived, he saw an old man standing at the front of the gate. Yawshah tried to pass, but the old man wouldn't move. Yawshah reached for a blade but the man stood still. He found out why when the blade shattered on the man's chest. The image of the old man shuddered and was replaced by that of Gerah Maugaine.

His fury instantly drained into fear and Yawshah fell to the ground face first. Gerah asked him why he had abandoned his family's Call to service. Yawshah honestly replied that the call was never his. Gerah replied that he, too, once felt that way, but a Call is not an option, nor something that can be ignored. Angry, Yawshah stood and as he looked at Gerah, he instantly knew that he had been wrong, and he allowed Gerah to draft him on the spot. After he graduated from the academy, General Frannel personally requested Yawshah be assigned as his assistant.

Yawshah was promoted to the rank of captain prior to being assigned to the royal ship carrying the First Queen.

USCHI

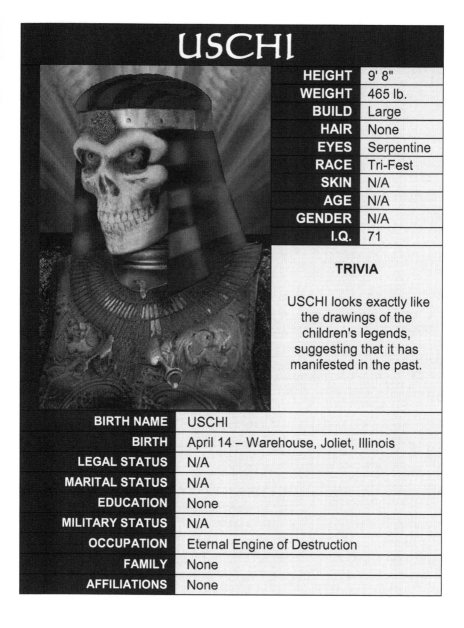

HEIGHT	9' 8"
WEIGHT	465 lb.
BUILD	Large
HAIR	None
EYES	Serpentine
RACE	Tri-Fest
SKIN	N/A
AGE	N/A
GENDER	N/A
I.Q.	71

TRIVIA

USCHI looks exactly like the drawings of the children's legends, suggesting that it has manifested in the past.

BIRTH NAME	USCHI
BIRTH	April 14 – Warehouse, Joliet, Illinois
LEGAL STATUS	N/A
MARITAL STATUS	N/A
EDUCATION	None
MILITARY STATUS	N/A
OCCUPATION	Eternal Engine of Destruction
FAMILY	None
AFFILIATIONS	None

USCHI

USCHI is the name of a fictional monster in Arterran literature. There are many stories, but all have the same description: a giant skeletal beast that fed on the hearts of children because it has no heart of its own. The tales are considered to be among the most horrific of all Arterran literature.

Tales of the USCHI go back to Jusinan himself, who spoke of a race of giants who "had less compassion than the USCHI". The first mention of USCHI dates to 3200 B.C. in some of the earliest stone writings still in existence. Due to the superhuman traits depicted in the stories, some Arterran historians theorize its roots come from an exaggeration of a Legion manifestation.

In Arterran culture, the first letter of Holy objects is always capitalized. The last letter of unholY objects is capitalized, but special spiritual objects are totally capitalized. USCHI is a tri-fest; a rare being who manifests power on both the physical and spiritual plane simultaneously.

Argus, a thirD tieR demon seeking sanctuary and new power on Earth, was baited to a warehouse in Joliet, Illinois, where the highest tech battle armor available was being housed. The Earth's version of the prisM of Edrah fused the demon into the armor, eternally binding the man in the armor, the armor itself and Argus into a new being: the tri-fest known as USCHI.

USCHI is bound by Brother Eternity's formational spells from directly or indirectly harming him or his property and is bound to follow his every order. While its intelligence is that of a small child, USCHI is anything but innocent. It is no exaggeration to say that the stories adequately describe it: An eternal engine of destruction whose presence is a disaster of Biblical proportion.

GEORGE WAGNER

HEIGHT	5' 10"
WEIGHT	215 lb.
BUILD	Medium
HAIR	Brown
EYES	Green
RACE	White
SKIN	Medium
AGE	53
GENDER	Male
I.Q.	119

TRIVIA

George belongs to a fiction writing group

BIRTH NAME	George Mason Wagner
BIRTH	November 13 – DeWitt, Illinois
LEGAL STATUS	US Citizen, no criminal record
MARITAL STATUS	Married (Lillian Irene Reynolds)
EDUCATION	BA, Engineering - Parkland College
MILITARY STATUS	N/A
OCCUPATION	Engineer
FAMILY	Three children: Julie, Shiloh and Tina
AFFILIATIONS	Deacon, Champaign Community Church

GEORGE WAGNER

George Wagner was always known as "the quiet Wagner boy." Unlike his outgoing and athletic twin Pete, George spent much of his childhood at the local library. Even his teachers urged George to put down his books and make friends, but George would just politely smile and grab another book.

It took his father's death when he was fifteen to change things. Both Pete and George dropped out of school to work at the local canning factory.

Pete immediately left for the military when he turned eighteen, but George stayed at home with his mother and his books. He met his future wife Lillian while working at the factory and they were married three months later, in time for Pete's return home.

Pete had married as well while he was overseas and brought his bride home as a surprise to his mother. The surprise was on Pete as his new bride ran away the moment she set foot on American soil. Pete returned home, broken hearted. He moved into his parents' home and remained there until his mother died. George invited Pete to come live with him and his family, but Pete left and hasn't been seen since.

George worked two jobs to put himself through college and graduated with a degree in electrical engineering at the University of Illinois.

George is an avid writer and he has had several short stories published in various magazines. He is currently working on his first novel, a mystery featuring a detective who gets clues by talking with dogs.

JULIE WAGNER

HEIGHT	5' 11"
WEIGHT	145 lb.
BUILD	Medium
HAIR	Brown
EYES	Green
RACE	White
SKIN	Medium
AGE	17
GENDER	Female
I.Q.	121

TRIVIA

Julie is the tallest
member of the
Wagner family

BIRTH NAME	Julia Diamond Wagner
BIRTH	July 26 – Champaign, Illinois
LEGAL STATUS	US Citizen, no criminal record
MARITAL STATUS	Single
EDUCATION	Graduate, Champaign High School
MILITARY STATUS	N/A
OCCUPATION	Student
FAMILY	Parents George and Lillian; two siblings: Shiloh and Tina
AFFILIATIONS	Varsity Basketball Player, Champaign High School, Salvation Army, First Birth

JULIE WAGNER

Julie Wagner is an outgoing girl who plays on the high school varsity basketball team and is a volunteer in her spare time.

When she was fifteen, her best friend became pregnant and after helping her friend at the local chapter of First Birth, an organization that assists pregnant teens, Julie began volunteering there after school.

She plays point guard for the girls' basketball team. Maria Phillips is her team mate and after Maria started dating Shiloh, she and Julie become good friends. Maria prides herself on giving Julie fashion tips, something Julie had almost totally ignored until that point.

She has been dating Cody Batson for the past year and after graduation, plans on going to the University of Illinois to major in architectural design.

LILLIAN WAGNER

HEIGHT	5' 6"
WEIGHT	141 lb.
BUILD	Medium
HAIR	Brown
EYES	Brown
RACE	White
SKIN	Medium
AGE	52
GENDER	Female
I.Q.	113

TRIVIA

Lillian provides the artwork for her husband's books

BIRTH NAME	Lillian Irene Reynolds
BIRTH	February 28 - Gibson City, Illinois
LEGAL STATUS	US Citizen, no criminal record
MARITAL STATUS	Married (George Mason Wagner)
EDUCATION	Graduate, Gibson City High School
MILITARY STATUS	N/A
OCCUPATION	Housewife, artist
FAMILY	Three children: Julie, Shiloh and Tina
AFFILIATIONS	Community Church Women's Auxiliary

LILLIAN WAGNER

Born in a small rural city, Lillian Reynolds learned the meaning of a hard days' work at a very early age. Her parents were factory workers, and money was hard to come by so she and her two brothers helped make ends meet by working in the corn fields of Illinois after school. To amuse herself as a child, Lillian began drawing pictures of local landscapes.

After graduating high school, she began work at a local canning factory where she met and fell in love with George Wagner. She wasn't looking for love, but when she started the job, she searched for a familiar face. She had graduated the same year George had but didn't really know him. They quickly became friends and then began dating. They were married a couple of months later.

Lillian gave birth to Julie three years later under great duress. Her doctors told Lillian that because of the trauma during delivery, she would never be able to have another baby. When Julie was eight, she and George decided to adopt a boy. Initially they looked for an infant, but chose a child closer to Julie's age, a young boy named Shiloh Mashal. Shiloh had been abandoned a few months earlier with an odd case of amnesia; he couldn't remember anything other than his name.

His medical needs were simple, mostly restricted to dietary concerns as well as watching his unique case of asthma. Shiloh became a part of the Wagner family in time for a shock: Lillian was pregnant! She delivered Tina ten months after adopting Shiloh.

After Tina started school, Lillian returned to her art, selling the occasional piece on eBay.

SHILOH WAGNER

HEIGHT	5' 9"
WEIGHT	160 lb.
BUILD	Medium
HAIR	Bronze
EYES	Blue
RACE	Arterran
SKIN	Medium
AGE	17
GENDER	Male
I.Q.	116

TRIVIA

Prior to learning how to fly, Shiloh had an extreme fear of heights.

BIRTH NAME	Shiloh Khane Mashal
BIRTH	Sept 10 - Throne City, Jusinan, Ehrets
LEGAL STATUS	US Citizen, no criminal record
MARITAL STATUS	Single
EDUCATION	Graduate, Champaign High School
MILITARY STATUS	N/A
OCCUPATION	N/A
FAMILY	Shiloh has family on both worlds
AFFILIATIONS	High School Yearbook Committee

SHILOH WAGNER

Destiny rides on the young shoulders of Shiloh Wagner. He was proclaimed Witness Regent at age eight after his elder brother Grayden was banished, but it was not meant to be.

Eythan sent Shiloh, his mother and other members of the family off planet just before Grayden attacked. Shiloh almost fell victim to an assassination attempt on his ship. The ship was damaged in the attack, and fell into a spacial anomaly.

Everyone thought Shiloh and those on his ship had perished, but Shiloh found out the secret of the anomaly: it was a borderless realm connecting Ehrets to its sister planet, Earth. Another attempt was made on his life after passing through the anomaly, so a failsafe to guard his life was triggered, killing everyone else onboard.

The ship was damaged and unable to house him until his powers would manifest, so Mattis blocked his memory to help protect him until the time of the manifestation and sent him out of the ship to be adopted by an Earth family. Shiloh almost immediately began displaying various symptoms resembling asthma and dietary defects. In reality, it was merely the difference between living conditions between Ehrets and Earth.

Mattis has attempted to train Shiloh based on historical records and Shiloh's father in particular, but didn't realize the effect that the anomaly would have. The anomaly is a place where spiritual beings go to increase their power. While mortals obtain no such benefit, Shiloh's abilities are spiritual in nature, so the manifestation of his powers are different than any Witness recorded.

Shiloh will manifest the full powers of the Witness Imperium when he turns nineteen, but by which calendar?

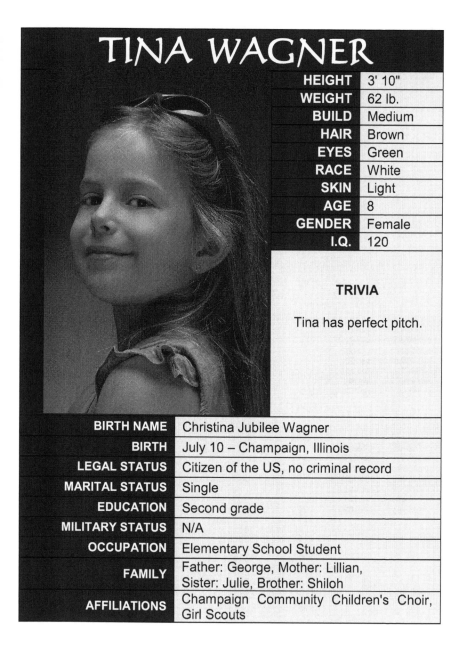

TINA WAGNER

HEIGHT	3' 10"
WEIGHT	62 lb.
BUILD	Medium
HAIR	Brown
EYES	Green
RACE	White
SKIN	Light
AGE	8
GENDER	Female
I.Q.	120

TRIVIA

Tina has perfect pitch.

BIRTH NAME	Christina Jubilee Wagner
BIRTH	July 10 – Champaign, Illinois
LEGAL STATUS	Citizen of the US, no criminal record
MARITAL STATUS	Single
EDUCATION	Second grade
MILITARY STATUS	N/A
OCCUPATION	Elementary School Student
FAMILY	Father: George, Mother: Lillian, Sister: Julie, Brother: Shiloh
AFFILIATIONS	Champaign Community Children's Choir, Girl Scouts

TINA WAGNER

The youngest member of the Wagner family is also proudly the loudest. A second grader at Champaign Elementary School, she is also a singer in the Community Church Youth Choir. Tina loves music and is taking piano lessons.

Her parents adopted Shiloh because Lillian Wagner was told that she couldn't have any more children after the trouble she had delivering Tina's older sister Julie, but Lillian became pregnant with Tina soon after adopting Shiloh.

Tina is now the light and heart of the Wagner family, bringing a new and sometimes nerve-wracking energy to the once placid household.

The long-plain refrigerator now displays new crayon art and the sounds of cartoons have replaced the news in the front room.

THE WORLD

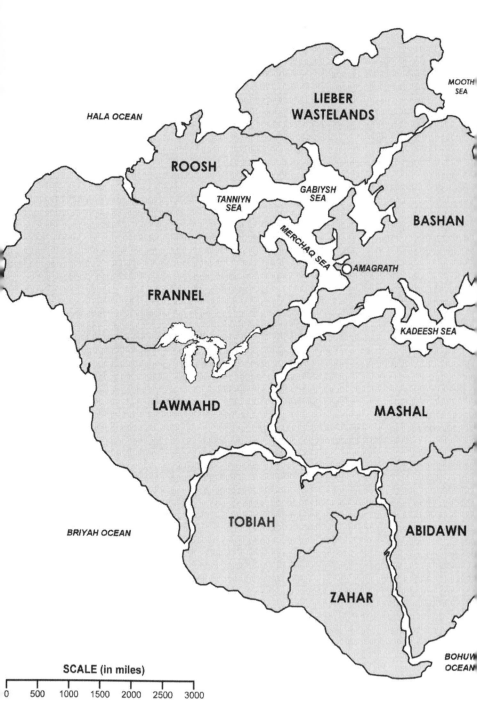

HALA OCEAN

MOOTH SEA

LIEBER WASTELANDS

ROOSH

TANNIYN SEA

GABIYSH SEA

MERCHAQ SEA

BASHAN

AMAGRATH

FRANNEL

KADEESH SEA

LAWMAHD

MASHAL

BRIYAH OCEAN

TOBIAH

ABIDAWN

ZAHAR

BOHUW OCEAN

SCALE (in miles)

0   500   1000   1500   2000   2500   3000

OF EHRETS

RHYGUS
VORTEX

VENTURA RUINS

MOOTH SEA

KHINYAN

BOKER
SEA

BASHAN

MLECHAW

MAUGAINE

OLD JUSINAN

JUSINAN

DAGON

THRONE CITY
TEMPLE CITY

QEDEM OCEAN

HILOOL

BIDAWN

ZAHAB SEA

PEYSHA
ISLAND

BOHUW OCEAN

SCALE (in miles)

0   500   1000 1500 2000 2500 3000

The Last Witness

GLOSSARY

YOUR GUIDE TO ALL OF THOSE CRAZY WORDS

AHVOAN

(618 - 433 B.C.) The Witness Imperium who tried to use the second prisM to amplify his powers, Ahvoan caused the cataclysm that resulted in the misnamed Rhygus Vortex (Ahvoan blamed the catastrophe on his assistant Rhygus). As the first member of the Zahar tribe to become Witness, Ahvoan nearly destroyed the line of Witnesses by his actions, and as a result, the Zahar line was forever banned from the golden throne. To this day, the Zahar line is blamed for shortening lifespans globally and their tribe is socially the lowest class on Ehrets.

AMAGRATH

An ancient coastal city located 300 miles northwest of Peysha Island. It is the city where a Witness Imperium was slain by the original prisM in 626 B.C. The Witness had ignored threats to the empire and realized the scope of the impending danger, but it was too late. Amagrath has come to symbolize naivety as well as a hopeless last stand.

ARTERRA

1. The name of the single continent on Ehrets, so called because it was united by the House of Arter in 312 B.C. .
2. The name of the worldwide theocratic empire that spans Ehrets. Citizens of Arterra are called "Arterrans".

ASSEMBLY OF MINISTERS

Created twelve hundred years ago, the Assembly was designed to assist the throne in matters by appointing the wisest citizens of Arterran society to specialized positions. It quickly became a clique for the powerful as well as a bureaucratic nightmare for Witnesses. The twelve ministries in the assembly are: Agriculture, Commerce, Education, Industry, Justice, Media, Religion, Science, Security, State, Territories and Welfare.

AWVEN

Originally, the highest skilled warriors of the Dagonite empire, the Awven were the first faction of Dagonite society to surrender to Arter. Today, the Awven are an order of Ehrettan monks who are best known for their bright red and black frocks and their studies of ancient Jusinan music and dance.

CITADEL

Originally a fortress built by Gentry to defend the new Arterran Empire from dissenting nations, the Citadel now houses the central command of the Arterran government and as headquarters for the Central Arterran Security Forces. The Citadel is located west of the Palace in Throne City.

DARTON

A small city located 150 miles southwest of the eye of the Rhygus Vortex. It was home of one of the secondary temples, where the Angel of Death routed the invading nations who attempted to drive a young Arterra into the ocean. Darton became infamous when it became home to the Tragedy of Ages which resulted in the misnamed Rhygus Vortex.

DESTEEN

1. (112 - 267) Considered by most Arterran historians as the greatest military commander who ever lived, Desteen saved the line of Witnesses from certain destruction at Amagrath by routing an attack that allowed the firstborn son of the Witness who died at Amagrath to take the Regency ceremonies. Desteen died during the defense, but his plan was a success. The new Regent defeated the incoming armies.

2. Class of sky vessel known for its brute force power. The Desteen is a black dreadnought class ship, designed for a medium sized crew and long missions.

EHRETS

Six percent smaller than Earth, Ehrets' cloud cover protects the surface from radiation. Inhabitants lived up to 500 years, but the cataclysm at Ventura nearly destroyed the planet's atmosphere. Inhabitants currently live to 200 years and are exclusive vegetarians. The culture is a mixture of ancient tradition and modern technology, where dinosaurs tread beside hovercrafts.

EMERALD THRONE

Located to the right hand of the Golden Throne, the ten foot tall throne of the Witness Regent is an assemblage of hundreds of emeralds, overlaid with gold and other precious gems, crafted the year before Gentry took the throne.

FIRST QUEEN

The mother of the Witness Regent, this position is granted to the queen who delivers the first legitimate male heir to the Witness Imperium. The position carries with it the title of Governess of the tribe she is from. This is the only official ruling position offered to a female in the Arterran government.

GENTRY

1. (924 – 708 BC) The first male born to Arter after becoming a Witness, Gentry became the first Witness Imperium when Arter's powers were handed down and augmented. One of the few early Witnesses who was literate, Gentry's extensive writings, though creatively dull, provide a rare glimpse into early Jusinan culture.
2. The Mattis unit assigned to Gerah.

GOLDEN THRONE

The throne of the Witness Imperium is a twenty-three foot tall statuary seat made of gold, platinum, silver and jewels. "Gentry's Baldachino" was built around it sometime after the death of Gentry.

HEALEY

1. (994-829 B.C.) Healey was Arter's third wife and the mother of Gentry. Her death caused political squabbles among Arter's other wives. The office of First Queen was established to prevent similar incidents in the future.

2. The Mattis unit assigned to Peri, Healey is located in Peri's staff.

IVORY (WHITE) THRONE

Located on the left hand side of the Golden Throne, the seven foot tall throne of the First Queen is carved from a solid piece of ivorystone, (a rare fine white marble that exists on Ehrets) overlaid with silver and precious gems. The throne was built at the direction of Gentry as a sign to the populace of the power of the First Queen.

JUSINAN

1. (1990 B.C. - 1667 B.C.) The Ehrettan counterpart to Abraham was given a promise of "one seed which will fill the world". Called by God, Jusinan moved from the comfort of his family home in the center of the continent and traveled east until he reached the coastline.

There he set up the small city-state Jusinan and his tribe prospered. His wife gave birth to thirteen sons and at the time of his death, Jusinan had seen four generations of grandchildren.

2. The city originally established by Jusinan in 1949 B.C., located on the eastern coast in the Maugaine Tribal region.

3. Any person who can trace his Jusinan heritage through his mother.

LEGION

A male manifestation of multiple possessions, the advent of a Legion brings massive death and destruction. A Legion is usually motivated by vengeance and hate and will destroy everything in his path until he is satiated, which usually occurs by killing the object of his hatred, at which point Legion expires. Forty-seven Legion manifestations have occurred on Ehrets, two on Earth.

LIEBER WASTELANDS

A region of land on the northwest coast of Arterra, home of the Veridian Mountains one of the only two mountain ranges that exist on Ehrets. Lieber's soil is too thin to support crops, but is rich in various ores, so most of its residents live in mining colonies. Their high pay is offset by the expense of importing nearly everything they consume and the high land rates set by the provincial governors to prevent people from taking their wealth elsewhere.

MALAK

Mistakenly referred to by the generic term "angel", which refers to any of the original spiritual beings created by God, Malak is the name given to the two-thirds of the host who remained faithful after Helel's War. The Malak killed the seditious umbrA (demons) in Helel's War and banished their spirits to roam the physical plane, Malak retain their spiritual bodies and as a result are much more powerful than the umbrA.

MATTIS

1. [1903 B.C. - 1544 B.C.] Mattis was the most beloved of all Arterran prophets. He protected the line of Witnesses at Amagrath by granting the Regency to the eldest daughter of the Witness Imperium after his assassination.

Mattis made a number of prophecies concerning the line of Witnesses, especially the last Witness.

2. Mattis Project: ordered by Eythan Mashal to provide a new level of computing power, there are four units: Mattis, Gentry, Healy and Sumac

3. The most powerful of all the Mattis units, housed in Eythan's helmet, currently in the possession of Shiloh Wagner. Mattis is the only unit with the complete protocol and as such, can control any of the other units.

QUORUM

A group of sixty priests formed after the Assembly of Ministers, the duty of the Quorum is to give spiritual advice to the High Priest, who guides the throne on spiritual matters. The Quorum was originally an ambitious attempt to make humans as much like angels as possible.

Candidates are physically and chemically castrated to reduce gender influences and lusts. Males and females are allowed to belong to the Quorum as long as they consent to total gender neuterization. Failing to consider the spiritual foundations of human gender, the majority of the Quorum are psychotic eunuchs with supremacist and sociopathic tendencies.

PALACE

Though it has since expanded to the size of a small city, the palace is the same building built by Arter and remains the official residence of the Witness Imperium. The surrounding structures were all built hundreds of years later as the size of the Arterran government increased and the rule of the Witness Imperium was reduced.

PEYSHA ISLAND

The only landmass fully separated from the main continent on Ehrets, only those condemned to life sentences are sent to Peysha. There is no rehabilitation at Peysha, just confinement. Crimes inside Peysha are not punishable, so the inmates have developed their own system. Any inmate attempting to escape from Peysha is immediately put to death.

THE PRISM OF EDRAH

The prisM is a five inch tall pyramid-shaped, ebony-enchanted marble built by the last surviving son of Nepheel in an attempt to destroy the world. It was used to assassinate the Witness Imperium at Amagrath. A similar prisM was built on Earth, but was lost sometime in the second century B.C.

THE PRISM OF QETEL

The second prisM was carved by a renegade priest with a shard from the original prisM, but where the first prisM which was constructed in only six years, the second prisM was demonically augmented for almost a thousand years.

It was moved to the original temple site in Rhygus, but was intercepted by then Witness Imperium Ahvoan, who tried to use the prisM to amplify his powers.

The direct interfacing of the powers of the Witness with the prisM resulted in a world-wide supernatural explosion. It caused havoc around the planet.

Among other things, it warped local weather patterns, causing the formation of the misnamed Rhygus Vortex, which has drained the Ehrettan atmosphere ever since.

PRIESTHOOD

The foundation of Arterran civilization, the priesthood is linked to every vocation on Ehrets. Since Priests are celibate, their numbers are maintained by ascetics and conscripts.

Ascetics account for about thirty percent of all priests. Conscripts come from the stock of orphans and illegitimate children.

Boys are given to the Temple after they are weaned to be raised as priests, servants or cenobites, while girls are raised to become maidens, courtesans or factotums.

Failure to pass any of the courses in the priesthood schools results in an immediate transferal to the Toad Squads.

ROAKESS

(548 – 712) The Witness best known for his philosophical writings, Roakess' arguments became the foundational basis for the Assembly of Ministers. His writings are housed in the Temple of Knowledge and are taught in all schools. He lived a relatively short life but was the only Witness to ever live in all twelve palaces.

RHYGUS

1. (557 B.C. - 498 B.C.) Chief servant of the Witness Ahvoan, Rhygus was blamed for the cataclysm that nearly destroyed Ehret's atmosphere, reducing lifespans to under 200 years. He was killed by a mob soon after the disaster.
2. The thousand year old vortex in the Ventura Ruins.
3. An Arterran curse word.

SUMAC

1. (122 B.C. - 70 A.D.) The Arterran high priest was martyred while defending the Temple from a group claiming to be from the newly formed Christian religion. Later investigations showed that the group was a cult trying to defame the newly formed Christians.
2. The only stationary Mattis unit, mounted in the Golden Throne itself.

THE TEMPLE

The grandest building on Ehrets, the Temple was built six hundred years ago on the site of the original site of Arter's Temple, Kawnon Hill. Daily sacrifices continue and draw people from all over Ehrets, but only priests can walk within the confines of its marble walls.

The annual sacrifice is the highlight of the Temple year with an estimated fourteen million penitents seeking to sacrifice.

THE CALL

A Divine Mission given directly to an individual by God or one of His messengers. Failure to heed a Call always will result in grave consequences.

THRONE CITY

Located east of the Kadeesh Sea, six miles above Temple City, Throne City is home to fourteen million people. Established by Gentry after he took the throne so the seat of the empire would be centrally located, it is home to the First Palace, the foundation of which was built on the tomb of Jusinan as well as other structures as the Court of Reconciliation and Court of Knowledge. Arter's sepulcher island, 'Arter Gawdeesh', exists just off the coast in a small island in the Kadeesh Sea and is considered to be a part of Throne City.

TIERS

To mock Heaven's twelve-tier structure, Helel (Lucifer) established thirteen tierS for his command structure. Each tieR has six lieutenants subservient to the tieR above it. The first tieR is subservient to the will of Helel (Lucifer); while the second tier is in charge of nations and is subservient to the first tieR, etc.

The number of tierS doesn't account for demons within each tieR.

TRIBES

The base social structure of Arterra, every aspect of Arterran society is divided into twelve tribes. Traditionally, a person has three names: their individual name, their family name and their tribal name. For instance, Fensid Az Khinyan is Minister of Finance. Fensid is his personal name; his father's family name is Az and he belongs to the Khinyan tribe. The only exception is for Ministers of Religion, who are not allowed to carry either a family or tribal name. Each tribe is represented in the Assembly.

TRIBAL STRUCTURE

SURNAME	AREA	MINISTER
Maugaine	Religion	Ahmahl
Bachan	Media	Kopher Akzahb Bachan
Frannel	Security	Khayle Shawmar Frannel
Mashal	State	Awvone Rah Mashal
Khinyan	Commerce	Fensid Az Khinyan
Lawmod	Education	Roah Awsaw Lawmod
Tobiah	Industry	Keseel Eviyl Tobiah
Hilool	Agriculture	Ornan Taphash Hilool
Abidawn	Justice	Chamac Avval Abidawn
Zahar	Science	Chazaq Briy Zahar
Mlechaw	Territories	Adan At Mlechaw
Roosh	Welfare	Tamah Nmibzeh Roosh

UMBRA

Commonly referred to as demons, umbrA are the third of the angelic host who revolted against God and were killed in Helel's War.

After their bodies were destroyed, their spirits were banished to roam the mortal plains. UmbrA retain the majority of their angelic power, but their lack of physical body makes them far weaker than Malak (angels).

Shortly after they were killed, their numbers were halved, with half remaining on Earth and half finding themselves on a new world called Ehrets.

UNION

The most powerful instance of multiple possessions, Union is a female multiple possession that is motivated by lust and jealousy. Union will destroy everything in her path until she is satiated, which only occurs by raping and killing the object of her hatred, at which point she expires.

Twenty Union manifestations have occurred on Ehrets, but are so powerful that only eighteen were successfully vanquished. To date, there have been no Union manifestations on Earth.

VALIANTS

The highest order of monks on Ehrets, the Valiants are a band of one hundred and twenty knights who are responsible for maintaining oral histories and standards of order.

The Valiants were established on strict standards of honor and self-sacrifice by prince Gawdal in 313, the only prince ever to refuse the Regency ceremonies. Their order is so respected that they have been allowed to continue their duties even under the reign of Grayden.

WITNESS IMPERIUM

The highest office in the land, the Witness Imperium is literally the ruler of the planet Ehrets. First established with Arter's eldest son Gentry, Witnesses Imperium not only have augmented physical abilities, they also have powers that stretch into the spiritual realm.

Most Witnesses Imperium don't know the true extent of their own power and rely on the more common abilities such as healing, and dispossession.

Few Witnesses Imperium know about, much less exercise, their abilities concerning planetary and animal control.

WITNESS REGENT

The designated successor to the office of Witness Imperium is not just a figurehead. As Governor of the Jusinan region, the Witness Regent possesses political power over the central region of the Jusinan Empire. The Regent also possesses most of the physical powers of the Witness Imperium, though they are not at the same level of power. The Witness Regent, for instance, is more vulnerable if he is not aware of an attack. Regents are barred from marriage, and any children sired prior to the Imperium ceremony are considered illegitimate.

THE STORY
BEHIND
THE STORY

OR,
HOW MAGICMAN
BECAME
THE LAST WITNESS

It was 1969 and I had just started school. My parents bought some comic books for me and I began making up some of my own characters. One day I came up with "Magicman". Yep, that's him to the left. He used "supermagic", whatever that was. This drawing doesn't show it, but there were several buttons on the front of his top hat that gave him powers. Did he want to fly? Easy; just push the button that says FLY. Super strength? Push the button that said STRONG. I don't know why he didn't just push all the buttons and have all superpowers, but I guess that's not how a five year old thinks.

As I grew into a much more mature eight year old, comic books became more important. I started drawing heroes like Batman and Superman. I didn't want to stop drawing Magic man, so I compromised and gave him a superhero suit! He kept the wand (He's not called Magicman for nothing!) I dropped the top hat for a cowl and placed a highly creative 'M' on his chest. Magicman the superhero was born! My best friend Frank Nelson could draw scenery and vehicles and I could sort of draw people, so "W&N" comics was formed when we were about ten. We drew two or three small comics and at twelve, I even saved up ten dollars by turning in pop bottles to copyright one of them, but I can't find a record of it anywhere on the Library of Congress' website, which really stinks, because ten bucks was a lot of money back in 1976!

My dad died the next year, so we moved away and I never saw Frank again. Life got pretty hectic during that period. Between late 1977 and early 1981, my family literally moved *sixteen times (that's not an exaggeration)*, leaving no time for friends or girls, but plenty of time to read, draw and teach myself guitar. Don't try to convince me it was worth it. It wasn't.

I started working several jobs when I was 14, one of which was at a radio station in Texas. My DJ name was "Gerah Weich". My voice hadn't changed yet, so I experimented with a guitar distortion box which made me sound like a robot, so I drew a robot character to match my voice. Voila! In 1980, Gerah Weich was born!

The drawing to the right is the earliest image of Gerah I could find ('85) Basically, at this point, he was just a smart alec in a pseudo Ironman suit. Wanna see some real creativity? Note the "G" and "W" cape clasps.

How original is that?!

My art was improving but something was missing with Magicman and Gerah (they were now a team). But who were they when they weren't fighting Butterboy (*I'm not kidding*) or the evil Wizard? I really had no idea. That's when I first thought about writing. Oh, Frank and I had teamed up on writing with our comics, but I wanted good writing, which meant actually working on it, but where to start? Gerah didn't have a secret ID, but Magicman finally did: Thoreau Wagner (Thor for short). And as for changes, well, I gave Thor a stylized M and changed Gerah's armor, but it wasn't enough.

Something was missing; that intangible element that makes your characters breathe. My plots were too cliche and stale even for me, so I began wondering what could be done for my guys to make them interesting and realistic. I discarded things like Magicman having a weakness to butter (aren't you glad?). I also began to define what specific powers they had, as well as what they could and couldn't do.

As a character, Gerah quickly outgrew Thor. Gerah was noble and selfless, though I still had no idea who he was! Thor quickly moved to the background while all my attention was spent on Gerah. Then I joined the Army, and spent the summer of 1986 in basic training at Fort Knox. I was a broadcaster in the Army (think Robin Williams in "Good Morning, Vietnam", but on TV).

I was sent to Ft. Ben Harrison, Ind. for training. I'd always done well in school, but for the first time in my life, I actually had to study. I have no idea how I found the time, but I finished Born A Warrior (my first book!) in February of 1987. I typed it up on an old manual typewriter. It was double spaced and only 125 pages long, but it was mine! Someday I think I'll type it out to print just to look at when I think my writing stinks.

This brought Thor to the forefront, but caused new problems. Thor was now 6' 4", 325 lb, with a 214 IQ! So perfectly... boring. ZZZZZZ So bringing him to the forefront only made things worse! The book was only 125 pages long, but it proved I could write a book!

It also established that Thor wasn't from Earth, but his powers were just as magically based as they were when I was five.

While I forget what the glowing hand thing was all about, I'm sure it seemed important at the time.

I was stationed in Korea for my entire tour (*thanks to my love of The Destroyer series. One of the main characters comes from Korea*) and had Shiloh's suit made into a real suit.

No, not a costume.

I literally paid someone to custom tailor a dress suit in the style of that costume to the right. I still have it in my closet, because I know that if I burn it, the ashes will ascend to Heaven and I'll be punished.

For a very long time.

After leaving the military, I moved to Texas where I've lived ever since. I re-read *BAW* later that year and decided that my main problem was that the book had no depth because the characters had no depth. I spent some real time on Gerah and he began to grow quickly. Thor again took a backseat as Gerah took over.

He had this cool suit of armor, so one day I decided that I'd draw a detailed breakdown of Gerah's armor. To do that, I first had to decide exactly what his armor looked like (*or 'armour' as I spelled it then. British spelling was just so cool!*)

There'd been so many versions of Gerah's armor over the years, I didn't even know what was official!

The drawing to the right is what I finally came up with as Gerah's "official armor".

Now all I had to do was draw the tech inside. Of course, I had no experience drawing electronics of any kind, but did that stop me? (If you know me, you realize that's not even a question.)

All I had to do was just create technology that didn't exist.

Can't be too hard, right?

I mean, it's fake technology! Who is going to tell me that I drew it wrong?

It ended up being the single largest project I had ever undertaken. I checked out every book I could find, only to find out that what I was looking for not only didn't exist, but even if it had, I wouldn't have been able to comprehend it.

So I just made everything up. That's right, there's no such thing as "Ramsedium IV" or "agium", and to be honest, I have no idea what I meant when I put "psychic imprint of eye".

On the next few pages, you'll see what I did. I broke down the helmet, chest plate, boots and gauntlets (front and back).
I didn't come up with what the technology was until *after* the art was done. I found out pretty quickly that putting the art first was a seriously bad decision.

Don't believe me? See for yourself...

GERAH'S ORIGINAL ARMOR

GERAH'S HELMET

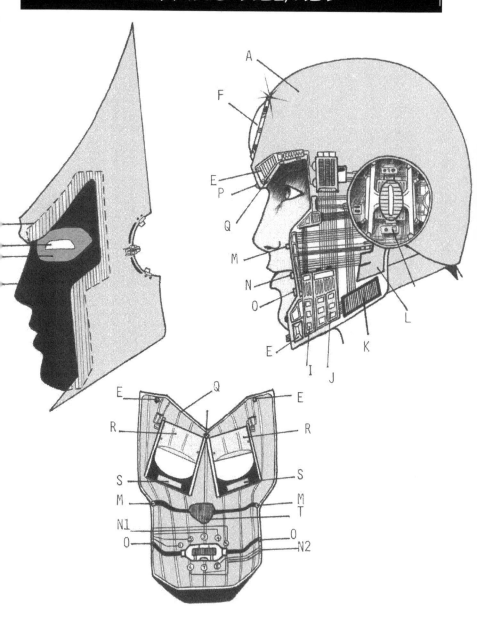

GERAH'S HELMET

A. Titanium ceramic shell (*yeah, you read that right*)

B. "Psychic" imprint of eye

C. Lens

D. Agium faceplate

E. Magnetic couplers

F. Energy diadem

G. Ear cuff

H. Power transformer

I. Receptacle / Battery

J. Receptacle / Battery

K. Synthesizer / Voice amplifier

L. Receptacle / Battery for ear cuff

M. Oxygen tubes

N. A series of tongue-activated controls

N1. Night vision

N2. Digital readout

N3. Oxygen on / off

N4. Radio channels open / close

N5. Activate / Deactivate magnetic fields

N6. Radar screens

N7. Amplifier / Voice filter

N8. Force fields

O. Microphone line

P. Direct line feed for faceplate power

Q. Heating / Cooling lines

R. Infrared lenses / Radar screens

S. Digital readout

T. Air filter

GERAH'S CHESTPLATE

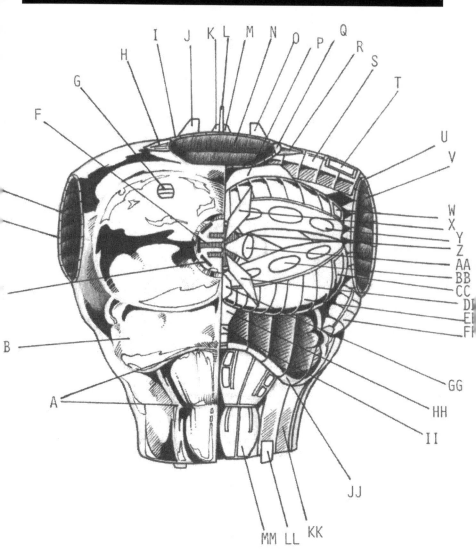

This thing wasn't just bulletproof, no, that's passe'. This had all kinds of power and broadcast capabilities in it.

GERAH'S CHESTPLATE

A. Armor flexor joints
B. Exterior coating (Tri-flex chain mail agium)
C. Chest diadem casing lock
D. Arm lock / Interface circuitry housing
E., V. Interior padding (Class A)
F. Energy channel valves
G. Cape buckler locks
H. Helmet / Neck armature locks, emergency interface
I. Neck armature lock
J. Bracer
K., O. Secondary relay
L. Primary digital relay for spine
M. Emergency relay
N. Interior padding (Class C)
P. Collar bone bracer
Q. Armature locks
R. Lock exterior coating of Ramsedium IV
S. Shoulder shell, Ramsedium IV
T. Shoulder sensor monitors
U. Arm locks/Interfacing circuitry housing
W. Upper chest musculature
X., DD. Energy channeler
Y. Sensors
Z. Diadem surface energy release matrix
AA., BB. Sensors
CC., EE. Lower chest musculature
FF. Side musculature
GG. Overload circuitry for diadem
HH. Sternum bracer
II. Energy banks
JJ. Secondary skin armature
KK. Waist armature (secondary, banded agium)
LL. Trunk locks and code interface
MM. Stomach musculature (standard)

GERAH'S GAUNTLETS

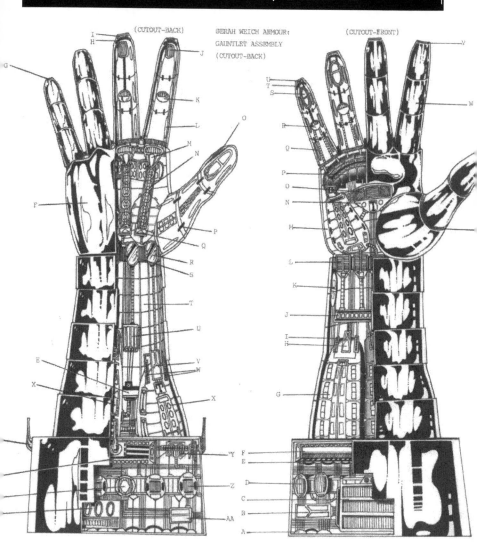

Admit it; you thought I was kidding about all this stuff, didn't you?

GERAH'S GAUNTLETS

FRONT

A. Initial input / output
B. Energy banks bypass
C. Electromagnetic generator
D. Main system energy banks
E. Signal input
F. Weapons patch bay
G. Musculature Assembly
H. Energy bypass controls
I. Signal I/O processor for "G"
J. Signal processing banks
K. Signal processor
L. Front concussion generators
M. Second skin armament
N. Manual bypass for hand cannon
O. Palm cannon
P. Exo-skeleton musculature
Q. Signal processor
R. Knuckle reinforcement
S. Finger interface
T. Finger pad
U. Finger laser
V. Opening filter for laser
W. Gauntlet casing
X. Joint reinforcement for digits

BACK

A. Finger interface
B. Energy processor
C. Laser generator / Bank
D. Cuff lasers
E. Weapons system circuitry
F. Gauntlet casing
G. Opening filter for laser
H. Finger pad
I. Finger laser
J. Finger interface pad
K., M. Knuckle reinforcement
L. Signal processor
N. Energy amplifier
O. Thumb sensor
P. Joint connection
Q. Concussion processor
R. Concussion generator
S. Battery lines
T. Second skin armament
U. Weapons signal processor
V. Energy bypass controls
W. Signal I/O processing for "X"
X. Musculature assembly
Y. Signal processing circuitry
Z. Energy banks
AA. I / O data processor

I have it on good authority that you can't build a good suit of armor without finger lasers. Oh, and knuckle reinforcements. When you run out of energy you still have to be able to punch, you know.

GERAH'S BOOTS

SOLE DIAGRAM

Pointy boots, aren't they?

GERAH'S BOOTS

A. Agium contact spikes
B. Inner skeletal plating
C. Energy banks
D. Structural framing
E. Ankle filter
F. Induction regulator
G. Guidance chip
H. Leg musculature
I. Boot casing
J. Skeletal sensor array
K. Internal armor plating
L. Inner framing
M. Coolant lines
N. Momentum discharge plating
O. Energy relays
P. Energy banks
Q. Signal processor
R. Inner plate venting
S. Signal processing banks
T. Musculature interface
U. Command lines
V. Power lines
W. Ankle filter casing
X. I / O for "V"
Y. Inner heel structure
Z. Heel reinforcement
AA. Heel casing
BB. Exhaust vents
CC. Guidance vents (the man's gotta steer somehow!)

1. Forward exhaust panels	**4.** Rollers
2. Gravimetric grip bar	**5.** Lumbar spikes
3. Adjustment exhaust	**6.** Primary heel exhaust

At this point, I realized that Gerah had to have an impressive foe. That's where Argus and USCHI come in. (1987) I didn't think much about it at the time, but Argus' creation was when the super-natural was introduced into the storyline. While at the Armed Forces TV station at Seoul, Korea, we had access to worldwide television feeds. On a German station I saw an advertisement for a TV special. I had no idea what was being said, but the way the guy said "USCHI" sounded powerful and evil, I had to use it as a name! I later found out that it is just a female German name.

Below is the original sketch of USCHI.

Originally, Argus was a demon and USCHI was his mortal pawn - a man who had stolen hi-tech armor but wanted yet more power, so he *yawn* sold his soul to the devil.

Then Argus (right) mystically amplified his armor and USCHI's greedy desires are then manipulated into murder and mayhem.

Thankfully, that all changed.

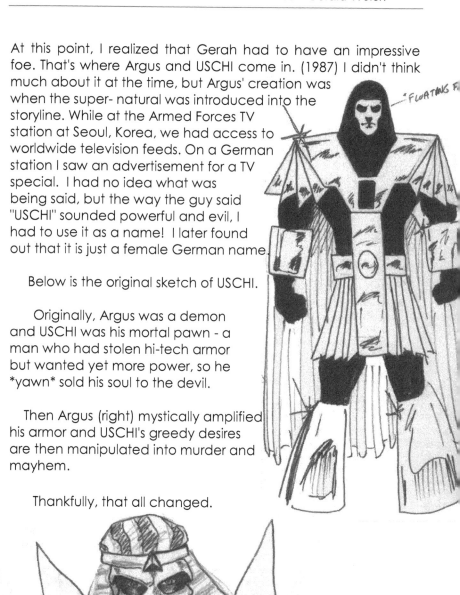

"FLOATING F

Ugh. Some the original cast as they looked in "Born A Warrior", circa 1987. Skarza is now thankfully called Grayden and you know Meltha as Malthus and King Arno is now Eythan.

I'd copyrighted *Born A Warrior* in 1990, and after playing around with various versions of helmets for Thor, I stopped working on it. I continued to draw, experimenting with various styles and shading patterns. John Byrne was my favorite artist at the time, if you couldn't tell.

When I started writing again two years later, I reread *Born A Warrior*. It was horrible! I wanted to rewrite it, but not until I threw out the entire premise of the book, starting over!

Another thing: I was a Christian, so why were Thor's powers still magically based when I was aware of another, more powerful source? Speaking of sources, the name "Thor" was the name of a pagan god. So, with much pain, Thor was no more. One day I was out driving around, looking for any kind of inspiration for a new name and passed a "Shiloh Ranch". Shiloh? I loved it!

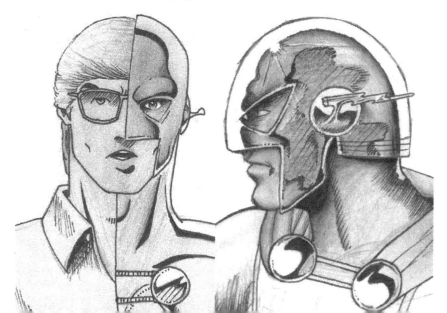

And since I was making this a supernatural story, I needed a title that was more indicative of the nature of the books. I can't tell you why I chose *The Last Witness* or else it would spoil the series' secret.

Remind me to tell you some other time.

I was equipped with a new name for my lead and a new series title. Originally, I was going to rewrite BAW, but it was so bad, I just started from scratch.

Early concept sketches of Gerah.

I had revamped Shiloh's look, so naturally I couldn't leave Gerah out! Even though I came up with what would be Gerah's helmet (previous page), I stuck with the original design for some reason, but I never forgot the cool wing/claw helmet design I came up with!

The first version of TLW was finished in the spring of 1994. At this time, I owned a video production company. I ran for Congress in 1996, but when a bad business decision forced me to declare bankruptcy, I withdrew from the race and TLW became the least of my concerns. Speed ahead to 1999.

I was working on software for my company, WAVE Corp and for test environments, decided to pull TLW out and get inspiration from one of the scenes. Unlike my previous experience with BAW, I enjoyed TLW and decided to start work on it again. I began drawing various characters in the series, not only so I could see them, but so eventually you could as well. It's always been my intent to make the ultimate behind the scenes book. The following pages will give you a peek at some of my early work and maybe a peek or two at the future.

So when someone asks me how long I've been working on *The Last Witness*, I smile and think back to the magic top hat and tell them "Since I was five."

As Gerah says, "Live to learn and then learn to question."

This is the first official full pic of USCHI as well as a promotion for book two where he first appears.

The words at the top left are what USCHI is thinking.

(LEFT) My original sketch of Eythan, detailing the braids and head dress which covers the center braid. I'm glad I changed the crown...

(BELOW RIGHT) Half-Life, a demon we first see in TLW #2. The visible half of him is intangible, the invisible half is invulnerable. He's going to be a fun one for Shiloh to deal with.

Gotta love that Pat Broderick style, eh? I know, his shoulder looks dislocated but shhhh and observe the cool.

(LEFT) Original drawing of Ahmahl. I still like the helmet and may use it elsewhere. I didn't keep this version of Ahmahl because he looks too strong here, and despite his personal belief, he's little more than Malthus' puppet. That's why I made Ahmahl's photo image look like you just want to slap him.

Well, at least I want to slap him.

(Bottom right) My original sketch of Brother Eternity.

Like many of my other original sketches, it ended up being an approximation of where the character is now.

That's how it works.

Besides, he looked too much like The Rock and I'm not about to give Hollywood any bad ideas.

(RIGHT) This is the moment when Skarza officially became Grayden. I call it the "disco era version of Grayden".

Note that the prisM at that time was a long crystal instead of the pyramid shape that it is now (BELOW) I changed it because the original prisM looked too much like the crystals from the Superman movies.

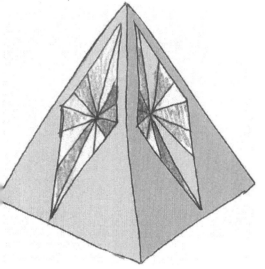

(RIGHT) First sketch of Shiloh's helmet. Mattis is mounted in the small rectangular boxes above his eyes. The oval between his eyes is a sensor.

Size comparison between Gerah and USCHI. Of course, this is Gerah's old armor, but it still gives you a sense of just how large USCHI is. Yes, they will meet. And no, it won't be pretty.

WARLORD'S "FACELESS ARMOR"

This is a test sketch of Gerah with some lighting effects. BTW, this is his current suit. Gentry is contained in the two boxes on his belt. Note, he is wearing a cape, not a mantle. Yes, it makes a difference.

(Right) USCHI has the "eyes thing" going on. I describe them as "serpentine". If he stares at you, it's like being hypnotized by a snake.

Well, a demonically-powered snake that wants to gut you.

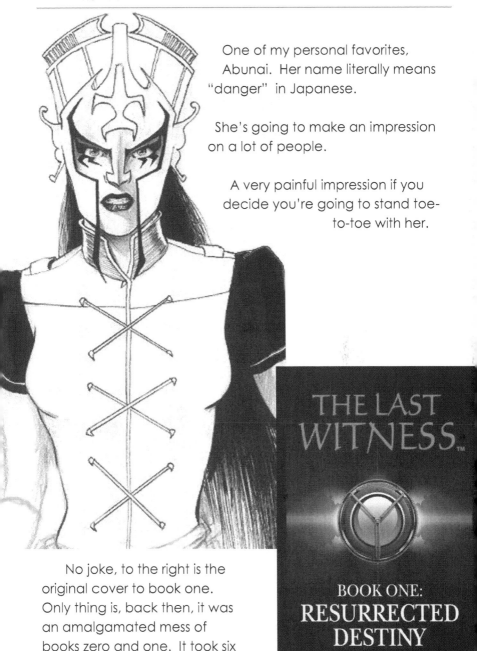

One of my personal favorites, Abunai. Her name literally means "danger" in Japanese.

She's going to make an impression on a lot of people.

A very painful impression if you decide you're going to stand toe-to-toe with her.

THE LAST
WITNESS™

BOOK ONE:
RESURRECTED
DESTINY
GERALD WELCH

No joke, to the right is the original cover to book one. Only thing is, back then, it was an amalgamated mess of books zero and one. It took six months to separate them.

This is a behind the scenes how covers work. I always try to work on future covers so I'm not forced to design a last minute cover, which almost never ends up looking good.

I'm currently working on several covers. Here's one. The original sketch to the left is from 1990.

Below left, you can see my photomanipulation; maybe this will become a cover, or maybe not.

I will tell you this: You know one of the two people here, but I'm not telling you which.

How's that for a hint?

Patience, we still have a lot of books ahead of us and a lot of ground to cover, so sit back and buckle up.
Me? I gotta get back to work.

-Jerry

MEET THE AUTHOR

Gerald Welch is a husband, father of three sons, writer and graphic artist. He lives in Texas and is one of only four people on Earth to ever be granted the title "Honorary Master of Sinanju".

(If you don't know what that means, I wasn't talking to you)

His website is www.jerrywelch.com where he's always blogging about something or other.

Catch his tweets! http://twitter.com/thelastwitness

A NOTE FROM JERRY:

I listen to music while I write and thought you might like to hear the "Noveltrack"™ to The Arterran Chronicles

Bryan Adams – *When You Love Someone*
Barlow Girls – *Psalm 73, Take Me Away, Never Alone, Thoughts of You*
Shirley Caeser – *Hold My Mule*
The Calling – *Where Ever Will You Go*
DC Talk – *Red Letters, Fearless, There Is A Treason At Sea*
E.S. Posthumous – *Isfahan, Menouthis, Ulaid*
Evanescence – *Hello, Weight of the World, Field of Innocence, Goodnite, Call Me When You're Sober*
Keith Green – *Asleep in the Light, Altar Call, The Prodigal Son Suite*
Sara Groves – *Stir My Heart, Breath of Heaven, Cannot Lose My Love, Painting Pictures of Egypt, He's Always Been Faithful, When It Was Over, Fly*
GS Megaphone – *Out of My Mind, I'd Rather See God's Face, Use Me*
The Kingsmen – *Old Ship of Zion, Love Lifted Me, I Made a Covenant*
The Lads – *Creator*
Annie Lennox – *Missionary Man, Cry*
Level 42 – *Something About You*
Toby Mac – *In The Air, Extreme Days, Yours, J Train, Momentum*
Rich Mullins – *The Robe, Awesome God*
Operatica – *O Del Mio Dolce Ardor*
Squire Parsons – *Family Reunion, He Came to Me, The Broken Rose, One Voice, I Sing Because, Old Ship of Zion*
Placido Domingo &Vienna Choir Boys – *Ava Maria*
Skillet – *Energy, Looking for Angels*
Richard Smallwood – *Holy, Thou Art God*
Michael W. Smith – *I Am Loved, Greater Than We Understand*
Russ Taff – *I Still Believe, Cry, Your Love Broke Through*
Steve Taylor – *The Finish Line*
Train - Ordinary
Jerry Welch – *Love, Unknown Soldier, Robot Girl, He Cares (inst)*
The Wilbanks – *Psalms 23*

and the following movie scores:

300, Batman Returns, Face Off, Highlander I, X-Men 3

Proof

Made in the USA
Charleston, SC
05 July 2012